LP
T7494b   06-

D0345462

N'APPARTIENT PLUS
À LA BIBLIOTHÈQUE
MUNICIPALE DE GATINEAU

BIBLIOTHÈQUE MUNICIPALE
AYLMER, QUÉBEC
MUNICIPAL LIBRARY

The Best of Friends

Joanna Trollope

The Best of Friends

COMPASS PRESS

AN IMPRINT OF WHEELER PUBLISHING, INC.

Copyright © Joanna Trollope, 1995
All rights reserved.

Published in Large Print by arrangement with Viking,
published by the Penguin Group, Penguin Putnam Inc., in the United States.

Compass Press Large Print book series;
an imprint of Wheeler Publishing Inc., USA

Set in 16 pt Plantin.

PUBLISHER'S NOTE
This is a work of fiction. Names, characters, places, and incidents either are the product of the author's imagination or are used fictitiously, and any resemblance to actual persons, living or dead, events, or locales is entirely coincidental.

Library of Congress Cataloging-in-Publication Data

Trollope, Joanna.
    The best of friends / Joanna Trollope.
        p. (large print) cm. (Wheeler large print book series)
    ISBN 1-56895-674-6 (hardcover)
    1. Friendship—England—Fiction. 2. Family—England—Fiction.
3. Large type books.
I. Title. II. Series
[PR6070.R57B47   1998b]
823'.914—dc21   98-39418
                                                          CIP

For Tuggy

CHAPTER
1

On their dawdling way home, Gus said he really needed a smoke. Sophy said, "Nobody of fourteen needs a smoke."

"I do," Gus said.

He stopped walking and sat down on the pavement, his back against the wall behind it.

"Get up," Sophy said.

Gus patted the pavement beside him invitingly, as if it were a sofa.

"Come on, Soph."

Sophy looked at the traffic roaring by. If Gus lit up, sure as hell, one of those cars would shortly contain all their parents, on the way home from this lunch party they'd been to.

"Not here," Sophy said.

Gus slumped back against the wall, aping collapse. His head lolled and his mouth hung open. He crossed his eyes. Sophy gave him an impatient nudge with one foot, and walked on. He might be so familiar to her that he was almost like a brother, but he wasn't her brother and she wasn't, when he acted the twerp, responsible for him. She had only gone with him to watch this football team thing at school on a Saturday afternoon because he'd nagged at her, with wasp-like persistence, until she couldn't stand him a minute longer. In her view, Sophy had done enough for Gus for one day.

She walked on down the main road into Whittingbourne. It was hot, in a threatening, thundery way, with purplish-grey clouds piling themselves up theatrically over the golden stone tower of the church, visible above the bleak brown roof of the sports centre. Sophy's Indian gauze shirt blew against her in the warm, dirty summer wind, outlining all the bits of her outline that she didn't like. As she got to the roundabout by the sports centre, she turned back to look at Gus. He was standing up now, spreadeagled against the wall with staring eyes, as if confronting a firing squad. No wonder his brothers called him The Fuckwit. Sophy, knowing the performance was all for her, and thus pointless if she was out of sight, walked on.

Beyond the sports centre—a brand-new one, with a vast plate-glass window in front, through which cavorting swimmers could weirdly be seen but not heard—the road curved sharply left, past a garage, and then right, to run into the medieval end of Whittingbourne past the wall of the Park. Whittingbourne Park contained an elaborate Victorian mansion— replacing a restrained neo-classical one—which was now a home for disabled teenagers. Two years before, when Sophy was fourteen, and fired with the idea of a life of voluntary service, she had worked every Saturday and a large part of the school holidays at Whittingbourne Park. The teenagers—mostly older than Sophy—had struck her as both bold and determinedly, cheerfully naughty. When she met them now, in Smith's or the market place, they ran their wheelchairs at her and shrieked triumphantly.

Just opposite the entrance to Whittingbourne Park was Sophy's house. It was, according to Sophy's father, Fergus, who knew about these things, medieval with seventeenth-century additions. A high wall shielded it from the road and the traffic in front, and behind it had a tiny quiet garden that Fergus had filled deliberately with medieval plants, hollyhocks and broom, mallow and mint and soapwort. There was a Gothic wooden bench in the garden, adapted from one in Winchester Castle, and a tunnel arbour of roses and vines, and a camomile lawn.

Sophy paused opposite her house, and considered it. She thought she wouldn't go in. It would be empty after all and might still be echoing disagreeably with this morning's quarrel. If she waited until her parents had returned, mellowed by a party, and had dispelled the reverberations of all that they had said, and shouted, earlier, she wouldn't feel so apprehensive about going home. George, Gus's eldest brother, had once told her how he envied her for living in a house with only three people in it.

"You wouldn't like it," Sophy had said. "Really you wouldn't. Everything shows, *everything*. There's nothing in our house, ever, that isn't a big deal. Not even where the spoons live."

There were thudding feet along the pavement, and wild cries.

"Don't leave me!" Gus shouted. "Don't! Wait for me! Wait!"

He fell against her, panting.

"I might have been kidnapped!"

"Nobody'd want you," Sophy said.

"Some pervert might. You going home?"

"No," Sophy said. She shoved Gus upright. "Get off. You're all sweaty."

Gus said, looking across at the upper windows of Sophy's house peering over the guarding wall, "Why's it called High Place? When it isn't?"

"Dad thinks it's metaphorical. It's the house where the Bishop used to come, to collect his dues."

Gus was bored immediately. He yawned. He took a crushed packet of Marlboros out of his pocket, flipped the lid open, and tipped a cigarette into his mouth.

"Jeez, do I need this—"

"Can I come home with you?"

" 'Course. Why ask?"

"I don't know, I just—"

"You practically live at my house, don't you, anyway?"

Something bulged and hardened in Sophy's throat. She picked up the blue bead she wore around her neck on a leather thong and put it between her teeth, and bit hard. Sometimes it was hateful to be the taker rather than the giver, hateful and humiliating.

"Actually—"

Gus lit his cigarette and drew a deep, elaborate breath. Then he exhaled gustily and eyed Sophy through the smoke. He wanted her to come home with him, badly.

"C'mon."

"Actually," Sophy said again, spitting out the bead, "I think I'll go round and see Gran."

"Why?" Gus said, drooping.

"You wouldn't understand."

"Why wouldn't I?"

Sophy released her long, rather thin dark hair from its band, shook it out, and fastened it back again.

"Because it's about a slightly complicated kind of pride."

Gus said, "I'll make you an ice-cream soda."

" 'Nother time."

He peered at her.

"You crying?"

"No!" she shouted.

Gus glanced again at High Place. It had never seemed to him a very likely house for Sophy. To his mind, Sophy looked more natural at school or in the odd, crooked flat where Gus and his family lived. Gus didn't like going to High Place; there were too many unwritten rules there that one was bound to break. He shrugged.

"Suit yourself."

"Bye," Sophy said.

He looked at her. He noticed the little hollows

at the base of her throat and the lines of her bra faintly visible through her thin shirt, and the blue bead.

"Bye," Gus said sadly.

Sophy walked away with great purpose until she was out of Gus's sight, and then she stopped walking altogether and leaned against a wall. It was a stone wall, rough with ochre crusts of lichen. Whittingbourne was largely built of this stone, and the older parts of it were roofed with it, too, and sprouted fat cushions of stonecrop. The Victorians had, of course, interjected plenty of red and yellow brick, and blue slate, and the twentieth century had put up its dull slabs of flimsy functional building, but for all that, Whittingbourne remained chiefly a stone town, grey and gold. Sophy had been born there, and so had her mother. Gus had been born there too, after his brothers. Gus's father had come to Whittingbourne when he was only three. He had been to school there, at the boys' grammar. Sophy's mother had been at the girls' grammar school. They had first met during a joint schools' production of André Obey's *Noah*, when Sophy's mother played Noah's wife and Gus's father was Ham, blacked up with burnt cork. They were sixteen then, in 1964, Gina Sitchell and Laurence Wood, wearing costumes made by their mothers and, in Laurence's case, a clumsy wig of black wool. There was a photograph to prove it, a cast photograph, from which Sophy's mother looked out composedly at her daughter with the same face, only prettier. Gina Sitchell's face had been perfect for the sixties, wide-eyed and wide-mouthed under a feathery fringe.

"I had false eyelashes for the play," Gina told Sophy, "and then I painted extra bottom lashes onto my cheeks. It made me look permanently astonished."

Sophy hardly ever wore make-up. Fergus said he didn't like it and Sophy said she didn't know how to use it. She always said that, deliberately, about things she was uncertain of. "I don't know how to listen to it," she said of modern music, or, "I don't know how to look at it," of non-representational modern art. Fergus approved of her attitude and commended her for her honesty. Leaning there, against the warm, rough stone wall, Sophy thought, briefly, about honesty. She had not been honest with Gus. To have been honest with Gus, she should have said, "I'd love to come home with you because I'd sell my soul for your home life." Instead, she had said she was going to see Gran, implying that that was what she'd prefer to do. Well, she had better try at least to make a truth of that fibbing implication and actually go and see Gran. She took her shoulders away from the wall and straightened them. A man watching her from an upstairs window across the street decided that, although she was too tall and too thin, she did have a certain something. Perhaps it was her neck.

7

• • • •

Vi Sitchell lived in an apartment in a new block of sheltered housing for the elderly. It was a square block, with a central courtyard blindingly planted with French marigolds and scarlet salvias, approached through an archway in an old wall across which, at night, an iron gate was stoutly locked. Vi was permanently indignant about the gate. It was locked before the pubs shut. Vi didn't necessarily want to stay in a pub until closing time, but she wanted to know she could if she chose to.

"Bleedin' Nazis," she said of the warden caretakers.

They were in fact a mild-mannered, middle-aged couple who seemed to believe, against all the evidence, that the inhabitants of Orchard Close were sweet old things, tranquilly accepting the sequestered twilight of their long lives.

"Twilight!" Vi said. "I'll give them twilight. Me best years are to come and they'd better not forget it."

Vi was eighty. She had had Gina late, by the standards of her day, when she was thirty-four. The father had been an American airman who had thought, after the end of the war, that he might make a new life for himself in England. The prospect of fatherhood, however, changed his mind and he went back hurriedly to Avenel, New Jersey, leaving behind nothing but a collection of gramophone records and a pair of his uniform trousers out of which Vi made Gina a stuffed pig.

8

"Looks like him, an' all," she said.

She had never married, nor pretended to be married. She had left London for Whittingbourne when she found she was pregnant and abandoned, largely, she said, because of the railway posters which showed a pretty water-colour image of the place above the slogan, "Gateway to the Heart of England." She got a job in Whittingbourne's main draper's and rose, despite never losing her robust, often raucous, London ways of thinking and talking, to be its assistant manageress, instituting both a coffee shop and a fashion department. Gina was born in Whittingbourne General Hospital and brought up in a narrow terraced house with neither view nor garden, to whose front door she had her own key. From the age of seven, owing to Vi's increased commitment to the shop, she had to use it. On winter afternoons, she told Sophy, she let herself into the house and took a book and a flashlight to the linen cupboard—the only warm place—to read until Vi came home.

"I read everything, everything I could lay my hands on, as long as they were stories. Dickens, Louisa M. Alcott, Tolstoy, Noel Streatfeild, Daphne du Maurier, Enid Blyton. Anything. And a magazine Vi took, called *Home Chat*. I read that, avidly, for the love stories, and when it folded, we had *Woman's Own* instead, and I read that too. And Thomas Hardy."

Vi had no books at Orchard Close. When Gina had married, she'd taken all her books with her, and it never crossed Vi's mind to replace them. She liked Gina to read, but for herself, she would rather *do*. Seven Orchard Close was stuffed with her doing, patchwork and macramé and crochet and knitting, bits of china awaiting her bold, unsteady painted flowers, half-finished fire-screens and pieces of embroidery, collages of landscapes with silver lamé lakes and green tweed hills, paintings—in bright acrylics—of the bunches of flowers she bought for almost nothing at the end of the day.

Vi loved colour. She also loved Gina and Sophy, boxing on television, a Saturday night glass of brandy and ginger ale, and Dan Bradshaw.

"The love of my life," she told Gina. "But I wouldn't tell him so."

Dan Bradshaw was a widower. He was seventy-seven and lived across the courtyard of Orchard Close in a flat as neat as a ship's cabin. He loved choral music—"Can't stand music," Vi said, "can't abide the noise"—and natural history and Vi. He was as much in love, Gus's father, Laurence, had pointed out firmly to Sophy, to impress the ageless seriousness of the emotion upon her, as if he had been a young man, a man of only twenty-seven, not seventy-seven. Vi seemed wonderful to Dan Bradshaw, fearless and exuberant. Sometimes, she went across the courtyard at seven in the morning to wake him up, wearing a red mackintosh over only her nightgown. It gave the occupants of Orchard Close plenty to talk about. Two of them had even taken their net curtains down, to get a better view.

When Sophy came through the arch from Orchard Street into the courtyard, she found Dan Bradshaw, on a kneeling mat, down among the marigolds. He smiled shyly at her, and tipped his straw hat.

"A plague of snails," he said, "a plague. I suppose it's all the rain."

He had a plastic bucket beside him. The bottom was covered with snails, clinging together.

"What'll you do with them?" Sophy said.

"Take them into the old Abbey grounds," Dan said. "Put them in the shrubbery there. I'll have to do it quick, though. Vi wants to try her hand at cooking them."

Sophy squatted beside him. He was a small man, with neat hands and hair.

"It's only a tease. She never would really. She hates foreign food."

"I couldn't let her cook them," Dan said. "I couldn't see them suffer. You at a loose end then, after the exams?"

"Yes," Sophy said. "At least, a bit. It's one of those days when everyone I know but me seems to have something to do."

"I thought you were a reader," Dan said.

Sophy reached into the bucket and picked up a snail by its shell. Two others hung grimly to it, from underneath.

"I am," she said, dropping them hurriedly. "I'm just a bit wordsick, after exams."

"I was a Boy Scout at your age. We had self-sufficiency tests, camping and that. It wouldn't be safe now, more's the pity." He began to scatter bright-blue pellets around the

11

marigolds, out of a plastic canister. "Hate doing this. Needs must, though. Sorry, snails."

Sophy stood up.

"I'll just go in and see Gran."

Dan chuckled, his face softening.

"Tell her—"

"What?" Sophy said.

"Doesn't matter," Dan said, suddenly overcome by private feeling. "Doesn't matter. I'll tell her myself, later."

"So they went to that party," Vi said. She was spreading thick swirls of buttercream icing across a chocolate cake. Vi was the only person Sophy knew who made cakes, seeming neither to fear nor to disapprove of them.

"They all went," Sophy said. "Mum and Dad and Laurence and Hilary. They tossed to see who couldn't drink because of driving home and it was Hilary."

"Should've got a taxi," Vi said. She held the spatula out to Sophy. "Have a lick. It'll be such a party too, crawling with ex-wives. Funny how some people have to celebrate their birthdays all over everyone else. Fifty! What's fifty, I'd like to know? Especially on your third marriage. Is that too sweet?"

"A bit."

"Can't be too sweet for me. It was the war that did it. Couldn't think about anything except hot baths and sugar. Dan still saving snails?"

"He's got about fifty, I should think. In a bucket."

Vi put the icing bowl and the spatula into the sink, and ran hot water noisily into it.

"Soft as butter, Dan is. He'd run rescue centres for rats and earwigs, given half a chance." She turned the tap off and looked at Sophy. "How's things?"

Sophy twisted her hands.

"Like usual."

Vi went across the tiny kitchen to where a mirror hung, a heart-shaped mirror framed in red plastic. She took a lipstick out of a cup on a nearby shelf and began to put it on, watching Sophy's reflection as she did so.

"Tell me."

Sophy sat down at the tiny kitchen table. She put her finger into a fallen blob of icing and squashed it.

"It was just a bit awful, this morning. They started before I got up. I could hear them. And then they wanted to go on, when I came downstairs—"

"Same old things?"

"Mmm—"

Vi capped her lipstick. She put her head on one side and considered the effect. Odd stuff, lipstick, when you thought about it. Victorian girls used to bite their lips to redden them, sometimes until they bled. She turned round to her granddaughter.

"You know, duck, it's just their way. It doesn't mean much."

Sophy said nothing. She knew what Vi meant, in a way, in that her parents' quarrelling was almost a means of communicating since

13

they had done it so frequently, for so long, but she also felt there was more to it than that. Her mother seemed to be getting more anguished, her father colder. And they were so angry with one another, even contemptuous.

"What you term disloyalty," Fergus had said, loudly and furiously that morning, "is simply a desperate attempt to have something of my own, to retain something of myself."

Gina had yelled that he was wilfully misunderstanding her. Couldn't he see, she screamed, that she was lonely, living with someone whose sole aim was to shut her out? She was wearing a dressing gown Sophy admired, of dark-green Provençal cotton patterned with little bright paisleys in red and yellow, and she had spilled coffee on it, by mistake. She was mopping at the spill in a kind of frenzy, with a blue disposable cloth, and crying out that to be lonely inside a relationship was far worse than not to have a relationship at all. Sophy had simultaneously ached with pity and longed for her to stop. She had gone out of the kitchen then, and upstairs, where she sat on the lavatory, pointlessly, for twenty minutes, staring at a book of Tintin cartoons.

Vi sat down opposite Sophy and took her wandering hand. Vi's hand was warm and capable, with a lot of big rings on it, in which cake mixture had lodged.

"Come on, now."

Sophy said vehemently, "I *hate* it."

" 'Course you do. And they should never do

14

it in front of you. But they've always done it, since they were courting." She gave Sophy's hand a squeeze and leaned forward to peer into her face, exuding a breath of baking and Yardley's Red Roses. "I remember when your father told us he'd changed his name. He was christened Leslie, after Leslie Howard, the actor, because his mother had a fancy for him. And then he changed it, when he met Gina; he put a little ad in the paper saying he was now to be known as Fergus Bedford. Gina went for him about that. Said she couldn't stand people who were ashamed of their origins, wouldn't even let him explain himself. I shut myself into the kitchen and let them get on with it. They went off in the end, all lovey-dovey, arms round each other, and I never heard it mentioned again."

Sophy said resentfully, "There isn't any lovey-dovey *now*."

Vi regarded her. She looked tired, but that could well be the aftermath of exams and Sophy being so conscientious, such a hard worker. And of course, she'd grown so, in the last two years, as well as starting on this daft vegetarian racket. Both Gina and Sophy assured Vi that perfectly good proteins lived outside red meat, but Vi couldn't really believe it. Sophy, pale and slender, with her long, narrow wrists protruding from the floppy, cuffless sleeves of her shirt, looked to Vi so much in need of a mixed grill with a proper pudding to follow that she felt quite faint with frustration. She squeezed Sophy's hand again.

15

"I could try talking to Mum again, duck, but I don't think she'd listen."

Sophy shook her head.

"She wouldn't. Anyway, I don't want it primarily for me, I want it for them."

" 'Course you do, bless you."

"It's just"—Sophy began wildly, conscious of the prick of incipient tears again, for the second time that afternoon—"I just don't want to be there when it's like this!"

"Can't you go away? A bit of a break?"

Sophy shook her head.

"I'd help you, duck—"

Sophy nodded, gulping. "I know, I know, thank you. But I've got a job, you see. To save up for travelling. Hilary's giving me a job. At The Bee House."

Vi snorted. "What kind of job? Washing up?"

"Sort of—"

"Three pounds an hour?"

"I'm only sixteen. And I do want to earn it, Gran, I—"

"Yes," Vi said. She gave Sophy a kiss. "It's better earned." She stood up. "Time to put the kettle on. Wonder what would happen if I had a little talk with Hilary—"

"About Mum and Dad?"

"And you."

Sophy thought. She fingered her bead.

"Mum's always talking to Hilary. I—"

"What, dear?"

"I—don't think you should talk to Hilary. I don't think Mum should. I don't think you and I ought to talk, either," Sophy said, gabbling faster and faster in her distress. "I don't think people ought to go on and on talking and discussing and analysing; it makes it worse, it makes it bigger, it makes me feel so *guilty*," Sophy cried, throwing one arm up across her eyes, "as if I'm *prying*!"

Vi put the kettle down and put her arms around Sophy.

"If anybody's innocent in all this, dear, it's you."

Sophy said, her voice muffled by emotion and the silky folds of Vi's vibrant flower-patterned Saturday afternoon summer dress, "But I don't feel it! I feel it's my fault!"

"Hmm," Dan said from the kitchen doorway. He held the bucket out in front of him, to show it was empty. Vi indicated Sophy's condition with a complicated grimace.

"There were seventy-seven," Dan said. "Would you believe it? Seventy-seven snails on sixteen plants." He came forward and put a hand on Sophy's shoulder. "I need you," he said. "I need you to help me with the jumbo crossword."

Burdened with cake, Sophy made her way home as the shops were closing. She took a deliberately long route, all the way up Orchard Street, to where it merged into Tannery Street and then opened into the market square. On non-market days, the square was a car-park down the centre, and, in the top right-hand corner, on the wide paved spaces around the

17

parish church, was a lounging place for what Vi called corner boys. Some of them were at school with Sophy, but at weekends, in their careful off-duty uniforms of oversized denim and undersized leather, they pretended, with group bravado, not to know her from all the other girls they jeered at, and catcalled. Sophy hardly heard them any longer. She had discovered that if she caught the eye of one of them, or, even more disconcertingly, looked pointedly at an individual pair of feet, she could deflect their attention. "Nice dose of National Service," Vi said; Vi who had voted Labour all her life. "That's what they need." She had thumped one once, a boy who'd cheeked her, with a carrier bag containing a swede and two pounds of onions, and had had her picture on the front of the local paper, as a heroine.

Sophy crossed the market square and looked with mild, mechanical interest at the window of the clothes shop which was, at the moment, the favoured one of her year at school. She chose, mentally, two garments she wouldn't mind as presents and a pair of heavy-soled shoes she would like if they were five pounds rather than thirty-five and a long, knitted waistcoat that was nearly, but not quite, worth saving up for. A girl from her class, hand in hand with a boy Sophy had seen collecting shopping trolleys from car-parks for the local frozen-food centre, went past and said, "Hi, Sophy!" with careless triumph.

"Hi," Sophy said.

Behind her, the great blue-and-gold clock on the parish-church tower struck a sonorous half-hour. She turned and looked up. Half-past five.

"You ought to get back," Vi had said. "They'll worry. Shall I give them a ring?"

"No," Sophy said. "No. They'll think I'm with Gus, anyway, they'll—" She stopped.

Vi had patted her hand.

"You can always come back. If you need to."

Sophy had nodded. It had been too hot in Vi's sitting room, the air heavy and scented with cake. She had done seven clues for Dan and he had been full of admiration, but he was too easy to impress, and she had despised herself, almost as if she had cheated him. When she left, he said, "God bless, dear," and she wished, unfairly, that he hadn't. She looked up at the sky above the market square.

The clouds were coming down now, fastening themselves like a thick, soft, dark lid over the roofs and chimneys and towers. Soon there would be more rain, and more snails would begin their silent, inexorable progress towards Dan's marigolds. Sophy took a deep breath, as if about to jump into a swimming pool, and set off towards High Place at a determined, uncomfortable trot.

The first raindrop, huge and warm, hit her like an exploding egg as she opened the heavy high gate in the wall, that Fergus had had specially commissioned. She let it fall shut behind her with a clang and fled round the house for the back door while further drops splashed over her head and shoulders, as big as if they'd been ladled. The glass door to the kitchen stood open, propped by an old stone Gina had found in the garden, carved on one face with a clumsy acanthus leaf. Inside, the kitchen was empty and tidy. The note Sophy had left lay exactly where she had put it, on the central table, weighted by a pink pelargonium in a white china pot.

Sophy closed the garden door behind her and listened. Silence. "Hello?" she said, experimentally.

There was still silence. She walked across the kitchen and looked at her budgerigar, hanging in his cage by the further window. She had won him, two years ago, at Whittingbourne Fair, and on his social days, he talked to himself animatedly in his tiny mirror. He seemed now to be asleep, or at least deep in thought, his tiny eyes unseeing in his green-and-yellow head.

"Where are they?" Sophy said. She gave the hanging cage a little push, but he took no notice. Sophy went out of the kitchen and into the hall, dark always because of its panelling, and darker still just now because of the rain-clouds looming at the windows. The door to the sitting room was open. Sophy looked in. Her father was sitting there, in the gloom, still dressed for the party, in a summer suit that he had bought when they all went on holiday once, to the Veneto, and had stayed two nights in Vicenza. He wasn't reading or anything; he just seemed to be sitting.

"Hello," Sophy said, holding the doorframe.

He looked up, towards her.

"Hello, Sophy," Fergus said. He never called her darling, even though she knew he loved her dearly. "Hello." He made a little gesture, as if he were about to hold his arms out to her but had then decided not to, after all. "I was rather waiting for you."

CHAPTER
2

In the badly printed guidebook that the Tourist Information Office in Whittingbourne gave out free, The Bee House was listed under "Buildings of Historical Interest." It wasn't, however, the building that was of interest historically so much as its associations. The building was a ramble, one of those amalgams of styles and constant changes of use that produce a feeling of intense humanity and even greater impracticality. Visitors, stepping cautiously around its odd corners and abrupt switches of floor-level, would murmur about its charm and eccentricity while uttering silent prayers of thankfulness that they were not responsible for either keeping it clean or repairing its roofs. Then they would pick up one of the leaflets that were kept in a wooden rack on the reception desk, and go out into the garden to see the bee boles.

The bee boles were what gave the house its

name and its place in the tourist guide. The long garden that stretched away to the north was enclosed, on its east-facing side, by a long and ancient brick wall which supported a number of espaliered fruit trees. It was also pierced a dozen times with neat alcoved recesses, each one wide enough and deep enough to have held a single bee skep made, said the leaflet, of coiled straw and, in medieval times, of wicker. Each skep would have had a wooden alighting board projecting in front of it, and the east-facing wall had been chosen in the hope that the morning sun would get the bees working early. Hilary Wood, Gus's mother, had tried to persuade modern bees to take up residence in these ancient dwellings, but they had resolutely rejected them in favour of white-painted chalet-style hives elsewhere and convenient for nearby fields of rapeseed.

In the bar of The Bee House hung several framed copies of historic documents. One was a fragment from the will of Adam Cullinge, in 1407, who bequeathed all his bees and bee boles at The Bee House to the church-wardens of Whittingbourne, "the profit of them to be devoted towards maintaining three wax tapers in the church, ever burning...." Another document was an inventory made by a subsequent owner of The Bee House, in the late sixteenth century, which included "8 fattes of bees: 16 shillings." A fatte of bees, said a note typed by Hilary and stuck on the wall below the inventory, was a hive of bees in good condition. An even later occupant of The Bee House, a tenant, had left a memorandum in a strong black hand to the effect that he managed to pay the rent solely from the sale of honey and beeswax. He had added an admonishing postscript to any aspirant bee-keepers: "Let your hives be rather too little than too greate, for such are hurtful to the increase and prosperity of Bees."

It was the bees, really, that had seduced them into deciding to make a home and a hotel business out of The Bee House. There was something about the industry and domesticity of bees which, combined with their appealing appearance and attractive history, made both Laurence and Hilary feel that they hadn't really a choice in accepting this odd bequest, that the choice had eerily been made for them. They'd only been in their early twenties after all, not married yet, and with Laurence full of yearnings about roaming the world before perhaps being an architect. Or maybe a furniture-maker. Something to do with design, anyway. And then along came this letter from Askew and Payne, Solicitors, of Tower Street, Whittingbourne, to say that Ernest Harrison, who had struggled to teach Laurence and his contemporaries Latin and Greek at the grammar school, had left Laurence the dwelling house known as The Bee House, which was in a very poor state of repair but which might fetch a reasonable price on the open market if sold during the summer months.

"I'll sell it," Laurence said, visualising air tickets to Australia and an open Ford Mustang.

"You can't," Hilary said. "At least, not without thinking. He left it to you."

"I wonder why—"

Hilary let a little pause fall and then she said, "I expect there was no one else."

Laurence remembered his classroom on summer afternoons, packed with adolescent boys who were all, in their turn, packed with exploding hormones, sitting in barely controlled rows enduring old Harrison. He was a stupefyingly dull teacher; most lessons, he'd have been more entertaining and instructive reading from the Whittingbourne telephone directory. Dressed in mouldering garments of fog-colour and brown, he maundered his way through myths and battles and poems and exhortations to the gods as if they were so many laundry lists. And yet Laurence had felt, in a way he couldn't have explained to himself nor dared to broach to his friends, that there was something there, in old Harrison, under the dinge and drab. He remembered two things particularly. One was old Harrison saying that none of them would ever encounter anything in all their lives as truly shocking, in the literal sense, as the *Iliad*. The other was his remark that almost any great work of art is bound to be subversive. Laurence had written that down, covertly, but old Harrison had seen him do it. His eyes had gleamed, faintly, briefly, behind his smeared spectacles.

Could it be that, for merely copying down a remark which was almost certainly not an original thought, one could be left a collapsing house with a twelfth-century cellar, miles of buckling hardboard partitioning, and an association with bees?

"What'd we do with it?" Laurence had said to Hilary. She was two years into reading medicine at Guy's Hospital in London, and they had met at a New Year's Eve party given by a mutual friend in a flat in Fulham. She had been the only girl there wearing spectacles and when, after midnight, he had tried to take them off her with alcoholic amorousness, she had said, "Oh you are so *depressing*," and had left the party in a huff. He'd found her the next day, after hours of persistent, hungover sleuthing. She had rented a room in Lambeth and was sitting up in bed, for warmth, wearing a green knitted hat and studying diagrams of the ear. It was only a year after that that Ernest Harrison had left Laurence The Bee House.

"What do we do with it?" Laurence had asked Hilary.

Hilary had looked at him sharply.

"We?"

He hesitated a bit, and coloured. Hilary went on looking at him for a while, wearing an expression he dared not analyse, and then she said, quite gently, that she had to get to the bank before it shut.

It wasn't only the fantasies of the beaches of New South Wales and a Ford Mustang that caused Laurence to hesitate. It was Hilary, too. He knew, although he hadn't yet asked her, that he badly wanted to marry her, and he also knew that, as the daughter and granddaughter of doctors, she was serious about medicine. He was also in slight awe of some of her views which she did not express loudly but with a quiet certainty that was alarmingly impressive. One of these views (and this made his courage falter just a little about proposing marriage) was about motherhood.

"We ought," Hilary had said one day, turning her characterful, bespectacled face on its long neck to look past him, "as a society, to admit that motherhood isn't *everything*. It's something, for some people, but it isn't everything for everyone. It's a lifelong relationship, but then so is having brothers or real friends. Mothers shouldn't have a monopoly on human wonderfulness. After all, babies are only what the machinery is designed for."

"Gulp," said Laurence. Briefly, he imagined Hilary pregnant by him and felt a little faint.

"I don't want," continued Hilary, retrieving her gaze from the distance and bestowing it on Laurence, "to be either some sacred Madonna or some exhausted freak who can't be expected to think a single coherent thought beyond the nappy bucket. Do you see?"

"Yes," said Laurence.

"Some of us should have babies and some shouldn't and those that don't should then be free to get on with something else."

"Yes."

"And not be told all the time that they are inadequate or incomplete women because of childlessness."

"No."

"If you're a child, you see, it's awful to be mothered all your life. Mothers should know when to stop."

"Yes. Why are you telling me all this?"

"Because it's in my mind."

I can't, Laurence thought later while roaming yet again through the musty, lopsided rooms of The Bee House, ask someone like that to marry me. I want her desperately but I also rather want normal things, like a baby. Sometime, anyway. Perhaps I'd better just flog this old heap and go and be a jackaroo for a while and see whether, when I come back, she's missed me.

"I'd miss you, if you went to Australia," Hilary said, two days later.

"Would you?"

"And it's a pretty corny thing to do anyway, going to Australia."

He took her hand and examined it closely as if reading her palm.

"What wouldn't be corny?"

"Doing something that wasn't just an easy adventure. Like—making something of The Bee House."

He pushed his face almost into hers.

"Like what?"

"Like—making a hotel of it? A little hotel?"

He closed his eyes.

"You could do a hotel-management course. We—both could."

"But you're going to be a doctor!"

"I was—"

She was smiling, a wide huge smile, and behind her glasses, her eyes were like lamps. Laurence, who hadn't cried for years and thought he had forgotten how, burst into tears. Much, much later, when they were quite bruised with kissing, Laurence said, "But what about babies?"

She looked up at the sky. He'd taken her glasses off without protest this time, and without them, her gaze was vulnerable.

"I wouldn't mind," she said, "at least, not one or two. As long as they're yours."

That was 1970: six years before George, eight years before Adam, ten years before Gus. It was also before Laurence told Hilary about Gina.

"Who's Gina?"

They were in the garden of The Bee House, raking up rubbish for a bonfire.

Laurence said, openly and seriously, "My best friend."

"What sort of best friend?"

"The person I talk to about what we want of life, borrow books from, go to the cinema with."

Hilary leant on her rake. She was wearing a red muffler and her short dark hair was tousled.

"Who is she?"

"What do you mean?"

"I mean how old is she, what does she do, why is she your best friend, what does she look like, why do we know each other for over a year and she never gets mentioned?"

"I didn't need to," Laurence said simply, "until I knew you'd marry me."

"Are you serious?"

"Of course."

"Were you keeping her as a sort of *reserve*? In case I refused you?"

"No."

"Laurence!" Hilary yelled suddenly, flinging away her rake so that it almost broke against a tree trunk, "don't you know anything about girls at all except that you are crazy to have one?"

Laurence said nothing. He ran his hands through his hair a few times. The gesture, Hilary noticed, wasn't remotely distracted but, instead, soothing, like someone closing his eyes while he collects his thoughts.

After a long pause he said, "Have you got a best friend?"

Hilary picked her rake up again and examined its tines.

"No. Not really."

"But you have two brothers and a sister. I haven't. I met Gina when I was sixteen and she was at the sister school to mine. She was an only child too and she'd never known her father. I'd known my mother but not very well because of her dying when I was six. So I suppose there was a sort of bond. And neither of us liked our home lives much. We realised we were friends on a joint-school theatre outing to see Paul Scofield play King

Lear. We sat next to each other on the coach on the way home."

Hilary began to rake again, vigorously, tugging up wet black roots and clumps of coarse, mud-clogged grass. She wanted to ask Laurence if he loved Gina but felt she couldn't because she had the sensation of being in an emotional landscape she'd had no experience of and where she might commit an ignorant *faux pas*, shaming herself.

Instead, she said crossly, "Why did you choose a girl?"

"I didn't," he said calmly, "I chose a person. She's in Montélimar, at the moment, teaching English and the piano at a *lycée*. She went just after we met. That's why I haven't introduced you."

"That simple?"

"Yes."

"No one else vital it's just slipped your mind to tell me about?"

"No."

"Damn," said Hilary, snatching off her glasses so that she could mop her eyes with her muffler. "Damn you, Laurence Wood, you've terrified me."

When, some time later, she and Gina met, Hilary had recovered herself a little. She was, by then, wearing an antique topaz engagement ring and had embarked upon a hotel-management course. Laurence had attached himself to a firm of architects who specialised in the restoration of old buildings. Both their fathers, who had expected much more traditional professional things of them than hotel-keeping, were deeply disappointed and wore their disappointment like uncovered and grievous wounds. This had the effect of making both Laurence and Hilary very certain indeed of one another and of their future. Gina, it turned out, was to be their first firm ally.

Hilary first saw her, by chance, sitting on the steps of the porch of Whittingbourne's great medieval parish church, tipping a stone out of her shoe.

"There's Gina," Laurence said. He sounded pleased, warm, but not ecstatic.

Gina was as dark as Hilary, but smaller. She wore her hair shoulder-length, with a fringe, and her face had a serene look because her eyes were set so widely apart. She greeted them both with affection, as if she had known Hilary for ages, which in a way, Hilary reflected, she almost had because of the letters she and Laurence wrote to each other, every week. "Dear Gina," Laurence's letters began; "With love from Laurence," they ended, absolutely above-board and obscurely unsettling.

"You're so right," Gina had said then, fitting her shoe back on and standing up, "about The Bee House. It's a wonderful idea. It's a *real* thing to do."

She came to help them occasionally with some basic clearance before she went back to Montélimar, for the last year of her contract. At the beginning, Hilary could not help feeling watchful, but soon she saw there was no

31

need because there was no conspiracy. There was instead an intimate acquaintance, a feeling that, above all else, Laurence and Gina wished each other well.

"We haven't been to bed together," Laurence said.

"Haven't you? Why not?"

"It didn't seem to be an issue. Sometimes it nearly did, especially with me, but that's all. And now, that really is all, because of you."

When Gina went back to France she said to Hilary, "Keep in touch."

"But Laurence—"

"Yes, I know. But you do it. Either as well or instead. And keep an eye on Vi for me now and then. Laurence means to, but he forgets."

After Montélimar, Gina went to Pau. While she was in Pau, The Bee House, courtesy of a mortgage, opened its first cautious doors to bed-and-breakfast guests. It was a mild success and emboldened Laurence to feel that, as well as acquiring the skills of a conservationist builder, he might also learn to cook. Hilary, halfway through a book-keeping course and much involved in plans for the hotel's steady development, asked where he would learn.

"Here," he said. "By myself."

"I'm not at all sure about this," Hilary wrote to Gina. "I'm not sure we really have the time for him to experiment until he knows what he's doing. And anyway, I need him to concentrate on what we already have for a while. I think I'm pregnant."

Gina did not reply. Hilary was upset about that, because her pregnancy ended in a distressing miscarriage and she needed someone to say something quite other to her than all the things her family was saying about working too hard for all the wrong goals and if only she'd stuck to medicine and a proper profession this would never have happened. It was only later that Gina's silence was explained. She had met a man in Pau, an Englishman called Leslie Bedford, rather older than her, and she had gone to Italy for two months. It was an utter impulse, she said, and she had never been so happy. She hadn't known how to look at things before Leslie, nor relish them properly. She said it was an enormous relationship in every way and that she felt absolutely released. Then she brought him to Whittingbourne.

"Well, he's handsome," Vi said. "If you like that sort of thing."

He was handsome, tall and fair, topping Laurence by several inches and making him look, and feel, more flung together than planned. He'd been brought up in European embassies, his father having been a minor diplomat, and he spoke French and German and Spanish and Italian. He seemed charmed by Whittingbourne, so charmed that when Laurence's father, a retired estate agent, mentioned that High Place, one of the town's most interesting houses, was coming up for sale shortly, he announced that he intended to buy it and move his business out of London to the country. It was also about this time that he changed his name. Fergus had been his father's name, he said. Gina looked his father up in *Who's Who*. Fergus had been his father's third name; the one by which he had been known was John.

"Why not John?" Gina demanded.

"Everyone is called John."

"Exactly!" Gina had shouted. "You're just a snob of the worst kind!"

Leslie had gone ahead and changed his name to Fergus. "Fergus Bedford Fine Arts" was printed on the new stationery and business cards above the new High Place address. In the same year that George was born ("This isn't glorious," Hilary said during labour. "I knew it wouldn't be. It hurts like hell") Gina became Mrs. Fergus Bedford and moved into High Place with a piano as a wedding present from her husband.

"Will we all be friends now?" Hilary said, scouring the jobs-wanted column of the *Whittingbourne Standard* for a local girl who might help her with George.

"I think so. Don't you?"

"What about Fergus?"

"I think I prefer him since he stopped being Leslie. Maybe we just have to get used to him being smoother than us."

"He's very nice to George. It must be a good sign in a man, being interested in a baby. Farmer's daughter, two O levels, seeks town position with a kind family. Worth a try?"

"Don't like the sound of wanting a *town* position. And she doesn't say she likes children."

"Do you think Gina will have children?"

"Oh yes," Laurence said. "Bound to. She's always wanted them. It was one of the things we used to talk about."

Sophy was born a few months after Adam, Laurence and Hilary's second son. They were both born in the newish maternity wing of Whittingbourne Hospital, within sight of the brown Victorian block where Gina herself had been born and where Vi had lain after her birth for five days without visitors except for a routine priest who kept his gaze severely on her ringless hand. Sophy's birth brought the two families much closer together because they could share so much, like birthday parties and chicken pox and the services of a plump, placid girl who never minded what she was asked to do since she seldom troubled herself to do any of it anyway.

It was also the time when a true friendship began to grow up between Hilary and Gina. It was a friendship based initially on both being in the same trade union of young motherhood, and the daily luxury they both looked forward to—almost, Gina sometimes thought, with a craving—was a long complain to one another, either face to face or on the telephone. The complaining session had several unwritten rules, of which one was that neither ever said anything really savagely unpleasant about husband or children, and another was that it was a requirement to be as hilariously funny about the day's disasters as possible. Later, looking back on those conversations, Gina knew that she would never have got through the inevitable squalor of Sophy's babyhood and little childhood—from which Fergus required, without question, to be shielded—without being able to rehearse, as she mopped up yet another little accident, as Vi would call them, the version she would later recount to Hilary.

Hilary's sister, Vanessa, a physiotherapist specialising in sports injuries, thought the developing friendship was hardly healthy.

"I mean, she practically *lives* here—"

"I like it. And she's incredibly useful."

"Hasn't she got a job to do?"

"Well, yes, she teaches piano and does some language tuition but not all the time."

"I suppose they have heaps of money. They behave as if they do. I say, don't you think you ought to have that damp patch attended to?"

Hilary looked up. The kitchen ceiling of the flat they had made for the family out of the attics of The Bee House had a long dark stain on it, just the same shape, Laurence pointed out, as a map of Italy except that Sicily was missing.

"We can't," she said, "it's the bar next. It's the most used part of the hotel and the paint's been kicked to pieces."

The map of Italy had stayed on the kitchen ceiling for almost four years, well after Gus had been born. They tried to decorate the hotel in the bleak winter months after Christmas, when demand for bedrooms dwindled to nothing, with one of them on bar duty and the other permanently speckled with emulsion. For their twelfth wedding anniversary, they bought themselves their first proper sofa, and all five of them sat on it, in a row, in ceremonial occupation, as if to demonstrate to whatever powers there were that they had at last achieved something that symbolised stability and a kind of, albeit shaky, success.

It was exasperating, Hilary sometimes thought now, to find herself looking back on those earlier days with nostalgia. She remembered them as noisy, dirty, anxious, and achingly exhausting, but only, as it were, technically. Like childbirth, she could remember that it hurt but not how much. Chiefly now, she remembered the anticipation of those years, the sense of adventure and of there being a future where they would all arrive, weary but triumphant, like mariners after a long and stormy voyage. The thing was, she supposed, staring unseeing at her unwanted, inevitable, post-lunch-party task of the weekly books, that she was now *in* the future, they all were, and it wasn't at all as she expected it. It wasn't a golden shore to a promised land but just somehow more of the voyage. The hotel was comfortable enough, successful enough, largely due to Laurence's increasingly admired skills in the kitchen, but Hilary could no longer remember—and was afraid to confess this because it seemed so much like letting other people down—what the whole enterprise was *for*.

She was very tired. The hotel had been full

all week and the restaurant was booked out all weekend, including a wedding reception in the room they had converted for such purposes ("We must have been mad," Laurence had said last night) two years ago. On her desk in this tiny office she'd had made out of a beetle-ridden boot hole lay not only all the accounts and invoices for the week, but a pile of requests for bookings and estimates, a particularly unpleasant letter from a man about an unrefundable deposit, and a seventy-page government directive detailing the new EEC regulations for kitchens in hotels and boarding houses of a certain category (up to three-star) in urban or semi-urban locations. There was also an in-tray labelled, in Hilary's mind, "Things I Can't Quite Face Today," including Gus's school report (poor) and a number of prospectuses from colleges and universities, in which she had so far failed to make Adam take even the slightest interest.

She yawned. She hadn't drunk anything at the party but orange juice—what a disagreeable, metallic, unsatisfactory drink orange juice was, when it was your only option—but still felt soporific from the effect of other people's champagne fumes and cigarette smoke. It had really been rather a grisly party, full of the exaggerated, strained jollity of middle-aged people pretending that they weren't middle-aged, and the poor third wife (whose navy-blue mascara had smudged) listening with bright-eyed anguish to a drunken speech, made by her husband's oldest friend, in which he blithely toasted "Johnnie and

Mags, and may they never grow older or wiser." The third wife's name was Marsha. Mags was Johnnie's first wife, a startling, six-foot brunette, who had left him for a much younger film director, but who had then taken care never quite to go away. She had dominated the party, in a scarlet dress, black gloves, and a cigarette holder. It was enough to smudge anyone's mascara.

And then of course there had been Gina and Fergus, not speaking. They had spent the party at opposite sides of the elaborate marquee (pink-and-white-striped canvas complete with french windows under fibreglass pediments, and Ionic-topped columns around which flowers and ribbons had been winsomely wound) being particularly polite to other people, as if to emphasise their refusal to be even remotely courteous to one another. Fergus looked frozen; Gina, haunted.

Stewart Nicholson, a senior member of Whittingbourne's largest medical practice, said to Hilary, "How long do you give that one?"

"Years," Hilary had said sharply. "Years. Quarrelling is as natural to them as breathing."

Stewart Nicholson had taken a huge bite of vol-au-vent, spraying Hilary with flakes of pastry.

"If you say so." He winked.

Later, in the car going home, with the prospect of her littered desk and a busy evening ahead of them, and soured by the party's falsity and too much orange juice, Hilary had given way to her temper. There had been an elaborate pantomime of who should sit where in the car, and, in the end, Laurence had, to settle it, climbed in beside his wife and left Gina and Fergus to sit, as widely separated as was possible, in the back. Something about the sight of them, glimpsed in her driving mirror, staring fixedly out of opposite windows, snapped a frayed cord of self-control in Hilary.

"If you two," she said, slamming the car into reverse, "can't behave like civilized beings in public at least, I can't think why you trouble to stay together one more minute."

There had been, then, a long and awkward silence, during which everyone looked away from Hilary and one another, and Hilary glared at the road. It was broken only, and finally, by Laurence saying, in a very thoughtful voice and as if Hilary hadn't spoken at all, "What a perfectly godawful party. Why the hell did we think we wanted to go?"

The door behind Hilary opened a crack.

"Mum—"

"Yes," she said, not turning.

"I think you'd better come—"

"Why?"

Adam slid into the narrow space between her desk and the wall. Hilary looked up. His hair, very short at the back, hung over his face in front, and his hands were hidden under long, crumpled, unbuttoned shirt-cuffs. Hilary sighed. She adored him, but felt that she was not, in the least, in the mood for him just now.

"Is there a crisis?"

"It's Gina. She's in the flat. She said not to

disturb you but she's crying. Gus made her a coffee."

"Gina? But I only dropped her home two hours ago—"

Adam shrugged. He lifted his front curtain of hair briefly and revealed his father's face, only young and sadly spotty.

"You'd better come. Shall I get a brandy from the bar?"

"Oh God," Hilary said, "is it that bad—"

Adam shrugged. He screwed up his face in an effort to express himself adequately and then he said, "She looks like someone's died."

CHAPTER
3

Dan Bradshaw lay in bed and watched the summer morning gradually brighten the daisies in the pattern of his thin cotton bedroom curtains. This, clearly, wasn't going to be one of Vi's mornings, because it was already twenty past seven and if she was coming, she'd have been and gone by now, bringing his tea, whisking the curtains open, sitting on his bed and giving him one of her Red Roses–scented kisses. Dan fought, briefly and unsuccessfully, with a sharp pang of disappointment. He'd wanted her to come this morning; what's more, he'd needed her to.

Something odd had happened in the night,

which he couldn't quite remember but which he was certain had happened. He remembered getting out of bed and knocking his bedside lamp over while fumbling for the switch, and he remembered not being able to find his slippers and, in consequence, noticing how cold the bathroom floor was under his bare feet. Vi always said he should have carpet tiles; practical, she said, and cosy. Then he couldn't remember anything else until he found himself waking up, or coming to, crouched on the bathroom floor by the lavatory with his pyjama trousers humiliatingly round his ankles and little patches of numbness all over him, as if he'd been pelted with ice cubes. He'd felt a bit dizzy for a while, and very cold, and as if his tongue had swollen so that he couldn't speak. It had all, however, passed off quite quickly, and he'd slept again, heavily, and woken, before his alarm clock went off, at five to seven, hoping and waiting for Vi. He thought he might tell her he had fainted. He thought also that he might not tell her about the pyjama trousers.

At twenty-five past seven, he sat up, gingerly, and considered himself. He felt reasonably normal, except for a weariness that could be explained by all sorts of things, not the least of them being seventy-seven. Cautiously, he put his feet to the floor—how he hated his feet now, bleached old feeble things, he thought them, like underground roots—and shuffled over to the window. Vi's curtains were open and he could see the glisten of newly sprinkled water on the blue lobelia and pink geraniums he'd planted in her window box. It was Friday, after all, WI market day, and as Vi said, if you were there after eight-fifteen, you might as well not bother, there'd be nothing left but rock cakes. Mostly, Vi bought vegetables at the market and jars of chutney to put into cheese sandwiches. Dan badly missed growing vegetables. He'd grown them all his married life, his docile, uneventful married life, in the garden behind the Edwardian terraced house where he'd lived for thirty-two years, only ten minutes' walk from Whittingbourne's council offices and his job as a rates officer. Vi called him names for his past profession and said the rates were wicked and the new council tax was worse. But then she wouldn't let him argue with her. Said she'd get bored if he started being logical. He gave in at once, couldn't help himself, didn't want, really, to disagree with Vi about anything, ever.

He went out to his tiny, shining, tidy kitchen and put the kettle on. He cleaned the kitchen himself—indeed, he cleaned his whole flat—using the methods he had learned sixty years before in the Merchant Navy. Vi said he'd polish the coal if he had any. Before Vi, he'd never had experience of a dwelling where things never got put away because their owner actually preferred to see them lying about. But then, before Vi, he felt he hadn't had much experience at all, of anything.

And now, just now, there was almost too much. Vi had had poor little Sophy staying for two nights because Sophy had said, quite quietly, in that gentle way of hers, that she didn't think she could actually bear to watch her father moving out. Vi had thought she ought to go with her mother to The Bee House for a few nights but Sophy had said she didn't want that.

"You'll upset your mother," Vi had said.

Sophy had looked mutely at the wall past Vi, at Vi's collage of a winter landscape with black embroidered fences running between fields of pale-grey and cream brocade.

"So where'll you go?" Vi said.

"Here, please."

Dan had expected Sophy to cry, but she hadn't much, at least not in front of him. He had wondered whether to take her to see his old friend Denny Pagett, who ran a swan-rescue service on the Bourne River, as a diversion, but had decided that it would be too childish. Anyway, swans were not really the thing to cheer you up, despite their beauty, what with their nasty manners and teeming bacteria. He taught her mah-jong instead, and she learned politely, but without real interest, as she did with his crossword clues. He felt, all the time she was staying, that he mustn't be at all demonstrative towards Vi, that it would seem, in front of the poor stricken girl, like bragging.

He wasn't surprised she was stricken.

"I'm going," her father had apparently said to her, "even though it breaks my heart to leave you. Your mother and I simply cannot live together any more. We would kill one another."

"Not literally," Sophy said to Vi, "but as personalities. I don't know really what he meant, but that's what he said. He said they'd changed and he was being stifled. Suffocated. He said Mum had lost all her independence and she wanted to live his life now instead of living her own."

He wanted to sell High Place, Vi told Dan, and move back to London. The house was in his name, because the business was there too, so that, although he'd have to give Gina half the proceeds, he could take the decision about selling unilaterally. Dan expected Vi to be stormingly angry, to snort and rage and call Fergus every name under the sun, but she didn't. She seemed oddly dispassionate about the whole thing and said that he'd been a good husband in his way, and that Gina was no picnic to be married to. She only showed her temper when she spoke of Sophy.

"I could crown them," she said, banging a pan down on the cooker, "for what they're doing to that child. It isn't as if she'd any more confidence than you could fit on a pinhead in the first place."

Dan made his tea, in a pot, and took it to the sitting room to watch a few minutes of breakfast television, which he loved for its absurd cheerfulness. Vi despised it, as she despised people who went to all the carry-on of making tea in a teapot when a teabag and a mug were to be had. He sat down on his settee, and poured himself a cup of tea, observing that his hand wasn't quite steady. He also observed that the settee's cover—an imitation crewelwork linen, chosen by Pam fifteen years ago from a pattern book in Chambers and Son, Furnishers, in the market place—needed a visit to the dry cleaner's. He looked round, sipping his tea, and regarded his furniture, all dark oak, all part of a matching set bought for his wedding in 1938, settee, sideboard, bureau, table and dining chairs. He thought of being without them and felt abruptly, fiercely possessive. Was that, he wondered, how Fergus Bedford felt about all those treasures he'd collected, all those hangings and carvings and pieces of furniture that made High Place feel more like a museum, or at least an antique shop, than a home? He was apparently going to take exactly half of everything in High Place to London. Exactly half. They were having an inventory made. Dan gave an involuntary shiver and put down his teacup. The coldness of the idea made him want to shut his eyes.

He dressed very slowly and carefully, knotting a tie round the collar of his short-sleeved shirt and clipping it to his shirt front with a gold-plated clip that bore his initials. He always wore a tie. He'd never, he thought, when out of uniform, gone without a tie. To him, these modern T-shirts looked like undervests, there was no self-respect in them. It was like these sports-shoe things that'd never take a polish. He polished his own shoes—and Vi's, if she'd let him—daily, before the eight o'clock radio news and his customary breakfast of cornflakes, three stewed prunes, and two slices of toast.

"You're an old woman," Vi said to him

46

sometimes. He never minded. He simply smiled at her. "I'm too old to swing through the trees," he said, not really meaning it, "even for you."

After breakfast, he crossed the courtyard to number seven. Through the sitting-room window he could see Sophy, wearing Vi's peacock-blue kimono dressing gown, watching television. Her attitude was huddled and forlorn, and she appeared to be eating chocolate biscuits out of a packet. Dan's heart went out to her and, at the same time, a compassionate delicacy forbade him to tap at the window. What'd he say to her, sentimental old fool that he was? And why should she have the burden of being nice to him on top of all the other burdens she had already? He'd wait until Vi was back, dumping broad beans and baby carrots on the kitchen table, helping him, as she did by her very presence, to help Sophy.

He went out through the open iron gate into Orchard Street, meeting the female caretaker, Mrs. Barnett, coming in with a carton of milk and a newspaper.

"Morning, Mr. Bradshaw. Lovely day."

"Morning, Mrs. Barnett. Let's hope it lasts."

Mrs. Barnett looked intensely confidential.

"We were so sorry, Doug and I, to hear of Mrs. Sitchell's family troubles."

"Yes."

"Such a sweet person, Mrs. Bedford. And

poor Sophy. I suppose there's no chance of a reconciliation?"

"I wouldn't know," Dan said miserably, edging away. "I really wouldn't know—"

"You tell Mrs. Sitchell," Cath Barnett said. "You just tell her she's not to sit alone, worrying. Doug and I are always here. For a chat, you know, not just for mending fuses. It doesn't do to dwell on things—"

Dan escaped, muttering farewell, into the street. Above him, the sky was a quiet pale blue with shreds of cloud and the air of Orchard Street smelled almost as it might once have done long ago when its ancient houses had indeed had orchards behind them, and pigsties and cabbage patches and brick outhouses where the lavatories and laundry coppers lived. Dan's mother had had a copper, in his childhood home in Preston, and it had seemed to him like a tyrant, dominating the start of every week with its dangerous caprices. If he lived to be nine hundred, Dan thought, he'd never think of Mondays as anything other than washdays.

But today was Friday. Friday was the day when the country magazine Dan liked appeared in the town library. He would walk down there, buying a newspaper on the way and maybe some of those Peruvian lily things that lasted so well, for Vi to paint. He would have liked to buy something for Sophy too, but he didn't know what and he didn't want to put the poor child to the effort of having to be grateful. No, he'd stick to the newspaper and the flowers, and then go to the library and read the piece about the ancient system of water meadows promised for this week in the magazine and then he'd go for a bit of a walk in the Abbey grounds, before going home. By then, with any luck, Vi would be back.

Whittingbourne Abbey had never recovered from Henry VIII and the ravages of the Reformation. Stripped of its lead, the medieval roof had sunk and rotted and soon the local people, seeing the decay, had expediently availed themselves of useful bits of masonry for their own purposes. All over Whittingbourne, strange pieces of carved stone appeared in walls and gardens, like the acanthus-leaf stone that served as a doorstop at High Place, and without them, the Abbey quietly sank into its green grounds until only a lonely, graceful arch was left intact among random fragments of wall and stairway. The Victorians had been delighted to find this picturesque disintegration, and had briskly re-pointed the remaining masonry and laid out, around the ruins, a deeply Victorian public garden of shrubberies and walks and stiffly planted flowerbeds. Along the walks, alcoves had been made in the leafy walls of shrubs for cast-iron seats, now bolted to concrete blocks for safety, and guarded, on either side, by ostentatious litter bins. Each bench had, as it were, its own social guild— one for old members of the British Legion, one for old men who were not members of the

British Legion, one for young mothers with pushchairs, several for the middle-years at Bishop Pryor's School who felt compelled to live every detail of their lives in public, one for the weird, the shifty and the unwashed, and two, in full view of the arch, which were used by people like Dan Bradshaw and secretaries from the town's solicitors' offices in the lunch hour, with their calorie-reduced lunchboxes.

At only ten in the morning, the park was quiet, save for a few truanting schoolchildren skirmishing with cigarettes and a purposeful woman or two, of the masterful kind Dan abhorred, walking small dogs on leads at a brisk pace. He carried his newspaper and a paper cone of flowers and, in his head, a great deal of useless but interesting information about how much we owed the Dutch, in this country, for their instruction, three hundred years ago, in the management of water meadows. Dan thought he would make for his favourite bench and sit there in the strengthening sun, long enough to read the front page of the newspaper, the editorial, and the letters. He liked arranging these orderly patterns, just as he liked planting things in rows and hanging pictures in dead straight lines. He walked briskly along the gravel path towards the space where the great arch reared up—a sight that never failed to move him—in its mown circle of grass. Then he stopped. On his bench sat two people. They had their backs to him but he was pretty certain that they were Laurence Wood and Gina Bedford, sitting a foot or two apart, but turned slightly towards one another. Laurence was leaning forward, elbows on his knees, in a position dear to Dan because it gave you, as a man, somewhere to put your hands. He hesitated. Should he speak to them? Was it manners to see them and then just walk away? What's cowardice, Dan thought, clasping his flowers and his newspaper, and what's kindness? Then Gina put her head in her hands for just a second and Laurence reached out and fleetingly touched her shoulder. Dan took a step backwards.

"God bless," he said, almost inaudibly. "God bless," and then he turned and crept away, back the way he had come.

"He said," Gina said, putting her face briefly into her hands, "that he just couldn't bear me any longer."

She felt Laurence's quick touch on her shoulder.

"He said the best surgeons cut very deeply but quickly and only once, and that's what he was going to do with me. He was going to tell me why he was leaving, why being married to me was impossible any more, and then he was just going to go, and not discuss it further."

She stopped. Laurence removed his gaze from her face, returned it to his clasped hands, and waited. He thought Gina looked terrible, absolutely terrible, as if someone had smacked her face so hard that they had almost obliterated her features. She was wearing jeans and a cotton jersey and red ballet shoes, but no make-up or earrings. Laurence thought he probably hadn't seen Gina without make-up since their schooldays, when most girls had kept a mascara wand and a frosted Rimmel lipstick in the cloakrooms, to put on for the all-important, full-of-possibilities walk home.

"He said I'd allowed myself to wither so that I'd not only not got any new horizons, but I wasn't interested in having any. He said I ran round after him and Sophy trying to claw out little bits of their lives and that I was showing every sign of becoming a hysteric with a craving for rows and scenes. He said I play emotional games and that my best energies are now devoted to manipulating people. He said—"

"Stop," Laurence said gently. He turned his face towards Gina. "Is there someone else?"

"He says not. Why?"

"Because all the things he's accused you of sound so utterly alien and untrue to me that I wonder if he's building himself a raft of excuses to sail away on."

Gina took off her wedding ring and began to slide it up and down other fingers.

"I have been a bit tearful lately, I know that, and I have kept demanding he pay me some attention because he wouldn't pay me any. I know it's undignified to go on like that but you don't think of dignity when you're desperate. Laurence—"

"Yes?"

"I—can't cope without him. I simply can't."

"Gina," Laurence said, with some exasperation.

"It's true. I really need him. He complements me, he stimulates me. And we've been really happy, Laurence, we truly have. The rows were nothing."

"Rows are never nothing."

"No, perhaps, but ours weren't cruel, really they weren't. They were just two strong personalities stamping out their own territory."

Laurence lifted his gaze and looked at the archway.

"Do you think there's any chance he'll come back?"

"No."

"Even for Sophy?"

"He said it was only for Sophy that he's stayed so long. He began wanting to go when she was twelve."

Laurence stood up and put his hands in his trouser pockets. Gina had been at The Bee House now for two nights, to avoid the presence of a huge removal van parked outside High Place. Hilary had been very patient, Laurence thought, especially for someone exceptionally busy and not given to much patience in the first place. It was only this morning, down in the kitchen checking menus for typing, that she'd said, "Do please take her out for an hour. Before you get busy. She's dying to talk to you and I really haven't got anything else to contribute just now. I think he's a heartless, selfish sod, but she won't let me say so."

"Of course," Laurence had said, feeling guilty. "Of course I will."

"Gina," he said now, rattling the change in his trouser pockets. "Gina, d'you think he's changed?"

She pushed her wedding ring back onto its rightful finger.

"Yes."

"Then," Laurence said slowly, turning to look down at her and feeling a rush of pity and affection, "then you must simply pretend that he is dead, the man you knew, and grieve for him. That is, Gina, if he is so changed that he is not now the man you married."

The removal company was one well used to moving things for Fergus Bedford Fine Arts. They had, over the last twenty years, brought many tenderly wrapped and boxed objects from salerooms and country-house auctions to Whittingbourne, and indeed, taken them away again to be shipped to America and the Far East. They had also moved a fair amount of stuff already into a house Mr. Bedford had bought, shortly after Christmas, in Holland Park in London. Mr. Bedford had told the foreman he was expanding his business, but moving a vanload of possessions out of High Place including a whole wardrobe of clothing and some very nice fishing rods didn't look like expansion to the foreman, but more like disruption. And there was no sign, either, of Mrs. Bedford who had always been so reliable for tea and sandwiches.

Fergus stood in the hall, with a list on a clip-board. Past him, ticked off like registered schoolchildren, went tables and cupboards and paintings and chairs and stools and screens. He looked entirely impassive. He felt absolutely harrowed. Having planned the whole operation for over a year, he had then bungled its execution, in a storm of trivial, wretched quarrelling, as if he had merely, instead, obeyed a sudden, violent impulse. He had meant, as he told Gina, to cut once, deeply, painfully and cleanly. "I am going," he had meant to say, "at once, now, because life with you has become intolerable," and then he had meant to go.

But he had miscalculated. He had over-estimated her awareness of the situation. He had made the mistake of not preparing her for her future by telling, at the least, both Laurence and Hilary, for whom he had an admiring affection and whom he could trust to give support to Sophy. And he had totally, cruelly blundered with Sophy whom he had supposed—perhaps, he writhingly admitted, because it suited him to—to be, at sixteen, beyond the security-craving dependence of childhood and well into comprehension of the fragile, complex webs of adult emotional life.

But she had been horrified when he told her. Horrified. And she had not seemed to be able to understand what he was saying.

"What d'you mean, kill each other?" she'd said, the day of Johnnie's frightful party when he had tried to talk to her as one adult to another. She made him feel like a murderer, and an exasperated murderer at that, because, all the time he was talking, she had the cheap blue bead she wore round her neck in her mouth, like a baby. She sucked it and gazed at him. It made him want to howl aloud with grief at what he was doing and with paternal irritation at the same time.

He said, out of an unthought-out impulse to get through to her, "Would you like to come with me?"

She stared at him, her eyes as blank as the blue bead.

"I can't," she said babyishly. "There's school."

"You could do your A levels in London."

Her gaze wavered, and blurred with tears. It was too much for her, he suddenly saw, too much to tell her that her whole life was to be changed in one way, without suggesting she might like to change it in all other respects too. Sophy swallowed, gulping air.

"I—I can't leave Mum. I mean, we can't *all* just walk out on her!"

Fergus flushed and looked down.

"No."

At the very end of the conversation, just as Sophy was going out, saying she thought she'd go up to her room, she had paused in the doorway and said, in a much sharper, more adult voice, with her back to him, "I suppose you have a girlfriend."

Fergus stood up.

"No," he said. "No, Sophy, I haven't."

She glanced at him, over her shoulder.

"I can't think of anything much more insulting," Sophy said, "than being left because just anything is better than staying. If you can't even stay for—" Her voice faltered, and then she said almost in a whisper—"Me, then you better go."

She had hardly spoken to him since. Whether or not she had talked to Gina, he couldn't tell because Gina, temporarily distorted by angry triumph after Sophy had chosen to stay, would tell him nothing. He had packed quite alone in a state of mind he never wanted to experience, even marginally, ever again, yet driven by an instinct to be gone that was stronger than anything. Moving through the house he had restored with such care—his respect for its antiquity had been meticulous, nobody could fault him there—he felt a surge of fury that all that achievement, all that *life,* could be written off by the wilful arbitrariness of human behaviour, personified, right now, by Gina. And then he would come upon a photograph of Sophy—aged two on a toboggan, aged seven in a straw hat, aged thirteen on a gondola with Gina—and feel as entirely wretched as a moment ago he had felt blazingly angry. Packing presents she had given him was pure torture. He wondered, briefly, and only once because he dared not wonder it again, so painful was it, if he was going to be able to bear not seeing her every day, not waking her every morning, not knowing all the routines and events of her life, from what

went into her lunchtime sandwiches to the sub-
jects of essays she had been set. She would turn,
he supposed, into a treat, something he would
be awarded every so often if he wasn't trou-
blesome and showed himself properly abject.
And he would turn from being "Daddy" into
"my father," and a mythology would grow
up about him to make the facts palatable and
manageable. The truth would become so
tamed by other people's psychological needs
that it would finally vanish, like a bucket of
water thrown into a river. Yet what was the
truth, for Sophy? The truth of the matter,
the true state of affairs that was driving him
from a house he loved and a daughter he
adored, was only really known to him and to
Gina, and only ever would be. That was marriage for you—even a broken one.

"Please carry them singly, with both hands,"
Fergus said to the removal man going past with
a blue-and-white Chinese jar in each arm.
They had sat, for ten years, at either end of
the deep sill of the landing window that looked
over the medieval garden. Sophy, aged six
or seven when they came home, had had
names for them.

"No need to shout, squire," the man said
without rancour, setting one jar down. "I
ain't deaf."

"No," Fergus said. "No. Of course not.
Sorry."

She'd said they were like two fat people, like
a mother and father, and their little round lids
were their hats.

"Get some other ones," Sophy had said, standing there in her red dressing gown with the ladybird buttons. "Get some little ones, why don't you? Get some little ones and then we can make a family."

CHAPTER
4

George Wood got off the train at Whittingbourne's small, desolate station carrying a sports bag with a broken zip and a carrier bag of dirty washing. He was home for the weekend, home from the hotel in Birmingham where he worked in the kitchens as part of the work experience of his hotel-management course. The kitchens were big, busy, and quarrelsome and George's week had been spent learning knifework from a chef who never spoke except to swear. Late at night, George and the other young commis chefs and chefs de parti went to a drinking club to grouse, smoke, and talk sex and soccer. Gulping a mouthful of Whittingbourne air, George reflected that this was the first taste of outdoors he had had for weeks.

He'd been thankful, nine months ago, to leave Whittingbourne. He had thought, his A level exams safely over, that he would now stride away from all the small-town values and people, the stifling repetitiveness and the petty interests, towards the great, airy uplands of the outside world. He had thought technical college would be full of people with wide horizons and that he would get a vision of the business of hotel-keeping that would show his parents to be, as he had long suspected, mired up to their necks in outdated habit. He now felt amazement, and even admiration, that they had stuck it all for so long. He also felt, and was uncertain how he was going to moot this, that he was not going to be able to stick it much longer himself. He looked down at the bag of washing in his hand. He shouldn't really have brought it, not at almost nineteen, even if the launderette in his hall of residence had been shut after being vandalised. And he certainly couldn't say, "Mum, I can't stand the course any more and I'm afraid I've got some washing, OK?" Perhaps the best thing to do would be to call in at the launderette in Tower Street and do his washing there, and, while he waited, rehearse the kind of things he might say to two parents who had said to him, over and over again when he was applying for the course, "Are you *sure,* having spent your life in a hotel, that this is what you want to do?"

He pushed open the door of the launderette. It was almost empty. A girl whom he thought he recognised from a year or two above him at school sat reading a magazine in a far corner, with a big baby strapped into a pushchair beside her. The baby was bald and was sucking idly on a huge pink plastic pacifier. George wondered whether to speak, swallowed, con-

60

sidered if his new haircut was a sufficient disguise and finally decided to use the machine as far from the girl and the pushchair as possible because the only thing he could think of to say was "That yours?" in tones of horror and disbelief.

"Don't," said all the instructions. "Don't overload, use too much powder, leave the machines messy, forget to collect your washing, wash items like bedspreads, fail to consider other patrons." George piled his clothes and borrowed chef's whites in a lump in his chosen machine. "Choose programme," the unsteady handwritten notice said, "THEN add powder. Dispenser only takes correct coins." He fished in his pocket. He hadn't enough change, only coppers, a single pound, a screwed-up fiver, a slot-machine token, and the cardboard flap of a cigarette packet on which he had written a telephone number and now couldn't remember why. He looked up.

"Got any change?"

The girl raised her eyes from her magazine. "Hi, George."

He grinned. "That yours?"

She nodded. "Remember Colin? Colin Weaver? We're living with his mum. He's driving for a brewery. This," she said without much interest, "is Emma."

"Wow," George said, "a baby."

"Not exactly planned," the girl said. "You at college?"

"Yeah. Thought I'd better not take my washing home."

"I see your brother around," the girl said, "Adam. He's in the same year as my sister."

George didn't want to talk about Adam. Adam would cackle with glee when he heard George hated his course. "You must be mental," Adam had said when George went off to Birmingham. "Totally insane. Hotels! Haven't you had enough of fucking hotels?"

"Got any change?" George said again. "For a fiver?"

She shook her head.

"Haven't got a bean. I'm waiting here till Col finishes work. I'm not going home without him. Not to that old cow."

"You married?"

The girl picked up her magazine again.

"You must be joking," she said witheringly.

George went back out into the street, holding his crumpled note. He would go for change to the newsagent where he and Adam always bought their music magazines and, in his case, the cigarettes he smoked with a kind of angry furtiveness out of his bedroom window. It wasn't that his parents had ever expressly forbidden him to smoke, but because Hilary especially treated him with such devastating contempt when she smelled smoke on him, it made him behave in a way that was both furious and secretive. Outside the newsagent, he almost bumped into Sophy Bedford. She was looking very pale, almost transparent, and when she recognised him her face suddenly became convulsed, as if she might faint or cry.

"George—"

He gave her a rough hug. Funny old Sophy, technically Adam's friend because they were the same age, but kindly patronised by him and adored by Gus for as long as he could remember. "Gus," Hilary once said, "has been in love with Sophy all his life."

George said, "Great to see you."

Sophy nodded. She had her hair twisted into some complicated plait and she was wearing torn jeans and a huge, faded T-shirt with a stretched neck and hem.

"I didn't know you were coming home."

"Just the weekend. I was—well, doing a bit of washing before I saw Mum." He grinned. "Diplomacy, you know. I was just going to Skinner's for some change."

"I've got change," Sophy said. "I'll lend it to you." She began to scrabble in the straw basket on leather straps that hung on one shoulder. "I'll come with you."

"No need," he said kindly.

"Yes—"

He peered at her.

"Soph? You OK?"

She produced a purple canvas purse and held it out.

"There—"

He took her by the wrist.

"What's up?"

"I'll tell you," she said. Her wrist felt like twigs in his grasp. "In the launderette. While we do your washing."

The girl and the pushchair had gone. Only

the magazine she had been reading, *Real Life Modern Romances*, lay on the orange plastic chair where she had been sitting. George pushed Sophy down into another chair opposite his machine, collected powder, poured it in, and set the machine in complaining motion. Then he sat down next to Sophy.

"Come and have a coffee."

"No. I'd rather be here. It's more—invisible."

He leaned forward.

"What's up, then?"

Sophy pulled her plait over her shoulder and began twisting the end.

"When—when you get to your house, you might find my mother there."

"Gina? Well, so what?"

"I mean—I don't mean just visiting, but maybe staying. Some nights she does, some she doesn't. If she goes back to High Place, I go with her. Otherwise I stay with Gran."

"Sophy—"

"Daddy's gone," Sophy said, twisting wildly. "Gone. Three weeks ago. He's taken half of all the things we had and he's gone to London."

George put his head in his hands.

"Oh my God."

"It was one quarrel too many, Gran said. Daddy said my mother had changed, that she wasn't the person he married any more and that they were killing each other. He said he hadn't got a girlfriend. He said he couldn't stay another day, not even for me."

George took his head out of his hands and looked at Sophy. She wasn't crying, but she looked as if she'd cried so much already she was all cried out, like a piece of waste paper, or an old rag.

"God, I'm sorry."

"Gus keeps giving me flowers. Like Daddy was dead. I don't know where to put them. I sort of don't know where home is."

George's washing machine began on a high whining spin.

"Mum never told me," George said. "I spoke to her last week but she didn't say anything."

"I expect my mother won't let her. I've heard them shouting. She won't let Hilary telephone Daddy, you see, she won't let anyone. I think my mother doesn't want to believe it's happened so she's pretending it hasn't, in a way. She keeps saying it's the end of the dream, the end of the vision. Your family are being so kind. Even Adam." Sophy gave a ghost of a smile. "If she drank all the brandy he brings her, she'd be pie-eyed."

George got up. He knelt down in front of Sophy and took her fidgeting hands.

"I'm so sorry. I don't know what to say, really, but I'm devastated for you. Poor kid. Poor Sophy."

"I'm just another statistic now, aren't I? One more divorce, one more single-parent family—" She ducked her head. "I never really truly thought this would happen. I thought they'd go on yelling and screaming for ever, like they always did." She extracted her hands and picked up her plait again. George noticed that her nails were bitten almost to the quick. "I'd give anything to have the yelling and screaming back again, *anything*."

The machine gave a final triumphant clank and whirred unevenly to a halt. George straightened up and wrenched the lid open.

"Will you come with me?" Sophy said suddenly.

"Anywhere. Of course. Where?"

"To my house. To see it. I can't go alone—"

George began to stuff sodden clumps of clothing into his plastic bag. Sophy sounded as she always had, all her life, pleading with someone to come with her in the dark, or to the lavatory, or on a school trip. "I can't go alone." It was what she always said. "Go with her," Hilary had always said to her sons. "Go on. She's an only child, you selfish louts, she's always alone." He turned back to Sophy. She was gazing at him, pleadingly.

"Of course," he said.

High Place was as quiet as a church. Sophy had turned the key in the glass garden door and let them into the kitchen, which looked like a show kitchen, shining and unnaturally tidy, except for the raw hole where the dishwasher had once been. Odd, George thought, to take a dishwasher. Tables, chairs, pictures, things with character you were fond of, yes, but a *dishwasher*. It was like choosing to take lightbulbs or spare lavatory rolls, a sort of deliberate, impersonal, cold thing to do.

"When did you last eat in here?" George said.

Sophy picked up the pink pelargonium in its pot from the kitchen table and carried it to the sink.

"Weeks ago. Mum and I have take-away stuff now if we're here, but she doesn't really eat it."

"Where's your budgie?"

Sophy ran water into the flowerpot.

"At Gran's. He loves it there. She talks to him all day. Go and look at the other rooms. Go and see what I mean."

George went out of the kitchen, into the dark panelled hall, and then into the sitting room. Sophy followed him, desperate he should have the same impression as she.

"Look."

George looked. The furniture in the room looked gawky and awkward. There wasn't enough of it and what was left was at odd angles and there were large blank spaces on the walls, and lamps on the floor, and no curtains.

"He took the sofa," Sophy said, "and some tables and chests and a painting of Rouen Cathedral. My mother won't let me put things back. She says it must stay as he left it."

"Why d'you keep calling Gina 'my mother'?"

"Well, she is."

"But you don't call her that, do you? You call her 'Mum,' don't you?"

"Not at the moment," Sophy said carefully.

George took a step towards the door. The room seemed to him to be full of pain and anger.

"When we're here," Sophy said, "we're like people trying to live in a house that's been half devastated by a bomb or something."

George leaned against the doorframe.

"Have you seen your father again?"

"No."

"Why not?"

"I can't yet. Because of my mother. She's sort of numb."

George had a brief and powerful vision of life at The Bee House at the moment—summertime, every bedroom full, his father almost permanently in the kitchen, his mother never still and particularly short-tempered, and in their midst Gina, numb with the devastation of Fergus's desertion. He glanced up the stairs.

"All the jars have gone," Sophy said, following his gaze. "The Chinese jars. When I was little I thought they were a family."

George moved from the doorframe and put his arm round Sophy's shoulders.

She said, "It's grim here, isn't it?"

"At the moment—"

"Nothing's the same. *Nothing*. One person does something they want and all the rest of us get knocked over."

"Perhaps when you have a chance to talk to him—"

"I don't want to," Sophy said, stiff in the circle of his arm. "I can't. I'm so angry."

"With him?"

"And her." Sophy slid free and began to pummel on the nearest wall with her fists. "How dare they? How bloody *dare* they? First they make me feel guilty and now they do this!" She whirled round and shouted at George, "They're just life-wreckers! That's what they are! Life-wreckers!"

George got back to The Bee House to find Don, the barman, unlocking the bar for the evening. Two residents were already waiting, making an elaborate pretence of lack of interest in the first drink of the evening behind newspapers and guidebooks. Hilary had had some trouble in persuading Don out of his penchant for tartan bow-ties and the invention of theme cocktails—"The Bee House Bombshell," "Honey Heaven"—but he still retained the chirpiness of a bartender from an old gangster movie.

"How y'doing, George?"

"Buggered," George said, forgetting the residents.

Don gave an enormous wink in their direction.

"Your ma's on the rampage. Water tank burst over number seven, new tank and all. Faulty, it was. Having a high old time in Brum, then?"

"No," George said. "It's knackering."

"No peace for the wicked," Don said, clattering

the protective grilles up. "You'll be on duty tonight. Full house in the dining room and Michelle's off with a migraine. Now then," he said, addressing the residents. "Sir and madam. What can I tickle your fancies with?"

George went through the swing door at the back of the bar, and into the narrow corridor behind it where Hilary's office was, and the staff washroom and the staircase that led up to the family flat at the top of the building. It was dark here, and shabby, and the staircase walls bore the marks of long years of boys and bags banging their way up and down it. "Home," Sophy had said almost savagely as she turned the key again on High Place. "Home! That's just a *house*!" George had wanted her to come back with him but she had refused.

"Ironic, isn't it?" she'd said. "I should be there, all this summer. Hilary offered me a job, but of course that's gone west, like everything else. I thought I ought to stay around Mum. Then I couldn't stand it. And I didn't know what to say to Hilary, so it all just sort of faded away."

George toiled up the staircase to the top floor. He thought it might be a comfort to see someone like Gus, or Adam, and just josh around for a while, but there was no music on, and no one in the kitchen, and their bedroom doors, though open onto a familiar chaos of clothes and sports things and dishevelled bedding, were empty. He paused by the sitting-room door and looked in. It was tidy, in

70

the slightly apologetic, unconfident way that all little-used rooms are tidy, and Gina was in there. She was lying on the sofa, on her side, holding a cushion against her in both arms. Her eyes were closed and her shoes—very small shoes, George observed—were on the floor beside a mug and a plate with an apple core on it. She didn't move. George hesitated, took a breath, and tiptoed on, down the passage to his own room, opening and closing the door with stealthy relief. Then he dumped his bags on the floor, kicked his shoes off, and burrowed immediately and thankfully under his duvet, head and all. Enough, George said to himself in the blessed, familiar-smelling darkness. Enough, enough.

"She *knows* it's not true," Hilary said vehemently. "She *knows* she isn't a manipulative hysteric with no purpose in life! She *knows* he has to give himself good reason for going! I don't blame her for wanting our attention, but I really can't take all this 'Woe is me because I'm all the awful things Fergus says I am' stuff. It's driving me nuts."

Laurence, pushing basil leaves under the breast skin of a row of chickens, said he didn't think Hilary was being fair.

"Not fair? What d'you mean, not fair? I've known both of them for almost twenty years and I've listened to Gina now solidly for three weeks and I'm not allowed a view, even?"

"Of course you're allowed a view," Laurence

said, not looking up. "I just think the one you have isn't quite fair. Fergus has made Gina feel a freak. That's the trouble. He's made her feel unwomanly and unsexy and neurotic and destructive. It's like being told often enough, cleverly enough, that you're mad. She's absolutely haunted by what he said to her. He did say terrible things, you know."

Hilary looked down at the chickens' pallid breasts now weirdly blotched with the under-lying leaves, like bruises.

"Of course I know. I keep saying only a disgusting person could say such things and then she says he isn't a disgusting person. I *ask* you."

Laurence looked over his shoulder to where Steve, nineteen, and Kevin, eighteen, were chopping vegetables.

"If she agrees that Fergus is a disgusting person," he said levelly, "then logically she then has to entertain the possibility that she's wasted the last twenty years."

"Heavens," Hilary said, thumping the clip-board she had clasped against her. "I mean, *heavens*. Why should Gina think there's any-thing novel in that, for God's sake? Don't we all think that? Why should that be Gina's prerogative?"

Laurence put the point of his knife into the wooden board under the chickens and pressed hard. He counted to five. Then another five. Then he said, as he was wont to do, in a voice that attempted to ignore the last thing Hilary had said, "I'll talk to Gina."

"What about?"

"Her state of mind. Getting some help."

"Good," Hilary said. She wanted to say, "Thank you," but somehow couldn't. Instead, she put out a hand and touched one of Laurence's.

He said, "Perhaps we don't know about grief?"

"Don't we?"

"No. We only know about disappointment."

"Yes," Hilary said. She left her mouth open to say she thought she was becoming quite an expert at that, but closed it again. She felt, obscurely, that some kind of mitigating apology was called for, so she said, clumsily, "The bloody water tank didn't help."

"No. Hil, I have to get on—"

"I know, I know. But it's so difficult to talk when the hotel's so busy and Gina's here."

"I've said I'll do something about that, I've *said*—"

"All right, all right, I know." She pushed her spectacles up her nose, red-rimmed spectacles that gave her, somehow, the look of a fierce imperious bird. "Just tell me one thing."

"What?"

"What do you think are the ultimate obligations of friendship?"

Laurence looked at her.

"I don't know," he said. "I've never tested them before."

• • • •

Gina woke to the sound of boys in the kitchen. The fridge door banged a lot and there was guffawing and a smell of toast. She hated sleep these days almost as much as she hated wakefulness. Sleep seemed, just now, either miserably elusive, or drugged and full of hideous dreams from which she struggled to consciousness feeling sick and dazed. It didn't much matter where she was except that waking here, in The Bee House, was easier, knowing that the building below her was full of people and ordinariness. She craved ordinariness at the moment. She looked at the holidaymakers in The Bee House, setting off for modest days out in their specially bought casual holiday clothes, clutching maps and mackintoshes, and envied them with the kind of hopeless jealousy usually reserved for princesses and movie stars.

She rolled over on to her back and stared at the sloping ceiling. She felt, at this precise moment, just desperately sad, sodden with sadness. Yet she knew the sadness wouldn't last but would drop down into depression or guilt, or might go quite the other way and rear up into a violent disbelieving anger and intense desire for revenge. She had tried to explain this to Hilary, this helpless feeling of being bound upon a wheel of conflicting emotions which spun for a while and then threw her off, without warning, into numbness again, where she lay, beached and disabled by Fergus's going.

Hilary had said, "I expect that's normal."

"Normal? *Normal,* to be numb?"

"In a situation like yours, I mean. I suppose it's a sort of instinctive defence against pain to come. Like the way people can behave beautifully at funerals and then fall to pieces."

But, Gina thought, I am falling to pieces. I can't even help Sophy. She held the cushion she had been hugging in the air and looked at it. It was covered in Indian cotton, with a pattern of stiff tulips, red and pink and green and cream, inside a zigzag border. She must think about its reality, where it had come from, who had made it, why Hilary—well, presumably Hilary—had chosen this one and not another one, with carnations perhaps, or roses. Her eyes filled with tears, quite unbidden. "How could he?" she whispered to the cushion. "How could he do this to me? How could he make me feel that it's all my fault?"

She sat up and hurled the cushion at the television set. She was suddenly seized with fury. How dare Fergus reduce her to this? God knows, in the endless nights she had gone over and over their marriage quite obsessively, looking for things she could blame herself for.

Yet would it be better if it was indeed all her fault? Would it help in any way to see Fergus as her victim rather than her as his? If she was to blame, then he became a lost prize, some lovely chance she had had all those years and then blown. Could she bear that? Yet could she bear hating him either? What, in fact, could she possibly, right now, this August Friday afternoon, bear for a single second without wishing to scream her head off?

"Hi."

Gina glanced towards the door. Adam stood there in jeans and bare feet and a tartan shirt open over a grey vest with "Cincinnati—The Whole Hog City" printed on it.

"Like a coffee?" Adam said.

She said, with difficulty, "I don't think so, but thank you."

"C'mon," he said. "George is home."

She stood up. She didn't, to Adam, look very steady. He didn't mind her like this. In fact, he preferred her weird and mixed-up to the Gina he'd known throughout his life, all pretty and nicely dressed and efficient. She was like someone who'd had a bit too much of the wrong stuff at an all-night party, and it made her more approachable. She'd stopped being a piano teacher and turned into a nice manageable mess like everyone else. He took a step forward and put a hand under her upper arm.

"Lean on me, madam."

"Oh, Adam, I'm so sorry, it's like having an invalid around—"

"Shush. It's OK. I'll get a brandy from Don to put in your coffee."

"No more brandy. But thank you. I'd forgotten about George. Where's Sophy?"

"At Vi's."

He led Gina unsteadily into the kitchen. George was sitting at the littered table, staring into a mug, and Gus was spreading margarine out of a plastic tub on to toast, with a spoon. George got up.

"Hi, Gina."

She smiled at him.

"Good to see you."

Adam pushed Gina into a chair.

"I saw Sophy," George said, sitting down again. "Just now. I'm—I'm really sorry."

She gazed at him. He had Laurence's face, Laurence's broad, humorous, attractive face. Adam had it too. Only Gus looked like his mother, darker, better-looking, with wonderful eyes. A sudden feeling of unspeakable comfort flashed through her, gone as quickly as it came, but blessed for a second—the comfort born of being here, in this cramped and crooked kitchen under the eaves with these three boys she had known since their birth and who were unchanged and unmarked by Fergus's leaving yet who knew her and felt sympathy for her. And they weren't angry with her. Not like Sophy. She smiled at Adam.

"I'd love that coffee," she said, "if it's still on offer."

CHAPTER

5

" 'The soul would have no rainbow,' " said the text hanging opposite Gina, " 'if the eyes had no tears.' Author Unknown."

Beside it was another, on a blue mount wreathed in painted almond blossom.

" 'A bird does not sing because he has an answer, he sings because he has a song.' Chinese Proverb."

The counsellor's offices were in small rooms at the back of a tall, bleak Georgian house behind Whittingbourne Hospital. The windows of the waiting room were curtained with bluestriped, tweed-like material and looked out on to the back of Whittingbourne's largest supermarket, designed to resemble, in roofline at least, some architect's Disneyland notion of a medieval manor house.

The windows were very clean. So was the waiting room, which had an atmosphere very much like a medical waiting room except for the texts on the walls and a blown-up photograph of a calm seascape in a coppercoloured sunset.

On the table in front of her, a low table veneered in plastic grain to resemble wood, was a potted plant—an out-of-season forced russet chrysanthemum that Fergus would have described, with curled lip, as "serviceable"—and a series of booklets arranged in fans. "Healing and Growing Through Grief," announced one. "Change and Loss." "Helping Yourself."

"That's what you must do now," Laurence had said, kindly but with the edge of impatient firmness felt by someone very busy and preoccupied by other things. "We can't help you any more, you see. Because what we do isn't helping, it's just keeping you where you are. You need outside help. The kind that shows you how to help yourself."

"I don't want help," Gina had said loudly, shoving away a glass of wine he had offered her. "I want *love*."

Laurence had looked at the kitchen ceiling, then at the fridge door on which Hilary had left a notice attached by a hippopotamus magnet, saying, "The unsalted butter is only for DISCERNING ADULTS," then at the unsteady stack of mugs in the draining rack, and had finally said, "But you aren't lovable. Not like this. You might be pitiable. But lovable, no."

Gina had been as shocked as if he had struck her.

"You *bastard*."

"No."

"Yes! Yes! What do you know about it?"

"A lot," he said wearily. "By now."

"Do you? *Do* you?"

"You're in love with it all," Laurence said, getting up from the kitchen table and emptying his glass. "You're in love with your situation. You think it's glamorous to be so distraught."

Gina had never thrown anything at anyone in her life. Living with Fergus, even at the height, or depth of their worst rows, they had known that most of their possessions were too cherished to throw. Now, she attempted to pick up her wine glass to hurl at Laurence, missed it and knocked the wine instead in a dark-red pool across the table and the local telephone book which was lying on it. Laurence began to laugh.

"Gina—"

She flung a tea-towel into the wine puddle. Laurence reached out and took her by the nearest wrist.

"Stop it. You're being an ass."

"It's real!" Gina insisted, wrenching herself free. "Can't you see? I'm not inventing anything! It's *real!*"

"I know," he said. "I know. But so are all *our* lives too, this hotel, Hilary, me, poor old George in a state about having made a mistake about college, breakfast for nineteen people tomorrow, a kitchen inspection next Tuesday—it's all real, it's all got to be lived. We can support you, Gina, but we can't carry you."

She had bent her head then, and began to wipe the phone book very slowly and carefully, smoothing the damp-puckered cover out under her fingers.

"OK," she said.

"Good. Good girl."

Don't ask me, he prayed silently, don't ask me now if you're more lovable if obedient. Don't ask. Gina picked up the fallen wine glass and took it to the sink.

"Sorry," she said in a prim voice. "So sorry to have been a trouble."

"You're not—"

"I'll do something. Next week. I'll definitely make an appointment. You'll see."

And then she had walked past him, out of

the kitchen with her head up, the way she used to at school when got at, as she often was, for not having a father.

"I suppose," Laurence said a bit later, slumping against Hilary in bed, "that Fergus has done just what her father did. Walk out on her."

But Hilary wasn't listening. She had just spent an hour talking to George during which George had said, over and over, that, although he knew he didn't want to do what he was doing, he didn't on the other hand know what he wanted to do instead, and she felt absolutely drained by the day and then by his unhappiness and inertia.

"Yes," Hilary said. "No."

Laurence put his face against her back, between her shoulder-blades, and inhaled.

"At least she said she'd go."

"Yes."

"This week."

"Yes."

"She tried to throw a glass of wine at me. At one point."

Hilary pulled herself free of Laurence's breathing face. George had knocked some coffee over during their talk. Black coffee on a corn-coloured carpet. He had been close to tears. He'd said, "Am I a failure?" At only eighteen, he'd asked that.

"Go to sleep," Hilary said. "Let's just sleep."

"But I thought you'd be pleased. I thought—"

He stopped. Why should she be? Why

should he feel she ought to congratulate him on doing something that normal considerate adults just do in normal considerate adult friendships, especially ones that last for a quarter of a century?

"Don't expect thanks and pats on the back from *me*," Hilary said, shoving her pillow about, "if that's what you're thinking. She's your friend."

"Ours."

Silence.

"Ours," Laurence said again, a little more loudly.

Hilary reared up briefly and looked at him.

"I didn't choose her. You did. I took her on, for you. Just don't forget that." She paused. "Please," she added with emphasis, and lay down again, closing her eyes.

On Monday morning, Gina had appeared quite early, dressed in leggings and a blue denim overshirt, and announced that she was going home. Hilary, checking laundry in a huge canvas hamper, stopped ticking items off a list and said, "Just as you wish."

Gina had looked at her hard. This was Hilary, after all, the Hilary who had been her greatest ally and sympathiser for all those years of Sophy's childhood and all those years—even longer—of mounting warfare with Fergus, yet who now, thinking about pillowcases and handtowels, seemed about as sympathetic as a barbed-wire fence. She remembered going to a play in London once, with Fergus, a comedy at the National Theatre, which opened to reveal a man lying groaning in bed with a bad back. His wife was standing over him. "Why," he said piteously, "oh, why can't you be sorry for me?" "I'll tell you why," the wife said sharply. "It's because I was born with a very small supply of sympathy in the first place, and you have now used it all up." Perhaps Hilary was like that.

"You've been so kind. All of you."

"No," Hilary said, "not at all. It's what we're here for."

"I hope you don't think," Gina said, striving to imitate Hilary's tone of forbearing politeness, "that I've exploited you."

Hilary paused. She stooped and shook a sheet out of the heap in the hamper.

"Maybe I'm not the best person to help you—"

"No," Gina said. This was very dangerous.

"But I gather," Hilary said, her voice constricted by stooping, "that you are going to get some help."

"Did Laurence—"

"Oh yes."

Gina looked down at Hilary's dark head above the tangle of white linen and green towels. She had a sudden, violent impulse to shove Hilary down, head first, into the hamper of other people's used bedding, and scream abuse at her. She put her hands behind her back.

"I'm very grateful. Really I am. I don't know what I'd have done without you all. Or where I'd have gone."

Hilary straightened up. The sentence "We were only too glad to have you" hung for a second in the air and then vanished, unspoken. Instead Hilary leaned forward. Her cheek brushed Gina's.

"God bless," she said. She sounded relieved.

Gina went back to High Place and let herself in. Sophy had plainly been there recently, because the pink pelargonium which she distinctly remembered as being in the centre of the kitchen table was in the sink, and an insufficiently turned-off tap was dripping into it, monotonous and maddening. Gina wondered if she would telephone Sophy. "I've come back," she would say. "I'm going to sleep here every night." She went over to the telephone and dialled Vi's number and then put the receiver back in its cradle. No. Not yet. Not until she had made her counselling appointment and could demonstrate, to Sophy and to the departed ghost of Fergus, that she was making one small step back from the edge of her life to the centre. She looked at the kitchen chairs, each one with its spotted cushion tied on, Swedish-style, with bows. She thought of sitting in one of them and putting her arms down on the smooth waxed surface of the table and then her head down on her arms. She mustn't. She mustn't think like that, nor give in to herself when she did. She turned round instead, roughly and mechanically, like a wind-up toy, and yanked the Yellow Pages off the shelves that Fergus had put up especially to hold telephone books, made of old elm boards he'd found at a reclamation site. God, how much easier it must be for women abandoned by men who'd had no more thought for their homes than as useful containers for their sixties record collections and vintage-car spares! The agony of seeing reminders of Fergus's commitment to the house while remembering his inability to feel, apparently, even a fraction of such commitment to her, a living being, a living, breathing being whom he'd promised to ...Stop this, Gina said to herself. *Stop* this. She put the telephone book heavily on the table and began, with every appearance of resolution, to turn the pages.

"It's very kind of you," Gina said politely, "to see me so soon."

The counsellor was called Diana Taylor. She looked about Gina's age, with a narrow face under curly red hair and clothes from which you could deduce nothing much—skirt, shirt, cardigan, string of beads, wedding ring. She sat by a table against the wall, but not behind it, so that she and Gina were facing each other. In front of her lay a pad, a big foolscap pad with nothing written on it, not even Gina's name.

"We had a cancellation," Diana Taylor

said, smiling. "And when you've decided to come to us, it's awful to wait."

Gina looked past her.

"I don't really want to be here."

"No."

"I mean, I don't want to be the kind of person who has to be."

"Nobody does."

"Is this how you're going to talk to me? All the time? Agreeing with me? Saying that everything I say or do or feel is perfectly all right to say or do or feel and that the whole bloody disaster is absolutely normal?"

Diana Taylor smiled again.

"Yes."

"Hell," Gina said. She leaned forward and put her head in her hands. "It might make me as angry with you as I am with Fergus."

"Fergus?" Diana Taylor said. "Who's he?"

"Are you married?"

"Yes."

"Your first marriage?"

"No," Diana Taylor said, "my second. To a man who runs a fish farm. Rainbow trout."

"Did your first husband leave you?"

"In a way. He died. And my mother, meaning to commiserate, said she was broken-hearted to think that I could never be happy again and I thought: My God, if that's true and I'll never be happy again I don't want to live another *minute*. But it wasn't true. It isn't."

Gina eyed her.

"Why is the waiting room full of texts? Like a Baptist mission—"

"Clients give them to us. Things that have helped them."

"Help," Gina said loudly. "Help! That's all anyone ever talks about. 'Do get help, Gina, proper professional help—I can't help you, not any more, and you aren't helping Sophy, are you?' And my mother's no help and nor is alcohol either, more's the pity—"

"Help only means," Diana Taylor said, rolling a ballpoint pen very slowly across the table, "to give someone the resources to do something. In our case, to heal themselves. That's all." She paused and then she said, almost casually, "To heal themselves from sorrow, mostly."

Gina gave a little grunt.

"Can you face one more text? My favourite, actually, and Shakespeare of course. 'Give sorrow words. The grief that does not speak knits up the o'erwrought heart and bids it break.' "

Gina said nothing. She looked down at her hands and then beyond them at her feet in the white loafers that Fergus had said were only suitable for naff golfing holidays in southern Spain.

"If you could tell me," Diana Taylor said, rolling her ballpoint pen, "a bit about Fergus and Sophy and your mother and yourself, then we could talk about it. I mean, how old is Sophy?"

"Sixteen. And I'm forty-six and my mother is eighty and Fergus is fifty-three and he's gone."

"Gone?"

"Yes!" Gina said, almost shouting. "Yes! Gone! Why on earth else d'you think I'm here?"

Diana Taylor said nothing. She picked her pen up and put it, with a little click, into a pottery mug already half full of pens. Then she folded her hands together on the table and waited. Gina looked at her hands, sensible, ordinary, slightly clumsy-looking hands. She imagined Mr. Taylor of the rainbow trout farm sliding the gold band on to the left-hand one and promising those promises of security and fidelity and comfort. She looked down at her own left hand. It wore the rings Fergus had chosen, a Victorian wedding band engraved with lilies and her engagement ring, an Edwardian half-hoop of big pearls and small diamonds, five big pearls for five words, "Will you be my wife?"

Gina said, "I do such stupid things."

"Like?"

"Fergus has taken half the furniture. Exactly half. The dishwasher but not the washing machine. The sofa but not the armchairs. The sideboard in the dining room but not the table. But I can't seem to see that these things are gone. It's one of the aspects of being in the house now that I hate. I walk round the things that are gone, as if they hadn't gone. I can't help it." She paused and looked at Diana Taylor. "I've been staying with friends. For over three weeks. But I think they've had enough. I don't know if the wife told the husband to tell me to go, or the husband just thought of it himself, but he did tell me really, anyway, in a roundabout way. I don't blame them and yet I do."

"Is Sophy there? With these friends?"

"No."

"Where is Sophy?"

"With her grandmother. It's where she chose to be, chooses to be. Isn't it terrible, isn't it *wicked*, not to be able even to help your own daughter?"

"No. Not for you, just now."

Gina stood up.

"Why don't you just tell me I'm a wicked, destructive mess and have done with it? Why are you sitting there oozing patience and understanding? Why don't you just tell me that this is conduct wildly unbecoming in a woman of forty-six?"

Diana Taylor stood too.

"Because you're in shock."

"Am I?"

"Life is accompanied by a series of losses. Loss of youth is perhaps the first. You've just lost something enormous. It'll change you but it won't kill you. Shock is often the first reaction to a loss like yours."

"Often? So I'm just like everyone else? So seeing my husband waltz off to live alone because *anything* is preferable to another hour with me is merely what happens to everyone?"

Diana Taylor leaned forward. Her eyes, Gina noticed, were clear hazel and unadorned with make-up.

"You're unique," Diana said. "So is your situation. It's only the feelings you share with other people, natural, turbulent, frantic feelings. It's grief. Grief at loss."

"Grief—"

"Grief. Sophy will have it too. Distress and mourning."

Gina said, "I think I've had enough. For the moment."

"Yes."

"I'll come back—"

Diana Taylor moved to open the door for her. She didn't seem to expect to be thanked but merely nodded. Gina nodded back. It was not a moment, she felt, of much social poise. On the way out, she saw that there was a young man in the waiting room, in jeans and sneakers, with a face like a skull and an almost shaven head. He was staring, furiously, at a card someone had left propped on the mantelpiece over the defunct and neatly swept grate. It said, "If life gives you lemons, make lemonade." He gave Gina a flick of a glance. "Bloody hell," he said.

Vi was making curtains. They were red, patterned with sunflowers, and to Sophy, who had watched their evolution for some of the afternoon, they didn't look entirely rectangular. More, she thought, sort of rhomboid. But she didn't say anything. Vi was working like a demon, wanting to get them finished, to hang them at the kitchen window in place of the old green checked ones, and see the effect, with the late sun glowing through the yellow flowers. She wasn't very talkative, because of the fever of the concentrated creativity she was in, and anyway the sewing machine was deafening and her mouth was full of huge glass-headed pins, so after a while Sophy stopped pretending it was amusing to watch her and drifted out. She might, she thought, go and watch Dan instead, who was having an afternoon with his stamp collection. Vi called it playing post offices. Sophy, who knew better, was allowed sometimes to handle the tweezers and sort these frail exotic fragments that so beguiled Dan.

"It's about mystery," Sophy had said to Vi. "It's nothing like collecting beer mats."

"Nothing's mysterious," Vi had retorted, "if you just collect it. It's got to be *made*, to be mysterious."

After Sophy had gone—Vi watched her trailing across thecourtyard—Vi wondered whether she should handsew her curtain hems. She ought to, really, more professional, gives a better hang, but it would take ten times as long as just to zip along them with the machine. She held a curtain up and shook it out. Bit puckered, on that side. She gave it a sharp wrench and there was the crack of breaking thread.

"Heavens," Gina said from the doorway. "Where are those for?"

"Kitchen," Vi said briefly. She glanced up. Gina looked no better. "Come here," Vi said. "Give us a kiss."

Gina stooped. Vi's cheek was as warm and powdery as a new scone.

"Mum, is Sophy around?"

"Just gone over to Dan's. Hunt the penny blacks. I was wondering when you'd come for her."

"Is she a trouble—"

"Sophy," Vi said, abandoning her brilliant curtain to go into the kitchen and put the kettle on, "couldn't be a trouble if she tried. It's you. You and her. You ought to be under the same roof."

"That's why I'm here," Gina said, following. "I've been to see a counsellor, and—"

Vi whipped round, the kettle in her hand.

"A counsellor? One of those psycho-shrink people?"

"Yes."

"You're mad," Vi said witheringly.

"Mum, I—"

Vi ran water loudly into the kettle. Then she thumped it onto the worktop.

"Typical," she said. "*Typical.* Me, me, me. All you lot, it's all you ever think of. What about my generation? How d'you suppose we managed fifty years ago without all those busybodies in white coats? We just got on with it. That's what we did. That's what I did. Got on a train, pregnant, with me suitcase and started a new life. Seventeen pounds I had, in the bank, and a case of clothes and a baby coming. What've you got? Damn great house, more things than you know what to do with, more'n enough money, qualifications, and that child.

That poor child. And what d'you do? Run crying to Hilary and Laurence who've got enough on their plates already and then to a bleeding *counsellor*. I'll give you counsellor, Gina Sitchell. What did he say, this counsellor? That nothing's your responsibility, I'll be bound. Oh no. *You're* not to blame, are you? I expect I am and Fergus is and so's the weather and the political situation—"

Gina put her hands over her ears and leaned against the kitchen doorframe.

"Mum, stop it!"

"Well, then—"

Gina came away from the doorframe and leaned on the table.

"Why are you so angry? What makes you so furious with me for getting help?"

Vi didn't speak. For some reason she felt abruptly a little tearful, so she concentrated on getting mugs out of one cupboard and a big cake tin, bearing a battered picture of Windsor Castle on the lid, out of another.

"Mum?"

Vi opened a brown pottery jar and took out two teabags.

"*Mum*. What is it?"

Vi put a teabag in each mug and then sat down heavily on a stool and put her arms on the table. She didn't look at Gina.

"You had a husband."

"Yes."

"And a home," Vi said. "And a baby with a father."

Gina sat down opposite her mother. Vi was

twisting her big rings, grinding them round one another.

"Then you let them go. You let this quarrelling go on and on and on and you let it all go. You had all those things, Gina Sitchell, and you didn't have to struggle for them, you didn't have to be lonely, and take all the decisions, did you, day after day, year after year—"

"Hey," Gina said, "wait a minute. I didn't leave Fergus. He left me."

"Takes two," Vi said fiercely. She got up to rescue the hissing kettle.

"So you can't forgive me for having what you never had and then losing it?"

There was a pause. Vi filled the mugs with a hand, Gina noticed, that was both shaky and freckled with old age.

"It's your *attitude*," Vi said. "Like you can't do nothing for yourself and shouldn't be asked to."

"Haven't you ever been depressed?"

Vi pushed a mug across the table.

"Why d'you think I keep so busy? Let that brew a minute."

"Mum," Gina said, "if that's true, is it really better to suppress depression and then take it out on me than to admit to it and get help?"

"I don't take it out on you," Vi said. "Don't make excuses. I'm just thinking about your life. And Sophy. What about Sophy?"

"Sophy—"

Vi reached over and fished Gina's teabag out with an apostle spoon.

"Yes. Sophy. She's your daughter, your responsibility."

"I'm—I'm a bit afraid of Sophy—"

Vi stared.

"What do you mean?"

"She adores her father," Gina said. "Adores him. Almost—romantically. So she's angry with me. Furious, really, and that makes me feel uncertain of myself and apprehensive of her. I don't know what to say to her. And if you add that to all the other things I feel, the guilt and the misery and the fear perhaps, you can begin to see why I went to a counsellor, instead of yelling at me."

Vi got up and opened the cake tin. She offered it to Gina. Inside lay half a cake, thickly iced in white and studded with big *glacé* cherries, like the jewels in a king's crown in a children's nativity play.

"No thank you, Mum."

Vi put the lid on.

"Me neither."

She stood, holding the tin.

"We're all alone in the end. Aren't we? We're the only person in our whole lives we can't change, that we're stuck with."

Gina waited.

"When your father left, I thought: Right, that's it, no more believing people for me, no more standing on anyone's feet but my own, not never."

"Did you really think that then? Or did you just think it later?"

"Then," Vi said. "Sitting in my room in

Chicksand Street, Bethnal Green, after I realised he'd gone. I said, 'Vi Sitchell, you're never going to let no one make you feel this bad again.'"

"This bad," Gina said, "is how I feel now."

Vi looked at her.

"My counsellor," Gina said slightly shakily, "isn't a man in a white coat. She's a woman called Mrs. Taylor in ordinary clothes and probably about my age. Her husband died, her first husband. She said I was in shock. She said the things I'm feeling are very normal things to feel. She was nice, very nice really. I was rude."

"Yes," Vi said, "you always were if people were too kind. Especially women." She looked down at Gina and then slowly turned her back and gazed out of the window at the tiny plot of garden where her bits of washing blew on a revolving line. "I think you've got to take Sophy back. Temper and all."

"Yes."

"She's got to see you care for her."

"Yes."

Vi turned back again.

"I'm your mum and you're Sophy's. For good and all. And we'd better not forget it."

CHAPTER
6

There was a moment, most afternoons, when, even for only half an hour, The Bee House kitchen was a sanctuary. Warm and quiet, the surfaces burnished, lunch over, dinner still to come, the room hung between accomplishment and anticipation with, briefly, nobody there to agitate the atmosphere. On fine days, the afternoon sun came in through the west-facing windows and lay peacefully on chopping boards and table-tops, touching lines of pans and knives and ladles as if ticking them off on some benevolent register. It was usually the only time of day when Laurence had any hope of remembering why he had devoted his life to this, and not to architecture or designing furniture or roaming round the Southern Hemisphere in a vagabond manner you could only afford to despise in later life if you had never done it.

He had a desk in the corner of the kitchen, a simple deal desk that had once been an Edwardian washstand, on which he kept a pot of lemon verbena to pinch for its fragrance while he organised menus and did, with much reluctance, the kitchen accounts. He drew a lot while he thought, doodling drawings with balloons of thought drifting out of people's heads, and played with a string of worry beads he had bought once in the harbour at Piraeus, on a brief holiday with Hilary, made of rough blue glass beads with little watchful black-and-white eyes set in each one. There was a grey marble egg too, and a wooden acorn which unscrewed to reveal a smaller one, turned from a different wood, and a red-painted clay dragon made by Gus at primary school, and then, in a row, his notebooks, battered, thumbed, scruffy with use and scribbles, the notebooks he had started when he had first said to Hilary, pregnant with George and not in the least responsive to much independence on Laurence's part, that he was going to learn to cook.

"Where will you learn?" Hilary had said, rubbing her spectacles clean on the hem of her red-drill maternity smock.

"Here," he said. "By myself."

He'd bought books, books by food scientists and food psychologists as well as books by cooks. He'd made endless lists of sensual responses to food. " 'Smell,' " his first notebook started. " 'Seven main responses. Flowery, peppermint, burnt, rotting, spicy, resinous and citrus.' *Pears Encyclopedia 1924.*" He'd bought seven knives and practised until he reckoned that with herbs and garlic at least he could get in five or six chops a second. He bought utensils in cast iron and stainless steel and copper and bamboo and china and glass and lectured Hilary on the difference between salting and brining, and marinading and macerating, while presenting her, at the most impossible times of day, with spoonfuls of bone broth or stewed venison or lemon chutney on which he demanded her immediate opinion. He read Eliza Acton and M.F.K. Fisher and Elizabeth David and Jane Grigson, covering the pages with fervent exclamations in soft black pencil, and when Adam was born he'd arrived at Whittingbourne Hospital not with flowers or champagne or the string of garnets Hilary had rather pointedly admired in a jeweller's window in the market place, but with a cake, a vast, soft, bread-like cake of his own invention full of Maraschino-soaked cherries with Adam's name written across the top in curls of crystallised orange peel.

He had loved those years. He had felt like an alchemist, and sometimes a sorcerer, and the kitchen was all at once a temple and a laboratory and an engine room. He was perfectly happy to let Hilary do what she wanted to the hotel and, in large measure, to the boys, who learned, very early, that if he was in the kitchen, their father was impenetrably preoccupied. The change came inevitably, with expansion. The hotel grew from seven bedrooms to twelve and the first of a series of Steves and Kevins had come, fresh from technical colleges, clutching their City and Guild qualifications, to do things in the kitchen at Laurence's instruction but never, quite, to his satisfaction. They joked and smoked and played football with empty Coca-Cola tins and, quite without intending to, took away the privacy and intensity of the kitchen as well as some of its magic. After six months, most of them drifted on, certain, out of some herd instinct, as George had been, that life, whatever it was, was not to be found in Whittingbourne but only in Birmingham or London. Then Laurence had to start all over again with two new ones, two new Steves and Kevins, taught by colleges to thicken sauces with flour and to cater, rather than to cook. Most of them told Laurence they'd chosen catering because there was always work in catering; however bad a recession, people had to eat.

In a long procession of them, Laurence thought, and not without a good deal of self-reproach, there had only been a handful who had worked with both comprehension and curiosity, one of them—a boy from a home, Laurence suspected, where the only cooking utensil was a frying pan—going off to learn French in evening classes. But most were simply getting by, chopping and boning and stirring, unable to see, despite Laurence's exhortation, that there was a difference between cooking, and just getting meals.

Sitting at his desk in the kitchen during the afternoon lull, Laurence had an intermittent nagging feeling that he, too, was inclined merely to get meals too often these days. He felt sometimes as he supposed inspired teachers to feel when promoted, because of unquestioned ability, to a headship where the teaching role had to bow before the infinitely less satisfying administrating, fund-raising, business-running ones. When the hotel expanded, it inevitably changed its character and became not merely a larger version of the same thing, but another thing altogether.

Yet he and Hilary were the same. They had allowed their life to change with the hotel but had not similarly allowed for themselves to change. Hilary had always been adamant that the hotel was a family hotel, a place that was the boys' home quite as much as it was a public business. She had always refused managers. Managers, she said, made hotels impersonal and injected another flavour, which might not be the flavour of the Wood family, which was, for better or worse, the essence of The Bee House. Yet there was too much for Hilary to do now, and inevitably, some of the things she had to do seeped over into his territory and troubled it. She had said several times recently that she envied him the completeness of his creative kingdom in the kitchen. Any minute now, she was going to sharpen that remark up and say, "It's all very well for *you.*"

Sometimes, Laurence wondered if she ever thought about her early ambitions. Did she regret not being a doctor? There was a time, a few years ago, when he could have asked her, quite easily, but now he discovered that he did not very much want to hear her reply. Obscurely, but unmistakably, he felt that she was subconsciously making a list of things to hold against him—The Bee House, Whittingbourne, his role as chef. And Gina: Gina

101

who had turned from a joint friend, it seemed, into Laurence's responsibility.

"She's your friend," Hilary had said childishly.

"Ours," he'd said.

"I didn't choose her. You did. I just took her on, for you."

I didn't choose her either, Laurence thought, crushing a verbena leaf; she just happened, exactly as I happened to her. It was a chance collision, as Hilary was later. I was never in love with Gina but I loved her at once because she was so pretty and neat, like a perfect little fruit with her glossy hair and clear skin and even teeth, and then I loved her because she was full of spirit and enquiry and used her imagination. She was going to learn languages and travel and I had visions of her eagerly devouring oceans and continents, always interested, always smiling. She once said to me she thought education was having lots and lots of doors open to you, with prospects visible through each one, and that you were beholden to yourself to go through as many as possible. But then she met Fergus. Perhaps she thought he was another open door. Perhaps, in a way, he was, except that he seemed to slam shut once she was through, and then he knocked her off balance. He only seemed able to keep his own balance, somehow, as long as she never kept hers; he depended upon destroying her equilibrium. Poor Gina, poor puzzled Gina, always struggling up the mountain and getting knocked off just as her fingers grasped the topmost ledge. And the worst of it is that Fergus didn't mean to. He just needed to; so he did.

Laurence looked down at his menu sheet. "Tapenade," he had written. "Grilled goat's cheese. Ceviche of scallops." Above him, in the reception area, which the crazy floor-levels of The Bee House made almost six feet higher than the kitchen, the telephone shrilled and shrilled. It was snatched up. Hilary perhaps, or Don. A car drove past the kitchen window towards the little residents' car-park behind the garden, so little that it induced terrible competitiveness among residents, some of whom had been known to come back early, even on a sunny day, just to be sure of a space. The back door opened, and Kevin came in wearing a red baseball cap, back to front, carrying a rolled-up copy of the *Whittingbourne Evening Echo*.

"Hello," Laurence said, without enthusiasm.

"Hi," Kevin said. He slammed the door and the kitchen jerked out of slumber. "We're gonna have a by-pass," he said. "And a DIY mega-store. Says so in the *Echo*. Great, innit?"

"Can I smoke in here?"

"No," Sophy said.

She was sitting at the work table in her top-floor bedroom, underneath the dormer window that looked down into the little medieval garden that Fergus had made. Her head was

103

bent in fierce concentration over a sheet of paper and her hair fell forward in a ragged curtain and obscured what she was doing.

"Oh, go on," Gus said.

He was lying on her bed, holding a green plush hippopotamus on his chest. The hippo had been a birthday present, when Sophy was seven, from Vi, who perfectly understood her craving for it, with its pink felt nose and whimsical, downcast, brown-and-white felt eyes.

"No," Sophy said. "It's my bedroom and what I say goes here and I say no."

Gus had brought Sophy more flowers, three pink roses, a small cloud of gypsophila and two sprigs of grey-green eucalyptus leaves. He'd chosen them with great care and Sophy had seemed quite pleased and had put them in a black glass vase on her work table.

"Soph—"

"Mmm?"

"What'you doing?"

"Writing."

Gus pressed his nose to the hippo's nose. "What? What are you writing?"

Sophy turned round in her chair.

"I'm writing down some of my feelings."

"Wow," Gus said. "Cool." He put the hippo on his stomach and propped himself on his elbows. "Adam's got some stuff. Rave stuff. He bought it from Kev."

"Adam," Sophy said primly, "is a fool."

"Don't you want to try it?"

"No."

He sat up further.

"You in a temper?"

"No," Sophy said. "At least, not especially with you."

Gus grinned. He threw the hippo in the air a few times. It was nice to lie where Sophy lay every night. She wore big T-shirts in bed, he knew that, extra-large men's ones. There was one hanging on the back of the door, dark green, with some writing on it in white he couldn't read. He rather wanted to say that he found the atmosphere in High Place a distinct improvement since Sophy's father went, but he sensed that this would not be a popular remark, so instead he said, "Your mum OK?"

Sophy turned back to her sheet of paper.

"I think so. She's going to see a counsellor. Your father told her to."

"Weird," Gus said. He looked round Sophy's room. It was white and blue and although it was very full of things, they were orderly and it looked as if you could find anything you wanted, any time. But it was somehow a lonely room, for all the books and pictures and ornaments and cushions, a room that only one person was ever in.

"You seen Maggie?"

"No," Sophy said, writing.

"Nor Paula?"

"No. I don't see them much, when it isn't term time."

Gus said suddenly, swinging his feet to the floor, "Soph, you need *friends*."

105

She said nothing but bent her head further over the paper.

"Soph—"

"I can't," she said tightly, "think about anything like that just now."

He stood up. He gave the hippo one last grin and chucked it onto the bed, where it lay, upside down, exposing a cream plush belly.

"I'm off."

"OK," Sophy said. "Thanks for the flowers."

"George'll be home soon."

"Will he?"

"Yeah. Chucking the course."

Sophy raised her head and looked out of the window.

"Everyone does that. Don't they? They don't like something, so they just chuck. It's—" She broke off. Gus waited for her to finish, standing by the door, fingering her nightshirt, but she didn't. She simply bent her head again and started to write at a furious pace.

"So long," Gus said.

He went downstairs, very carefully. Despite the traffic outside beyond the high wall, the house felt very quiet, unnaturally quiet. The carpet on the stairs was thick and clean and new-looking and all the white doors on the landing were shut. He rather hoped he wouldn't meet Gina because ordinary conversation—like "Hi"—was not somehow appropriate just now and any other kind of conversation he felt way beyond him. It was different with Sophy because, even when she was cross, he wanted

106

her to be a) with him and b) moderately happy. In that order. But Gina was a mum. Making a mum happy seemed to Gus an impenetrable and incomprehensible business; bad enough with your own, totally out of the question with anyone else's. He paused at the foot of the stairs. Gina was on the telephone in the sitting room. He could see her, through the open door, sitting on the floor in a big space of carpet, wearing jeans. Hilary almost never wore jeans. She said having three sons had given her a profound allergy to denim.

"Just to say thank you really," Gina was saying. "I've been three times and I'm beginning to like her. I thought she was repulsively sympathetic at first, but I don't now. I think she's kind and quite removed and professional. And I do feel a bit less helpless—"

Gus swallowed. This was definitely the kind of talk to be avoided, the kind of talk that had gone on in the family kitchen when Gina was staying, all those long three weeks, crying or sleeping all the time she wasn't talking. He edged, like a burglar, along the wall to the kitchen doorway, eeled round it, and fled.

It was raining when Hilary reached the cash-and-carry warehouse car-park, warm, sticky summer rain that made the asphalt surface greasy. She did a little nifty manoeuvring to deprive a man in a van from the last space near the check-out door, and then turned the radio

107

up for a few seconds to drown out his fury. She'd have been just as furious in his place, she reckoned, but only if she were a man. Men were amazingly irrational about anything to do with driving; cars reduced them once more to cavemen, all snarls and clubs and prowess. She got out, locked the car smartly and gave the van driver a wave and a smile.

She didn't mind these visits to the cash-and-carry. It was partly that the shopping, though profoundly utilitarian, was straightforward and manageably packaged, but chiefly, she suspected, because it got her away from the hotel while still being, to comfort her sense of obligation, hotel business. Her sister, Vanessa, had come with her once and been amazed at the world it revealed, a world of monster tins of baked beans, of giant rolls of kitchen paper, of soap-powder boxes as big as paving slabs, of bacon slices apparently packed a pig at a time. Like all Hilary's family, Vanessa had been amazed that this life could really be what Hilary wanted. Laurence was rather a dear, they all agreed, but not really a go-getter. And what of Hilary's brain? And her training? In her family's eyes, a wasted professional training was a sin so black it was hardly to be contemplated.

Hilary fed her plastic membership card into the meter by the entrance and pushed her way through the turnstile. There was music playing, the kind of soft, bland, unmemorable music that is supposed to lure you into believing that household shopping is not a repetitive chore but has instead a warm-hearted glamour all its own. Ahead of her, the neon-lit aisles of the warehouse stretched away, as tall as cathedrals, dwarfing the shoppers and the shopping and patrolled by immense fork-lift trucks, picking packs and bales off the steel shelves as delicately as giraffes picking the topmost leaves off trees.

Hilary had no list. After almost twenty years there was no need: a roll-call of necessities lay in her mind like a card in a card index. She remembered Vanessa being impressed by that, and saying if only she could remember patients' details so precisely, and then there being a little pause while both of them reflected on the contrast in their lives, Vanessa with her orderly practice and manageable hours, Hilary with her ceaseless commitment to something Vanessa could not see as a career but only as an occupation. Hilary had spoken to Vanessa the night before, not for any specific reason except that she had suddenly, and uncharacteristically, wanted to.

Vanessa was married to a solicitor and had two diligent daughters, one a dentist, one training to be an accountant. The dentist was married and it was the trainee accountant, still living at home, who had answered the telephone.

"Oh, Aunt Hilary! How are you? Well, fine, I suppose, except for these exams. I'll swing for myself if I don't pass them, I swear it. No, she's right here, doing the crossword, not busy at all. Sure thing. I'llget her."

"Hilary," Vanessa said, coming on the line, "I will not be misrepresented. I was not doing the crossword, I was composing an enormously strong-minded letter to the *Telegraph* about the scams in medical insurance. What can I do for you?"

"I'm not sure," Hilary said. She visualised her sister in her comfortable Putney sitting room with its bird prints and ample armchairs. "I think I may just need to complain."

"Ah," Vanessa said. "Anything specific?"

Briefly, Hilary had wondered if calling Vanessa was an idiotic thing to do, given Vanessa's forceful practicality. But then, Vanessa was her sister and there was no one else, just now, to say these things to and they needed, Hilary felt violently, to be said.

"Well. Sitting comfortably?"

"No," Vanessa said. "Hang on a tick. There. Fire away."

"The hotel is full and has been for five weeks. Staff problems are pretty grim. George has decided that we were all right in advising him not to go into hotel management and is throwing his course up, after a year. Adam has made no attempt to get a summer job and is driving me mad. I don't like the company he keeps, either. Gus is fourteen, which he can't help, but he just seems to exacerbate the Adam thing. Laurence declines to do anything much about anything except cook and Fergus has left Gina and we've had her here for three weeks until I blew and said she had to go and live her own life, not ours."

"Good Lord!" Vanessa said. "Why did he go? I thought they had the perfect life."

"He's behaved disgustingly. He said she'd changed into someone he couldn't stand. She's devastated and the awful thing is that I'm terribly sorry for her and can't take another minute of her, all at once."

"I see," Vanessa said. "Isn't there another friend who could help?"

"Not really. Not of that closeness. I don't know why. The hotel business is hopeless for making friends; there's no time and you don't seem to meet people in the right way. And Gina and Fergus weren't everyone's cup of tea, always needing to fight in public and the house being too precious to entertain smokers or drinkers in. I suppose I'm just tired."

"Yes," Vanessa said. "You sound it. And Laurence?"

"I told you. Stays in the kitchen. To be honest, it makes me as cross as a bag of cats."

There was a pause. Hilary waited for Vanessa to remind her, in an elder sisterly way, how she, Hilary, had been impatient since childhood and prone to easy exasperation, with plenty of examples of Hilary's behaviour on family holidays or at family Christmases.

Instead, Vanessa said unexpectedly, "A bit of hearty dislike now and then, Hil, doesn't damage real love, you know."

"What!"

"You're having a bad patch. Laurence reacts one way, you another. That's all. He mightn't be mad keen on you just now, either."

"Lord," Hilary said. "Do you talk like this to your footballers?"

"No. We talk about their knees. Their knees are the centre of their world. Your centre is different. Poor old George."

"I know."

"Is Adam doing anything really silly? Drugs?"

"Flirting, I think."

"Nip that one," Vanessa said. "Sharpish."

Hilary gripped the telephone.

"There's always so much, isn't there? For one person."

"That's life, Hil. Let me know if I can do anything about Adam. I know a bit about it from one of the boards I sit on. You don't want to let it get too far, that's the thing."

Hilary thought of the two white tablets she had found wrapped in foil in the pocket of a pair of Adam's jeans, while sorting the laundry. Confronted, he'd said they were just a bit of buzz, party poppers; he'd never taken anything heavy, promise.

"How much did you pay for these?"

"Not much," he'd said, staring at her, but she'd noticed a considerable tenseness in him as he flushed the tablets down the lavatory under her instruction.

"You're a perfect fool," Hilary had said. "A stupid, childish, bloody *fool*. And the only minute thing that redeems you is that I slightly suspect you meant me to find them and get you off the hook. Well, you may be off the legal hook, but you aren't off *mine*."

"Thanks," she said to Vanessa. "Thanks. I'll let you know. And thanks for listening."

There had been another slight pause then and for the second time Hilary had waited for Vanessa to say, predictably, that none of this unsatisfactory problematic complexity would have come about if only Hil-ary had stuck to her proper priorities in the first place. But Vanessa only said, "Ring any time, Hil. I'm always home by six, except Thursdays."

It was the closest, Hilary reflected, dumping a shrink-wrapped twelve-pack of bathroom cleaner in her trolley, that Vanessa had ever come to affection. She had never been affectionate, as a child or an adolescent, nor shared clothes or experiments with hairdye in the bathroom. She was punctilious in doing things for people, in remembering birthdays and hospital visits and good-luck cards for exams, but she didn't want to be thanked for them. Long ago, Laurence and Hilary had speculated with much hilarity on Vanessa's sex life with Max, her solicitor husband, who grew fuchsias in his spare time and was fanatical about maps. Did they do it at all? And if so, how could you manage it with the minimum of touching? By using a chair? Or a stepladder? Or a trapeze? Some of the suggestions had become pretty disgusting, Hilary remembered, adding aluminium foil and a five-gross box of guest soaps to the bathroom cleaner, and they'd laughed themselves sick. A bit sad, now, to think of all that laughing.

She pushed her trolley on down the aisle

towards tissues and lavatory paper. She should have brought Adam with her, to help carry, but she'd left him with the mowing and Gus with the job of neatening the lawn edges with shears. She'd agreed to pay Gus two pounds and Adam two pounds fifty an hour. Was it mad to give Adam any more money, or if she didn't, would he then seek to acquire some by illicit means? She sighed. There was no white lavatory paper, only pastels, the colours of fruit yoghurts. Perhaps green was the most bearable, forty-eight rolls in two bales. And I must do something about Sophy, Hilary thought. I promised her a job this summer and then her wretched father chucked this giant spanner in the works and I clean forgot to do any more about it. Poor Sophy, dripping about that house, with Gina either moping or trotting off to her counsellor. She can help wash up and do the bedrooms a bit, I don't suppose she'll mind what. Poor Sophy, Hilary said again, half aloud and suddenly grateful for Adam's robustness even if it did lead to waywardness, poor little Sophy. Sweet really, and a good girl, but such a drip. She stretched up and retrieved a giant box of scouring pads. It wouldn't be any good, ever, expecting anything dramatic from Sophy.

CHAPTER
7

"It's all right, dear," Dan said. "I'm just a bit tired."

Vi parked a bright-blue jug of orange gladioli on the occasional table in his sitting room.

"Can't think why. You haven't done nothing all morning."

He was sitting in one of his chintz armchairs with a newspaper, neatly folded, on his knee.

"It's the heat. Just seems to flatten me."

"You haven't got a pain?" Vi said, peering at him. "You got a pain you're not telling me about?"

He shook his head, smiling.

"No pain."

"I could bring you a bit of lunch. A slice of pie and a bit of salad—"

He shook his head again.

"No thanks, Vi. It's the heat. Can't fancy anything much but lemonade. How's Sophy?"

Vi sat down opposite him. She was wearing a summer dress patterned with emerald and yellow splashy flowers, and she began to pleat the skirt of it over her knees.

"Not talking."

"Oh dear."

"It's not that I think she should go on and on about it, but I just wish she'd say a bit. About her father. I mean, good or bad, he's her dad and he isn't dead, for heaven's sake."

"Has he been in touch?" Dan said, unfolding the newspaper and then folding it up again exactly as before.

"Gina says he rings every few days, but Sophy won't speak to him. She says she's writing him a letter." Vi snorted. "Letters! Letters are a load of trouble, if you ask me; you can never take nothing back that's in a letter."

"When I was in the Merchant Navy," Dan said, "I lived for letters from Pam. But I dreaded them too because she wasn't much of a handat feelings, wasn't Pam, and sometimes a letter left me feeling worsethan no letter. I thought she was hiding something or leaving something out."

"I wouldn't have been like that," Vi said. "I'd have told you straight."

Dan put a hand out to her. It felt cold.

"I know. I know. But you're a very different kettle of fish, thank God."

"You're cold," Vi said, dropping his hand.

"No—"

"Let's get you in the sun. We'll put you in a chair and I'll get my sewing."

Dan said, "I'm happier here, dear, honest. It's the light. It's a bit bright for me today. And I'm not cold. I'm never cold when you're here."

She looked at him, sitting there so tidily in his pale-green shirt with a paisley-patterned tie and a fawn sleeveless jersey.

"If anything happened to you—"

"It won't," Dan said. "We old sailors are tough as old boots. Pickled in brine. When have you known me to be ill?"

"Always a first time. Did you sleep last night?"

"Like a top," Dan said, too heartily. "Anyway, you asked me that. When you came in with my tea."

Vi giggled.

"Fancy my new nightie?"

He smiled.

"Bit bright—"

It had been fuchsia pink, with white lace round the yoke; a dramatic sight under her mackintosh.

"Oh, you and your bright. Anything other than beige and you put your sunglasses on—"

"I love you," he said.

She was suddenly still. He leaned forward a little.

"I've never loved anyone like I love you. Didn't know I could."

She thought she might cry. She scrabbled about in the sleeve of her dress, hunting for a tissue.

"Oh Dan—"

"You've changed my life," he said. "Brought the sun in. Honest."

She blew her nose fiercely.

"What about you?" he said.

She blew again.

"Same," she said in a hoarse whisper. "Same."

"What a thing," he said. "Us old crocks."
He was smiling at her.

"Doesn't matter—"

"No. 'Course it doesn't. You going to get us some of that lemonade?"

She stood up, creaking a little.

"I'll get my sewing."

He looked up at her, his gaze soft.

"Which sewing?" He knew about everything she made.

"The firescreen. The collage. You know. The Owl and the Pussy Cat."

He smiled at her again, full of contentment.

"You and me, dear," he said. "You and me."

The man from the estate agency said he would be as quick as possible, but he did have to measure up, he was sure Mrs. Bedford could see that. He waved a slim cardboard folder at her.

"I have my instructions, you see."

"From Mr. Bedford."

"Yes."

"It would have been *nice*, wouldn't it," Gina said, knowing she was being unfair, "if Mr. Bedford had had the courtesy to issue his instructions through me?"

The man said nothing. He wore a blue suit and a tie, she noticed, patterned with tiny penguins. He looked deeply uncomfortable. It wasn't his fault, poor fellow, that Fergus, having only once casually mentioned putting the house on the market, should then have the insensitivity to take decisive action without a further word.

"Sorry," Gina said. "Not your fault."

"Not exactly," the man said.

"Would you like coffee?"

"If it's no trouble."

Gina led him into the kitchen. He looked round. She could feel his admiration.

"The cupboards are elm," she said. "And the table is beech, made by a pupil of Ernest Gimson's."

The man wrote down, "Split-level cooker, plumbing for dishwasher, dimmer switches."

"And the floor is Bath stone, waxed. My husband found the flagstones in a house that was being demolished."

"Western aspect," the man wrote. "Fitted cupboards with shelves over. Door to garden."

"Are you going to say something," Gina asked, getting the coffee-filter machine out of a cupboard, and then changing her mind and finding the instant-coffee jar instead, "about how perfectly the house has been restored? Because whatever my private feeling, it has."

The man said, "We will emphasise that it's a very well-maintained period property, of course."

Gina thought, spooning coffee into mugs, that there was a hor-rible satisfaction in hearing High Place described so after all Fergus's dedicated commitment to it. It was somehow proof—and this a small if disagreeable comfort—that Fergus had got his priorities wrong, that no house should take the dedicated consideration that properly belonged to people. She wondered if his new house, his new London house, was getting the same loving, focused interest. He'd bought the house, he said, with a business loan, a big mortgage. When High Place was sold, they'd divide the proceeds, exactly as they had divided the contents.

"Don't go to a lawyer," Fergus had said on the telephone. "Don't start all that. Meddlesome and expensive."

"Why not?"

"There's no point."

"Isn't there?" she said, beginning to shout. "Isn't there? Don't you want a divorce?"

"No," he said, and again, "there's no point. Is there? Not until you want to marry again, I suppose."

"And you?" she yelled. "And you?"

"Oh, I won't marry again," Fergus had said with emphasis. "Not me. Anyway, a divorce would only upset Sophy."

She had banged the receiver down then, and missed the handset, and it went clattering down to the floor on its springing cord while Fergus's voice called for her without much urgency out of the mouthpiece. It was intolerable; he seemed to have trapped her in every way, parcelled up like a fly in a spider's web, with no lever to use on him in retaliation.

"Here," Gina said, holding out the coffee mug. "I'll show you the house."

At the top, outside Sophy's bedroom door, she paused.

"My daughter's room."

The man, coiling up his steel measuring tape, nodded. Gina knocked softly.

"Soph?"

"Yes," Sophy said.

"Can we come in?"

The door opened. Sophy, wearing her Walkman headphones like a hairband, said, "What do you want?"

"This is Mr. —"

"Ellis," the man said. "Mr. Ellis from Barton and Noakes. Estate agents."

Sophy said nothing. She turned away from them both and stared out of the window at the high grey sky.

Mr. Ellis said, making an effort, "Charming room."

"Yes," Gina said.

Sophy said nothing. She was wearing one of her big, gauzy Indian tunic shirts over her jeans and her narrow silhouette was visible through it against the light from the window.

"Mr. Ellis has to measure it, darling," Gina said.

Sophy shrugged. She leaned across her table and drew a magazine very deliberately across the surface to cover a sheet of paper that Gina could see was densely covered with her handwriting.

"Double aspect," Mr. Ellis said. "Very nice."

"Sophy—"

121

"Yes."

"When—when we've sold this house we can go, together, and find another one. Perhaps you could have a whole floor to yourself, not just a room."

"Excuse me," Mr. Ellis said, sliding his tape under Sophy's table to the walls. "Thank you. Twelve foot, ten inches."

Sophy said, without turning, "It's rather difficult to get worked up about another house right now."

Diana Taylor had said to Gina, "Try not to stoke the fires of your resentment. It's so negative. Use your energy to do positive things, things that will take you forward."

Easier said than done. Gina said, too quickly, "It's not my fault we have to, you know."

Sophy whipped round. She glared at Gina, wrenched the earphones off her head and flung them towards the bed. Then, barging past the kneeling Mr. Ellis and Gina, she marched out of the room, and slammed the door. There was a tiny silence. Mr. Ellis retracted his tape, very slowly.

"Sorry," he said.

Gina looked at him. Thirty-two or -three, perhaps, bony, poor skin, unbecoming haircut, caught up in some disconcerting whirlwind while he tried to do as he had been told, and measure a room.

"Me too," she said. "Really."

When Mr. Ellis had gone—"I will have to check with my colleagues, of course, but I think

122

we can estimate an asking price of two hundred and twenty-five thousand pounds—Gina went into the sitting room and sat at her piano. She hadn't touched it for weeks, hadn't even thought about it. There were almost never any pupils in the summer holidays anyway, and the few who had rung in the last weeks she had told, untruthfully, that she was just off on holiday. She played a bar or two of a Mozart Fantasie, a piece much beloved by Grade VI examiners, but there was no heart in it. She couldn't recall, just now, the slightest interest in music nor in those children whom, up to now, it had been her pride to get to such a standard by the time they were thirteen that they didn't *want* to give up. "I want you to get Grade VI," she would say to pupils, "by your tenth birthday. OK? And then by your twenty-first you'll be playing whole Beethoven sonatas."

She sighed and took her hands off the keys, seized by a wave of nostalgia for those now powerfully appealing days of piano lessons, Sophy at school, Fergus at a sale, the ingredients for supper in the fridge....

"Be careful," Diana Taylor had said. "Be honest about the past. Don't put haloes round things just because they're gone. You'll exhaust yourself with regret. And longing. Longing's a killer."

"Can I come in?" Laurence said.

Gina turned round. He was standing in the doorway of the sitting room, dressed in cotton trousers and an open-necked blue shirt with the sleeves rolled up, holding a dish.

"Brought you something."

"Laurence!"

She spun off the piano stool and rushed over to give him a kiss.

"Chinese pancakes," he said. "Purely veggie so Sophy can eat them too." He looked at her. "How are you?"

She took the dish and lifted the covering foil. Six little pale half-moon pancakes lay in a pool of shiny brown sauce.

"How sweet of you."

"Not very. I thought you'd prefer it to flowers, which I remember you saying once you thought outright macabre on the wrong occasion."

She looked up at him, smiling.

"Did I? I was dead right. These look delectable."

"And you look a bit better."

"I think I am."

"That's really what I came to see."

Gina went past him into the kitchen and put the pancake dish into the refrigerator.

"Come into the garden. I'm sick of the house. I've just had an estate agent here, measuring up. It was quite extraordinarily discouraging. Sophy walked out."

"I know. She's at The Bee House."

Gina turned in the doorway.

"Is she?"

"Yes. Hilary's going to give her a job. Always meant to, but somehow the summer has rather overtaken her. It'll give Sophy a month's worth of work before school."

Gina climbed the two shallow steps to the camomile lawn.

"Sophy never said."

"Didn't she? Do you mind?"

"I don't know. We lead such an odd life together, so silent and difficult. She *blames* me, you see. For Fergus going. She thinks that if I'd held back on just one remark or just one tear, he'd have stayed. But I pushed him over the edge."

Laurence sat down on the Gothic wooden bench. "I won't take the seat," Fergus had said, as if making a huge sacrifice. "I long to, but it was made for this garden and here it must stay. Mind it gets its proper price."

"They ought to see each other, Gina. Remind each other of their real selves and not these idealised ones they've made of one another since he left."

"I can't talk to her about it. She won't talk about anything except which kind of soup for supper. And to be honest, I can hardly bear the thought of her seeing him, of her being in his new house and having a life with him, however tiny, that I can't share." She sat down beside Laurence and added, with a sudden fervour, "It *is* so good to see you!"

He said gently, "I didn't mean to be a brute, you know. Throwing you out of The Bee House. It was just a rather bungled attempt at that American thing called tough love."

"You weren't a brute. I was awfully angry with you at the time but I'm not now. And you were dead right. I've got what Mum calls a psycho-shrink. I told you on the phone. She's rather good."

He leaned forward, elbows on knees.

"Describe her."

"Oh, mid-fortyish, reddish curly hair, safe blue and grey clothes, but not like that inside. Rather cool, quite detached. Kind like a teacher or a nurse rather than a friend." She grinned. "I love the talking."

He grinned back, over his shoulder.

"I bet you do."

"And I can be rude if I want to."

"Also true to form."

She nudged him.

"You're a pig."

"A pig who's known you a very long time. And who is deeply relieved to see a glimmer of humour returning. You looked as if you'd been smacked in the face."

She ducked her head. He peered at her.

"Gina."

"Mmm."

"D'you still want him back?"

There was a pause. She laced her fingers together, then unlaced them and put them in the pockets of her cotton jacket. She said, very carefully, as if they were words that were being taken down and might well be used in evidence against her, "Not quite as much. As I did."

Laurence grunted. He stood up.

"Back to the hot stove. Fourteen covers last night, besides the residents."

"How's Hilary?"

Laurence frowned.

"Fed up."

"I'm afraid," Gina said, standing too, "that I really got up her nose."

"No, you didn't. Or at least, if you did, everything else does too. She caught Adam with a couple of Ecstasy tablets and then found twenty Marlboro under Gus's mattress."

"Mum would say bring back National Service."

Laurence smiled.

"Right now, Hilary would agree with her, wholeheartedly." He stooped and kissed her cheek. She smelled as she always had, sharp and citrusy. Hilary smelled warm and dark, of spices. "You take care. I'll be back very soon with more meals to mend a broken heart. Drop in when you're passing."

Gina hesitated. She thought of Hilary, stretching over the laundry basket, briefly warm with relief at her departure.

"When it's less busy—"

"No, any time—"

They smiled at one another.

"You used to say, 'Oh, buzz *off.*' "

"Well, buzz then."

He crossed the little lawn, descended the steps to the wide stone path that circled the house, and made for the gate in the wall to the street. When he reached it, he turned and blew Gina a kiss before unlatching it and vanishing through.

• • • •

On Friday afternoons, Whittingbourne Market only had two clothes stalls; Monday was the day for clothes, stall after stall selling limp, bright tracksuits and T-shirts, flapping from the rails in long rows above thin white cardboard boxes of sneakers, made in Asia, and reeking of rubber. Friday was food day, with a cheese stall and a fish stall, and a stall much beloved by Sophy, selling dried fruit and nuts and pulses, and a hideous butcher's shop, in a high white van, with whole beasts, hacked into great hunks, swinging from hooks in plastic sacks. The men in the shop were red, to match the meat, and they bawled out their prices and bashed at bones with cleavers. Sophy used to go by with her head averted. A boy in her class had a Saturday-morning job in a Whittingbourne butcher's and she used to look at his hands, turning over the pages of his Shakespeare, with a revolted fascination.

"I want you to buy a dark skirt," Hilary had said. "Not dowdy, but decent, and a couple of white blouses. No frills. Don't spend much, as the customers or Kevin will only spill things down you, and bring me the receipts. Try the market first. There's often something all right there among the tat and then we neither of us need get worked up if it gets ruined."

She'd shown Sophy all round the dining room, all the cupboards and shelves where the cutlery and napkins lived, and how the tables were to be laid, green cloth diamond-wise over white, white salt and pepper next to a slim white flower vase. "Never put napkins in the wine glasses. And don't tell them to enjoy their meal or Laurence will strangle you."

After that, she introduced Sophy to Lotte, a Swedish girl who had married a boy from Whittingbourne, and who now cleaned the bedrooms with the help of someone else, called Alma, who had seven grandchildren and a bad back.

"About as reliable as the weather," Hilary said. "But works like a dray horse when she's here."

Lotte had pale-blue eyes and pale-yellow hair drawn back into a fabric-covered elastic band. Her voice was low and flat. She told Sophy she had been born just south of the Arctic Circle, in a place called Boden, and she was never going back, not for a million pounds. She showed Sophy how to make a bed so that the sheets stayed tucked in.

"Some of them leave the bathrooms horrible. And smoke in bed. Smoking in bed is not allowed, but they do it anyway."

In the kitchen, Steve said, "You know me brother."

"Do I?"

"Yeah. Alan. He's your year."

"Alan?"

"Skinny bloke. Big teeth. A right idiot. Alan Munns."

Sophy nodded.

"You'll be washing up here. You and Kev. Kev's a laugh."

"I think I'll be doing a bit of everything," Sophy said. "It depends where Hil—Mrs. Wood—wants me. Or who's got a migraine."

Steve was shaping bread dough into rolls.

"It's not bad here. Old Larry's OK. Got these fancy ideas but he's OK. You living in?"

"Only when I'm waiting in the evening."

Hilary had said she could use the spare room if it got so late she didn't want to walk home. It was only five minutes to High Place, for heaven's sake, but Sophy understood that Hilary was saying she was welcome to stay, if she wanted to, for other reasons, and the walk home could be her cover.

"I'd send a boy with you," Hilary said, "only I don't always have one to hand. So it's better if you have the option."

Sophy was pleased. The spare bedroom at The Bee House had crazy ceilings and an elderly, squashy brass bed with a patchwork cover so old that some of the patches had just quietly frayed away into the backing. She had spent quite a lot of nights in that bed in her life, revelling in its depth and squeaks and in the fact that through the wall, either side of her, a boy lay, Gus and George, snoring under a mound of duvet and discarded clothes. At High Place, she was the only person on the top floor; the only other room was merely a cupboard, for suitcases and the discarded items of her baby- and childhood. She didn't mind being up there alone, but there was definitely a charge in lying, for a change, between two people. Even snoring ones.

The stallholder was a Sikh, his hair entirely covered by his exquisitely wound turban of fine blue cotton.

"Mick Hucknall sweatshirt," he suggested to Sophy. "Simply Red. Lady in Red. Chris de Burgh."

She shook her head. The clothes riffled in the breeze above her, cheap and thin, made in circumstances which, to think about, gave her much the same feelings as the butcher's shop. There had been a Sunday-paper supplement about it with terrible photographs of squalid, ill-lit, unsafe sweatshops full of people working illicitly, for almost no money, fearful and exhausted. She reached up and touched a black skirt.

"Do you have this in a ten? Or maybe an eight—"

He grinned.

"You like me to measure you?"

"No," Sophy said. "I wouldn't. I can tell by looking."

He unhooked the skirt with a long pole and held it out to her. It looked dull and very suitable.

"No slits," Hilary had said. "And no buttons undone and no minis. Sorry, Soph, but there it is. Just like school."

She fingered the skirt. It felt harsh and fragile.

"And two shirts, please. As plain as possible. Size ten too."

He reached up again and unhooked a blouse made of blue-white silky stuff. It was buttoned in black and the buttons were shaped like little stars.

"There," he said. "Eight ninety-nine. Best polyester. Lovely job."

"I think I'd better have a word," Cath Barnett said.

She stood at her sitting-room window in the warden caretaker's flat, and looked out into the courtyard of Orchard Close where Dan's flowers blazed in rows like primary-coloured soldiers.

Doug Barnett was doing his racing selection from the newspaper for the afternoon meeting at Wincanton.

"Aw, don't, Cath. Leave them be."

Cath hesitated.

"I've had some complaints. That's the thing. I mean, she goes over in her nightie about seven and often she doesn't come back for an hour or more."

Doug put an asterisk beside Double Trouble in the three-ten, and Mantra in the three-forty-five.

"Cath. Don't be daft. They're eighty if they're a day. What can they get up to? And if they do, what the hell's it matter, and if they die doing it, it's a great way to go."

"It's not them, Doug. It's the others. Mrs. Hennell's a retired headmistress and Mr. Paget was Town Clerk. They're respectable people, Doug. They've got their standards. They don't like seeing Vi Sitchell traipsing through the

132

garden in her flimflams every morning like a floozie."

Doug grinned.

"Great old flimflams."

"I think I'd better have a word. I really do."

"She'll eat you for supper, Cath. She's got a tongue that'll strip paint if she wants it to."

Cath came away from the window and sat at the table, folding her hands on the seersucker cloth. She looked severely at the newspaper.

"Don't you go mad, now."

"I won't," Doug said. "Two quid each way on two races and a fiver to win on the big one."

"I wonder," Cath said, "if I could talk to Mr. Bradshaw. He's such a lovely old gentleman. I mean, I wonder if she's bothering him? After all, he might think she's an intrusion but has too many manners to say so."

Doug shrugged.

"You could try."

"Can't do any harm. Not if I do it very gently."

She stood up.

"You going down the betting shop?"

He glanced at the clock.

"Ten minutes."

"Get us twenty Silk Cut, would you? I feel I'm going to need a smoke, after this."

Dan ushered Cath Barnett into his sitting room. It was very tidy and dim, with the curtains half pulled. A soprano was singing somewhere, a tune Cath recognised, lilting and romantic, a tune that made you think of crinolines and ballrooms with crystal chandeliers.

"Excuse me," Dan said. He hurried across the room and took the arm off a record on an old-fashioned record player. *Merry Widow*," he said apologetically. "One of my favourites."

"Lovely," Cath said. "How are you bearing up with this heat?"

"Pretty well," Dan said. He indicated a chair. "Please sit down."

"I've come, Mr. Bradshaw," Cath said, settling herself, "about something a bit delicate."

He stared at her. He'd never liked her much, believing her to be one of those people who mean well and are therefore a busybodying load of trouble. He sat gingerly on the edge of a chair opposite.

"Well?"

Cath shifted. She'd always thought him a mild little man, but he didn't seem to be, all of a sudden, either mild or little. But she'd come to do a public service for the residents of Orchard Close, as was her duty, and she must struggle on.

"It's about Mrs. Sitchell, Mr. Bradshaw."

He went very still.

"What about Mrs. Sitchell?"

"I've had some—complaints, you see. From some of the other residents."

"Complaints?" Dan said, his voice rising. "And what would they presume to complain about?"

"Well, it's this. The thing is—and I'm not speaking for myself, Mr. Bradshaw, but for the other residents—that Mrs. Sitchell is causing some offence coming over to your flat every morning in her nightclothes and remaining here for an hour."

Dan stood up unsteadily. He was shaking.

"How dare you—"

Cath rose too. She held out a placatory hand.

"Now, Mr. Bradshaw, don't upset yourself. It was kindly meant. If we live in a happy community like ours, we have, don't we, to—"

"Get out," Dan said. "Get out, you and your dirty mind."

"Mr. Bradshaw—"

"Leave my flat, Mrs. Barnett. Leave my flat and tell all those dirty-minded, foul-mouthed old buggers out there to mind their own bloody business!"

"I'm sorry, Mr. Bradshaw, I'm sorry, I never meant to upset you—"

"Well, you have. I won't have a word breathed against her, do you hear me? Not a word. She's worth a thousand of you or anyone else here. She's got more life and goodness in her little finger than you've got in your whole meddling body. Now, get out and stay out."

When she had gone, he felt his way across the little room to his accustomed chair, and sat down. He was still shaking and he felt sick, sick and strange, as if he couldn't hear quite properly, nor see.

135

Vi, he thought. Oh Vi.

Disgusting woman, disgusting, prying, interfering woman who couldn't see a lovely thing right under her stupid nose. Mucking up something good and right, something *decent*. He'd have cried if he could, but he didn't seem able to do anything much just now, and there was a kind of mist in his mind, a black mist. Then a pain came, very sharp, in his left arm, and his hand went numb.

Oh my God, Dan thought. Oh Vi.

CHAPTER

8

"I'm not sure," Diana Taylor said slowly, "that I buy the woman-as-victim angle." She had given up the table in her interviews with Gina and now sat opposite her, with her writing pad on her knee. "The thing is, victims get so greedy. They allow their needs to develop to such a pitch that they make bottomless demands on other people. They fall in love with themselves."

Gina had her arms up, with her hands locked behind her head.

"Are you talking about me?"

Diana regarded her.

"Do you think that I am?"

"Sometimes," Gina said, unlocking her hands and leaning forward, "I could sock you."

"But do you think that you're a victim?"

"Of course I am! Of course if you live with someone for years who can only exist themselves by undermining the person closest to them, that person becomes a victim whether they like it or not."

"But that person doesn't have to stay a victim. You don't have to *collude* with the victimiser. Now's your chance to stop."

Gina sighed noisily. She ruffled her hair. "How?" she said.

Diana said, "By changing your conversation." She sat very still, feet—in blue suede loafers—together; striped skirt pulled over her knees. "By not referring to yourself as a victim in your own mind. By beginning to see yourself as an individual, not just as someone relative to someone else. Victims have to be the victim of someone, after all, and in your case that someone has gone. Use your maiden name, perhaps? Look for another house. Do things for yourself, little things."

Gina thought about this. She got up and went to the window, which had the same view as the waiting room, of the supermarket roof, and a packed car-park, and a long snake of shopping trolleys, linked by a security chain. She leaned her forehead on the glass.

"What did people do before there were people like you to talk to? People like my mother—"

"Some went to priests, I suppose. Most just got on with it."

"Change my conversation," Gina said

dreamily. "Gina Sitchell. Gina Sitchell, language and piano teacher. As I was."

"No," Diana said, "as you now are."

Gina took her face away from the window. She turned round.

"Why do you say that?"

"Because you must go forward. And you must ask yourself why you do things. If you feel you want to go back, you must ask yourself why and be honest about it."

"Do you do that?"

"Yes."

"Such as?"

"Such as why I'm here talking to you instead of doing what my husband would really like me to be doing, which is running the office at the fish farm."

"And?"

"I need to do this," Diana said simply. "I need to try and help other people in order to get my own life in perspective. And now that I'm experienced, I'm interested, so I'm hooked. And I don't want to be part of the fish farm. I don't like it."

Gina leaned on the back of the chair she had been sitting in, with crossed arms, her silver bracelets chinking slightly.

"Do you feel guilty about that?"

"No. Not now. I did, but that may have been because he quite wished me to. Or it may have been because I wanted to *want* to do everything and didn't wish to face the fact that I couldn't, that no one can. But the fish farm is his choice. Being here with you is mine. Now *you* have to choose."

"I think," Gina said, "I've rather forgotten how. I've got so used to reacting, I've rather lost the art of acting. I'm doing it to Sophy now, just tiptoeing round her feelings and moods, until I truly don't know if I'm being respectful or plain wet."

"Talk to her."

"I can't. I mean, she won't. Perfectly polite but not an atom of communication."

"Keep trying."

Gina came round the chair and sat down again, as physically composed, Diana thought, as a cat or a dancer.

"I don't want to hear, you see, how much she loves her father. I can hardly bear even to think about it. And I'm afraid she might, for reasons of her own, want to tell me about it in great detail and with great emphasis."

There was a small silence. In it Diana wrote something down, quickly, on the pad on her knee, and then she said, in her cool voice that had no persistence in it but which always seemed nonetheless to require an answer, "Why?"

Gina said nothing.

"Why? Why can't you bear to hear how much Sophy loves her father?"

"In case—"

"In case what?"

"In case," Gina said, her head bent, pushing up the sleeves of her cream cotton jersey, "in case it turns out that she loves him more than she loves me. And—and because that love will be returned. He loves *her* more than he loves me. Probably has ever loved me. Because," she said, suddenly gathering speed and energy, "because I absolutely don't want evidence that I'm the loser in all this, the one who is only ever loved, if at all, as second best. I don't want to be loved on *sufferance*."

"What do you want, then?"

"To be loved. For myself. Warts and all. Is that so very much to ask?"

Diana gave her wristwatch a fleeting glance.

"No. No, that's what we all want, men, women and children, whatever we may say. I suggest you make that part of your new conversation. I think love is a very good place to start." She smiled at Gina, the smile that indicated the end of the hour. "I'll see you on Tuesday."

There was no one at home when Gina got back to High Place except the budgie, whom Sophy had brought back from Orchard Close and hung in his accustomed window where he skulked, deprived of Vi's company and non-stop Radio 2. Sophy was at The Bee House, serving lunches, dressed in clothes from the market that managed to make her look utterly ordinary.

"But I'm supposed to look ordinary. Waitresses aren't competition, they're supposed to be completely background. People are

140

meant to look at their food, not at me, or Laurence will get in a temper."

"Laurence never gets in a temper," Gina said. "Or at least he never used to."

"Well, he does now," Sophy said rudely, slamming the fridge door on her deliberately, separately chosen shelf of vegetarian food. "Hilary says so and she knows better than you."

Gina opened the fridge now and looked inside. She wasn't achingly hungry but she felt that food would somehow make her feel comforted, less restless. There was Sophy's pallid slab of tofu, some plastic bags of vegetables, a carton of designer soup—spinach with nutmeg—and various ends of things, cheese, a bit of salami, half a can of beans, a couple of spoonfuls of hummus in a plastic pot. It all looked sensible and deeply unappetising, like the cold buffets in department-store restaurants, where everything in the end, all twenty or thirty things on offer, tastes exactly the same, of cheap dressing with too much vinegar in it. Gina shut the fridge. She would make toast, like Hilary's boys did, the ultimate comfort food, and eat it with butter and jam spread very generously indeed. "Do things for yourself," Diana had said. "Little things. Choose." Well, she was choosing. Toast and jam instead of hummus with carrot sticks and cucumber slices. Not exactly an earth-shattering choice, but one had to start somewhere.

She dropped two slices of bread—brown, seeded, bought firmly by Sophy from the baker in the market place where Fergus had always insisted it be bought—into the toaster, and pressed the switch. The telephone rang. She went across the kitchen with a light step. It would be Laurence, she just knew it, ringing as he did every few days, just to check that she wasn't backsliding, his voice warm and full of friendship.

"Hello," she said, smiling into the receiver.

"Come quick," Vi said. "Gina, come *quick*. Dan's in hospital."

"What—"

"He had a heart attack. An hour ago. I've been trying to get you, trying and trying. I found him in his chair, just sitting there, couldn't remember nothing. They wouldn't let me go in the ambulance. Next of kin only, they said. I want you to take me there. I'd walk, I could walk easy, but I want you to come with me. I want you to speak to the doctors."

"Oh Mum, of course I will, of course—"

"Quick," Vi said. Her voice sounded unsteady and suddenly old. "Quick, Gina. He'll be waiting. Every sound that passes, he'll be wondering where I am."

Dan lay in a high, narrow bed in a curtained cubicle. He seemed to be in pyjamas he didn't recognise and his left arm and side were all wired up to some contraption that looked like the Roland Emmett inventions in *Chitty Chitty Bang Bang*. He'd loved that film, gone three times. It had been a happy film, that was the thing, happy and mad. Pam didn't like it, though. She only liked love stories, American love stories, preferably with Fred Astaire, but then Pam had had no sense of humour really, and especially no sense of the ridiculous. When he laughed at things in life, she used to look at him without much affection and say, "You're cuckoo."

He felt odd and weary now, but the pain had gone and he could see a bit better even though his breathing didn't feel too good. He couldn't remember how they'd got him here, or on to this bed or into these pyjamas. He didn't like to think of strange people putting him into pyjamas, seeing him naked. Last time that had happened had been at sea, years and years ago, when he got dead drunk one night in Port Elizabeth and his shipmates, the other engine-room ratings, had carried him back on board like a sack of swedes. That was different, though, all men together and a bit of a lark. And he didn't mind people seeing him naked years ago—at least, not so much. He'd fitted his skin better then, he'd had a muscle or two. He'd given Vi a photograph of himself in uniform on the deck of the *Clan Ramsay*, hair slicked back with Brylcreem, shoulders square.

"Well," Vi had said. "You were a right little popsy, weren't you?"

Where was Vi? He wished she'd come. Two young men had been, one white, one Asian, doctors, he supposed, quite nice and polite but remote and official. They'd looked at all this tackle he was tied up to but not much at him and muttered things to each other about aortic incompetence and degeneration of the heart. He was in a big ward, he thought, and he could hear old men coughing and snuffling beyond his curtains and the sound of a television set somewhere and rubber-wheeled trolleys being pushed about. He didn't want to be here. He didn't want to be in this big, strange room full of sickness and old men, helplessly shackled to all these tubes and pumps. He wanted to be at home, in his own bed with his own privacy and his own dignity. And he wanted Vi. Above all else, he wanted Vi. Where was she?

It took ages to settle Vi. Gina had gone across to the Barnetts' flat and got them out of bed in search of some brandy or sherry.

"It's to put in some hot milk for her. I'm really sorry, but the pubs are shut—"

Doug Barnett produced an inch of Tia Maria in the bottom of a bottle. He was apologetic about that, an apology rendered more heartfelt by being seen by Gina in the worn-out mustard-yellow towelling dressing gown Cath had long since decreed only fit for the dustbin. It wasn't even clean. Doug clutched it round him, to hide the vest underneath, and grinned at Gina, thanking God she'd caught him just before he took his teeth out for the night.

Vi lay in bed in her fuchsia-pink nightgown. She still had her earrings on, and all her rings, and she was tearful and fretful.

"Filthy," she said, pushing away the mug of milk. "Whatever did you put in it? Paint stripper?"

"Tia Maria."

"Can't abide Tia Maria," Vi said. "Can't *stand* it."

She humped over on her side.

"Them bloody doctors."

Gina said nothing. The doctors had been quite helpful really, saying that it was Dan's age on top of an aortic weakness caused by rheumatic fever in childhood, but that it needn't be fatal. He might become rather excitable and have some breathing problems, but a quiet life should help, no need to despair. Vi had been rude in reply. She'd been crying a good deal and her make-up was a bit smudged and she told the doctors they were too young to know what they were talking about and no one could get better in a madhouse like this anyway. Gina had tried to shush her, but she only said it again, louder, and the young doctors looked very much as if they'd heard it all before.

"Don't you shush me," Vi said then, too loudly in the middle of the ward, turning on Gina. "Don't you shush me, madam! You've got no right to shush me at a time like this!"

Dan had had tears in his eyes when they'd appeared. Gina had left Vi and him together for a while and toured the shiny-floored corridors, looking into day rooms where invalids sat in the vulnerability of their nightclothes, holding cups of tea and staring at blaring televisions. After an hour, a sister had said that Dan must sleep, and Gina had had to take Vi away, holding her by the hand like a recalcitrant child. Vi wanted somebody to blame, somebody to punish. She started on the nurses as Gina towed her out of the ward, then she had a go at two passing porters with a stretcher trolley on which a young man lay, chalk white, with his eyes closed, and then focused on Gina.

"It's not my fault," Gina said, over and over again. "I'm as upset as you are. I love Dan too, remember."

"Love!" Vi snorted, trying to tug her hand free. "Love! What do you know about love, except how to love yourself, I'd like to know?"

Gina made her scrambled eggs on toast, but she wouldn't eat them. She said the eggs were too set. Gina offered to make some more but she flared up at the wastefulness of the suggestion and then scraped her plate ostentatiously into the kitchen wastebin. It was an interminable evening. Vi rang the hospital constantly, demanding to know how Dan was. He was asleep, the ward sister said, he would probably now sleep till morning, they'd given him a little sedative. Don't ring again till the morning, Mrs. Sitchell, don't worry yourself, he's fine, you get a good night's sleep.

"Cow," Vi said, crashing down the phone.

"Why don't you believe her?" Gina said. "Why don't you believe what she says about Dan and go to bed? She's the professional, she's on the spot. She knows."

"He hates it in there!" Vi shouted. "Can't you see? He hates it. It humiliates him among all those ga-ga old wrecks. Why should he be there? Why should he have to stay there and be treated like a baby? 'Dan, darling,' that nurse called him. Could have sloshed her, patronising madam. I'll look after him, I will! Let him come home where he belongs and I'll look after him!"

Gina got her finally into the bath and then to bed.

"I'm not taking me jewellery off. I'm not. S'pose I have to go round there in the middle of the night?"

"Would you like me to stay? I easily can—"

Vi glared.

"I see. First Dan's not competent to do what he wants, now I'm not. I've got a perfectly good telephone, haven't I? You take that filthy drink away and you scarper. I'll ring you in the morning."

Gina stooped over her. She smelled of distress and Red Roses dusting powder.

"I wish you'd let me stay, I don't want you to be by yourself—"

Vi closed her eyes.

"But I do."

"You promise you'll ring—"

Vi nodded. Beside her bed, in the clutter of nail-varnish bottles, portable radio, embroidery things and bags of sweets, was a photograph of Dan, taken perhaps two years ago, jaunty in a summer linen jacket. Behind it was a bigger frame, a double one, with a picture of Gina and Sophy taken in the garden at High Place. Both of them wore big smiles and big straw hats. There was no photograph of Fergus. Gina kissed Vi's cheek.

"Try and sleep."

Vi grunted.

"He'll be home soon. Promise."

Outside, in Orchard Street, the air, after the hospital and Vi's little house, smelled wonderful. Gina stood for a moment, in the quiet, glimmering summer darkness, and breathed it in. She had telephoned Sophy earlier in the evening, to explain where she was, and about Dan, and Sophy had asked if she could go and see him.

"I don't think so. Not until tomorrow."

"Gran, then. I'll come round to Gran's."

"I'm going to try and settle her," Gina said. "She's awfully angry and confused. Perhaps it would be better to wait till the morning. Till she's had some sleep, till the shock's worn off a bit."

"In that case," Sophy said, sounding cold and cross, "if I'm not allowed to see *anyone,* I'll go to the cinema. With George."

"Darling, I'm not trying to stop you, I'm only thinking of them, I'm just—"

"Don't worry," Sophy said in the same voice, "I'll go to the cinema. And I'll probably sleep here." She put the telephone down then.

"Is that Sophy?" Vi had said.

"Yes—"

"Is she coming? Is she coming round?"

Gina fought the desire to defend herself by saying Sophy was going to the cinema, won and said not, actually, until the morning.

"What'd you tell her?" Vi said, sharp with suspicion.

Gina turned her face up to the sky. It was deep, gauzy blue and scattered with stars. She never knew what they were, had never learned despite Fergus's fascination with the constellations. She felt absolutely drained and yet restless, and the thought of going back to High Place and letting herself into its quiet, clean, empty spaces was tremendously unappealing.

"Drop in when you're passing," Laurence had said. "Any time."

She peered at her wristwatch, its dial glowing in the faint light like a tiny echoing moon. Half-past eleven. Was that any time? And what about Hilary, severe with fatigue at the end of another long day...Perhaps she would just walk past The Bee House, and look in and see if there were still any signs of life, lights on, people in the bar spinning out their last drinks while Don polished glasses and beer taps with meaningful finality. If there was a glimmer of life, she would venture in; if there wasn't, she would go home and finish making the toast she had embarked upon nine hours before.

From the street, only one light shone on the ground floor, the spotlight above the bar which illuminated a painting a guest had once done, a not very good water-colour of The Bee House garden showing the long wall—all out of perspective—with the bee boles set in it and darkly shadowed. Gina peered in. The tables were cleared, the bar grilles were down and a black plastic bag of rubbish sagged by the door down to the kitchen, waiting to be taken away in the morning. There was a line of light under the door to the kitchen. Gina went round into the yard at the side of the building and saw that some of the kitchen lights were on, throwing great oblongs of pale colour on to the cobbles the Victorians had laid, square and even and blue-grey. She stood outside one of the oblongs of light and looked in.

Laurence and Hilary were in there, sitting either side of the big central table with its battery of knives sunk in slots down the middle. Laurence had a glass of wine in front of him and Hilary a mug of something. Her hands were folded round it and her spectacles were pushed up on top of her head, ruffling her short hair like thick dark feathers. Laurence was still in his chef's apron—he never wore full whites—over his usual clothes. All around them the kitchen lay tidy and quiet, a tray of eggs ready for the morning at Hilary's elbow.

Gina stepped forward to the kitchen door and knocked. There was a sudden little silence and then the sound of a chair being pushed back and Laurence's footsteps.

"Who is it?"

"Me," Gina said. "Gina."

"Good God," Laurence said, throwing the door open. "Are you all right?"

"Yes," she said, blinking at the light. "It's Mum, really. I'm sorry to come so late but it's been a bit of a day and I felt I couldn't go home—"

Hilary got up, settling her red spectacles on her nose. She came forward and gave Gina a quick kiss on the cheek.

"What's up?"

"It's Dan. Poor old Dan. Something to do with his heart. He fainted and Mum found him, pretty groggy and not able to remember anything much. He's in hospital and Mum's in as bad a state about that as she is about him being ill. It's taken me all evening to get her to bed."

Hilary held the kettle up.

"Tea?"

"Or wine," Laurence said. "The end of a very nice bottle of South African Merlot. Poor old Dan. Poor Vi, too."

"It's all right," Gina said, "I'm not staying. I just wanted to see someone, for a moment."

Laurence put his hands on her shoulders and pushed her down into the chair Hilary had occupied.

"Don't talk daft. Of course you're staying, at least long enough to drink a glass of something. We were only having a parental anxiety about George."

"Let's be honest," Hilary said, putting the kettle down. "*I* was. You were just wombling about as usual saying don't bully him, let

151

him decide. But he doesn't know *what* to decide, can't you see? He needs our help, he needs suggestions." She glanced at Gina. "What did they say was the matter?"

Gina said, "Something to do with the aortic valve."

"But he didn't have angina, did he?"

"I don't think so—"

"Odd," Hilary said, and then, in an instructive tone, "It's serious, you know."

Laurence slid a glass of red wine towards Gina.

"Don't," she said. "I've been trying to persuade Mum of the opposite all evening."

"Even only twenty-five years ago," Hilary said, "anyone with aortic disease might be advised not to marry."

"Hil," Laurence said gently, admonishingly.

She gave him a quick look.

"They love each other," Gina said suddenly. "They really do."

"Yes."

"Mum yelled at everyone in the hospital. Then at me. She's *terrified*."

"Of course."

Hilary came forward and leaned on her hands on the table. She yawned.

"So's poor old George in his way. Terrified of not knowing what he wants, of not being anything, becoming anything. I'm really sorry about Dan. And Vi, of course."

"Yes."

"I'm awfully sorry too," Hilary went on, "but

I'm dropping. Quite apart from George, we have some pure horrors in number two, all smarm on the surface, but relentlessly complaining. They're here for a week and nothing's ever right, with all the grizzles wrapped up in 'I do hope it's not too much trouble to change rooms, or pillow, or bath-towel size or bedside-lamp wattage or morning-tea variety.' I'd really rather they were rude." She leaned sideways and put an arm briefly round Gina's shoulders. "I have to go to bed. You stay and talk to Laurence. And try not to worry. Everything will look better in the morning."

"I'm not staying long," Gina said. "Promise. I just needed an interval between Mum and High Place."

Hilary blew them both an approximate kiss, and went out of the kitchen, letting the weighted door swing to behind her. Laurence untied his apron and threw it over a nearby chair. Then he sat down opposite Gina, as he had been sitting opposite Hilary.

"It's pitiful. It's one of the best relationships I know. They just love each other for what they are, not for what they need or want."

"I know."

"Are you jealous?"

Gina turned her glass by its stem.

"Yes. I suppose I am, in a way. I know Mum deserves it after the life she's had, but she's so impossible in so many ways and Dan isn't put off by anything. He just cried when he saw her in the hospital."

Laurence spread his hands out on the table

and looked at them critically, as if they were someone else's hands altogether, and he had been asked to assess them.

"They've got their priorities right." He glanced away from his hands at Gina. "How're you doing?"

She smiled.

"Quite well. Tiny bit better most of the time, except for Sophy, where I haven't even started, being paralysed with terror about getting it wrong and then alienating or damaging her."

"Rather as I feel about George. It's so hard being young now. You'd think having a thousand choices made you free as a bird but in practice it seems to be only alarming and confusing."

Gina said, "He's so sweet."

"George?"

"Yes. George."

Laurence smiled with a deep pleasure.

"Yes, he is, isn't he? Sweet. Probably that's what makes him vulnerable. Adam's much less sweet, and although he makes us furious we don't agonise over him the same way."

"We were like them not very long ago. Don't you remember? Resenting our parents, hating home, determined to do everything in a new, fresh, imaginative way and sure that we could. My counsellor always wants me to look forward, but I think that sometimes you have to look back just to remind yourself where the story began, how things came to be."

"The story—"

"Yes."

She picked her wine glass up and took a swallow. Laurence watched her.

"We've got a story. Haven't we?"

He said nothing.

"I mean," Gina said, "that when I'm desperate, when I don't know where to turn, I come to you. Don't I? Because we go back a long way, because I trust you. I suppose it's an instinct to come to you."

She looked across at him and she smiled.

He said, "You've had such a rough time—"

"I think maybe you're the only person—"

"No."

"You're so kind, Laurence," Gina said. "Such a kind man. You always have been. Kindness is such a lovely quality in a man."

He stood up and looked down at her. She looked back at him.

"Could I ask you something?"

"Anything—"

"Would you—would you hold me? Just for a moment?"

He came round the table, holding his hands out to her. She stood up, ignoring his hands, and put her hands on his shoulders. He looked down at her, at her dark head and brows and lashes, at her arms with the thin silver bracelets, and considered her. He had known her all those years, how she looked, how she thought and felt and behaved, a whole catalogue of facts that you do know, almost by osmosis, about another person over long years, facts that he, Laurence, had known fondly, but unexcitedly, for ever. And as he looked down at her,

155

he felt all those facts that he knew, and all those things he could observe, cohere in his heart most powerfully and mingle with his relief at her appreciation of him and the sheer pleasure of feeling her there in his arms until he could hardly breathe.

"Gina," he said, and his voice was hoarse. "Oh Gina."

He pulled her to him and held her there, his face against her hair, his eyes closed.

"Oh Gina," he said again, and slid his face down to hers to kiss her on the mouth.

CHAPTER
9

"Just go," Adam said. "Just bloody go. We'll cover for you."

Sophy looked at them all.

"I ought—to tell someone. Oughtn't I?"

"No," George said.

Gus, lying across the end of the sagging brass bed, said, "There'll only be hassle."

"You've got every right," Adam said, "haven't you? I mean, he'syour dad."

Sophy had pulled out the hem of her waitress's shirt and was fiddling with it.

"Mum's worried about Gran and Dan, you see, already, and I—"

"She won't know," George said. "She'll think you're here. You're here heaps anyway."

Adam yawned.

"Just do it. Why's it such a big deal anyway?"

"Everything's a big deal in my family," Sophy said automatically. "Always has been. You know that. We have to talk about how we *feel* about things, even about how the washing machine's loaded—"

"No, you don't," Adam said. "Not now your dad's gone."

There was a small silence and then Sophy said savagely, "Shut up about my dad."

"Sorry. I only meant—"

"You don't know him," Sophy said. "No one does."

Gus sat up and looked at her. She'd been in a pretty steadily bad mood for days, all twitchy and silent and difficult the way girls seemed to get. They made it violently plain that something was badly the matter and then wouldn't talk about it. Sophy looked really tired. When she looked like that Gus wanted to buy her flowers or make her one of his Egg Tango Specials, in a bun, with ketchup. He said, awkwardly, because his two brothers were there, "I think you should just do what you want."

Sophy nodded. She tied the two front corners of her shirt hem in a knot, and pulled them tightly in to her waist.

"Go on," Adam said, "go for it. Our mum'll think you're there and your mum'll think you're here and we'll let them both go on thinking it."

Sophy flashed a look at George.

"Will—will you come with me?"

He shook his head.

"Nope."

"But I can't—"

"You *can,*" he said. "You must. This is you and your dad."

"What'll I do if he's got a girlfriend?"

There was a pause. They all considered the idea of Fergus Bedford and a girlfriend, the very word suggesting the kind of airbrushed lovelies who adorned Gus's bedroom walls, advertisements torn from magazines.

"Jeez—"

"Don't think about it, he probably hasn't—"

"I'd die," Sophy said. "I'd just go mad."

Gus slid off the bed, rucking the patchwork spread into deep furrows.

"It's another reason for going, isn't it?" he said. "I mean, just to make sure he hasn't?"

Adam picked up a pillow off the bed and hurled it at him.

"You fuckwit," he said. "You *utter* fuckwit."

Whittingbourne Station was virtually deserted except for a hunched girl in black biting her nails and a neat elderly woman with a labelled suitcase. A dead, mid-afternoon quiet hung over it all and nothing stirred except a sparrow or two, down on the line, busily bobbing and pecking between the rails.

Sophy chose a bench at the opposite end of the platform from the girl and the woman, under a poster for family-excursion railway fares and another for a Tina Turner concert. She was wearing jeans and a white shirt under an indigo linen jacket Fergus had bought her, saying that he did rather crave, sometimes, to see her in something tailored. She'd hardly worn it and the linen still felt smooth and new, crinkling into sharp creases, like paper. It smelled lovely, better than cotton, almost of outdoors, of the fields where the flax had once grown, blue under a blue sky.

On her way to the station, she'd been to see Dan. She wanted to see him anyway, but he was also part of her alibi that she was still in Whittingbourne this afternoon and evening, and not in London, having supper with Fergus. Fergus had been astounded when she rang, then delighted, almost rapturous. He wanted her to come at once, right now, stay the weekend. No, she said, just supper and the night, this time.

"Does Mum know?"

Sophy paused.

"No."

"Should you not tell her?"

"No."

"I would rather you did—"

"*No,*" Sophy said. "Not this time. I don't want to be asked things afterwards. I don't want her—thinking about it."

Dan had been very sleepy. They'd sedated him, because he had become rather wild and excited and full of determination to get out of bed. Vi's sewing bag—red silk, embroidered with dragons, on a wooden handle—hung on the handle of his bedside locker drawer, and there were unmistakable flowers from her, orange and russet, in a moulded glass vase. She was there all day, Dan said drowsily, except for little breaks, stitching and talking and reading to him out of the newspaper.

"She's no reader," he said lovingly. "Hopeless, really. Breaks off halfway through every sentence to comment on what she's reading. Drives me potty."

He looked very small to Sophy, and fragile, lying there so neatly under the unwrinkled bedcover. She couldn't help noticing how well kept he was, nails and hair trimmed, chin smooth, pyjamas clean and buttoned up neatly.

"Did they say when you can come home?"

He rolled his head a little on the pillow.

"No, dear."

She wanted to ask him if he hated it in there, in this room full of beds and old men and the helpless, off-putting noises of illness, but felt she couldn't because even if he did, he had no option but to stay.

"You all right, dear?"

She nodded. It was on the tip of her tongue to tell him where she was going.

"Yes, I'm fine. Hilary's given me a job, waitressing mostly but a bit of cleaning bedrooms and washing up too. I've made forty-two pounds so far."

"Good girl," he said. One hand roved about in search of Sophy's. She took it and it was cold and small. "Good girl. That's the ticket."

"That your granddad?" a nurse said to her, on the way out.

"Sort of—"

"Lovely old gentleman," the nurse said. "Lovely manners."

"Will—" Sophy said, and then stopped.

The nurse began to flick through cards on the ward's reception desk.

"He's doing very nicely," she said. "Slept like a baby last night."

Vi hadn't. Vi had woken Gina and Sophy at two in the morning demanding they all three go to the hospital right now and get some sense out of someone. Gina had gone round to Orchard Close and Sophy had lain awake on the top floor waiting for the sound of her car returning. She must have gone to sleep in the end because she never heard it and in the morning Gina's bedroom door was shut and there was a note on the kitchen table: "Darling, don't wake me. Didn't get in till five. See you later?" "No," Sophy had written at the bottom. "You won't. I'm working tonight. I'll probably stay there." And then, in contrition at the end, "I hope you slept OK."

The train was only half full. Sophy chose a seat opposite a black woman who was asleep and a boy with headphones on, reading a computer magazine. She had her soft straw basket on her lap, in which her sleeping T-shirt and toothbrush lay concealed under her Walkman, a clutter of tapes, her purple canvas purse, and a copy of *Sense and Sensibility* which Fergus had given her and which she had never read. She didn't much feel like reading it now.

"Jane Austen," Fergus had said, giving her the book still in its smooth paper bag from the Whittingbourne Bookshop, "is remarkably good at teenagers. As you will see."

She jerked her head sideways and looked out at the fields they were passing, nondescript fields with the odd despondent animal here and there, and a road beyond and then a cluster of houses and a church tower and behind that another tower, the silver column of a grain-silo. It was impossible to reconcile, somehow, that Fergus could give her a book that he had loved with a kind of teasing intimacy, and then just go, as if the intimacy had meant nothing, had just been a game. George said it wouldn't have been like that. He said that, in order to break up something you couldn't bear any longer, maybe you had to damage something else you really liked a lot merely because the two were associated. He said he felt like that about college. He hated his course and had to leave it but in doing so he'd made things awful in other ways, with his parents, with the lives they led. He'd held Sophy's hand very briefly in the cinema and had then put it firmly and politely back on her knee as if returning a borrowed handkerchief.

"I may not want to do something normal," George said. "I don't know. I may just want to drift. But not here. Not in Whittingbourne.

Not where everyone's expectations are just like everyone else's."

Sophy closed her eyes. While Fergus had been at home, there had been expectations—his, constantly, of himself, of Gina, of Sophy, of the house. Fergus had driven them, goaded even. He had made Sophy feel that there were goals ahead, and treasures and dangers. Particularly the latter. Fergus was not a safe man, not a safe father, not like Laurence. You always knew, Sophy thought, that Laurence would be there, reliable, steadily and quietly working, thinking away as he worked, whereas if you opened a door—correction: *had* opened a door—and found Fergus behind it, it was a surprise and your heart lifted. Nothing could provincialise Fergus. Nothing. That was probably why High Place, bereft of his presence, had lost its air of mystery and power. It was now a lovely old house, a lovely, well-kept old house, but it wasn't the place of Sophy's childhood any more, the place that had to be revered and cherished because of its age and the intensity of its associations, a magic castle. For the first time in her life, Sophy could see what George meant about Whittingbourne, why he wanted to leave. There was no romance to Whittingbourne, no possibility of a life that might pass, and then soar, beyond the limits of the ordinary. Perhaps, Sophy thought, opening her eyes and seeing the backs of suburban terraces slide by, the lines of laundry, the sheds and alleys and yards, her father had felt that and had seen it in Gina too. Perhaps he had really seen the wide blue yonder that George kept hoping he'd see, and known that that was the only air he could breathe.

Outside Holland Park Underground Station there was a flower seller beside a newspaper vendor. Sophy paused. She had a strong and sudden impulse to buy Fergus some flowers accompanied by an equally strong shyness about doing so. If she gave him flowers, that would mean something, wouldn't it, but what? She didn't want it to mean the wrong thing, like I absolutely forgive you, because I absolutely *don't*. She stood for a long time looking at a bucket of tight, improbably perfect little yellow roses, neat as cabbages, imprisoned in tubes of cellophane. Poor things, grown not at all for what they were but only to sell. Above the flowers were several baskets, balanced on brackets, baskets of avocado pears and small melons, neatly striped. She would, she decided, take Fergus an avocado as a kind of compromise—a present but a practical one. Nobody could read anything into an avocado pear.

Fergus had given her directions from the tube station. It was ten minutes' walk, he said, towards Shepherd's Bush, and do look about you, there are some lovely houses. There were trees too, tall, country-sized trees, and a few shops of a sophistication quite dazzling to Sophy, a butcher's she could actually bear to look at, a chemist's with its window full of scent bottles, a French *pâtisserie* with fruit tarts reminding Sophy of those childhood holidays in France, of the white dust roads and the smell of herby hillsides and musty hotel bedrooms and the feel of breakfast bread in her mouth, sopped in milky coffee.

"Keep walking," Fergus had said. "Keep on, due west, counting the streets. There's a pretty square and a good crescent of houses. Then turn right."

The flower seller had given Sophy the avocado pear in a brown paper bag. It also had a label stuck to it saying "Large" in red letters. Sophy peeled off the label and threw it and the bag into a nearby litter bin. Better to give him the pear just as it was, unadorned, shove it into his hand at the moment he bent to kiss her, to help that moment, divert it a little.

There was his house. Sophy stopped on the opposite side of the street and looked at it. It was in a terrace, flat-fronted and three-storeyed, with basement steps and black railings in front and a glossy black door. It was painted white and there were curtains at the windows as if he'd lived there for a very long time, real, heavy curtains with linings. One pair had cords round them, looping them back. Sophy swallowed. The house looked so—so *settled*. There was even a tub of geraniums by the front door, dark-red geraniums with a white eye and trailing leaves, like vines.

She crossed the street very slowly and stood at the foot of the two steps that led to the front door. She could see a little into the main room from here, could see the big looking-glass from the hall at High Place, and a corner of the sofa. Late sunlight was coming into the room from the far end, where there seemed to be another window, giving everything a golden bloom. Even from here, standing a little below on the pavement, and only able to see details and fragments, the house had exactly the kind of assurance High Place had once had. Sophy wondered, briefly and with intensity, if she could bear it.

She reached into her basket and took out the pear. It was faintly warm, and felt friendly. She went up the two steps and looked for a door-bell. It was to the side, made of brass, with Fergus's business card slipped into a tiny frame above it and above that another card, "Anthony Turner: Fine Art Restoration." Who...

The door opened.

"I don't want to startle you," a perfectly strange man said, "but I saw you from the kitchen and I knew you must be Sophy. From your photographs, you see."

Sophy stared. He was short and perhaps in his late twenties or early thirties, with curly dark hair and an easy smile. He was wearing a red shirt, white jeans, and espadrilles.

"I'm Tony Turner," he said, holding his hand out. "Fergus has just gone to get some strawberries."

"Yes," Sophy said. She clutched the pear.

"He'll only be a moment. Come in."

She followed him into the hall. It ran the length of the house and was floored in big black-and-white squares. There were mirrors and a statue. She peered at the statue. It turned out to be the stone girl who had stood all Sophy's life in the tiny Gothic summer house at High Place because, Fergus had explained, she was made of gypsum and, if exposed to the rain, would simply melt, like sugar.

"Hello," Sophy said to the statue, putting a hand on her.

"She's lovely," Tony Turner said. "So discreetly coy."

"She was mine," Sophy said. "Till recently. She was in my garden." She put the avocado back in her basket.

There was a tiny beat.

"Of course," Tony Turner said, and then, in a brisk, hostly voice, "Would you like to see our garden?"

Our? Sophy shook her head. "I think I'll wait for my father."

Tony said patiently, "Your father suggested I show it to you."

"He can," Sophy said, "when he comes."

She was full of rage. She turned away from Tony and went into the room she had seen from the street and held on to the comforting, familiar padded back of the High Place sofa. Her sofa, Fergus's sofa, *their* sofa. Tony watched her for a moment, her narrow back curved over the sofa with the thin braid of hair lying down the centre of it.

"I'll leave you then," he said, "until Fergus comes. You'll see him from here, in the street. He won't be long."

"I'm sorry," Fergus said, "I just had this last-minute impulse about strawberries. I even thought I might meet you, on the way."

He held her against him, still clutching the strawberries, and she could smell their queer, evocative, almost synthetic smell through the paper bag. He felt very familiar, exactly the same shape and density and scent, but he was wearing a new shirt, a dark-green shirt with buttons that looked as if they were made of bone.

"Who's he—"

"Tony? He's my business partner. I couldn't have bought this house without him."

Sophy pulled away.

"He said 'our' garden."

"It is. The house belongs to us both."

She said childishly, "I don't know about him."

Fergus said, "No. But soon you will. He's very nice. He's been restoring things for me for five or six years and then his mother died and left him some money and he invested it in half this."

"Your voice is very *reasonable*," Sophy said crossly.

Fergus took her hand.

"That's to counteract yours, which isn't. Come and see the house. Come and see how many photographs there are of you. Look, there are even two in here."

Sophy turned. There she was, at three and

about seven, in this perfectly strange, weirdly recognisable London drawing room, smiling stupidly away because she didn't know, did she, what was going to happen later.

"The kitchen's in the basement," Fergus said, "with steps up to the garden, then I have the first floor and Tony has the top one because of the stairs and his more youthful legs. We thought we might get a cat."

Sophy said nothing. She went to the far window and looked out. There was a tiny garden, full of plants already, with a round white table and four white chairs standing on a circle of paving stones in the middle. Beyond it was a building like a grand garage.

"That's why we bought the house, you see," Fergus said, coming up behind her. "Workshop for Tony, small warehouse for me. Burglar-alarmed to the hilt, mind you. The alarm cost as much as the building."

Sophy said, not looking at him. "It all looks as if you'd been here for *years.*"

"Of course," he said. "You know me. Houses, the way one lives in them—it's my priority—"

"Oh!" she cried furiously, whirling round on him. "I know *that*! I know that better than anybody, after what you've done!"

He put the strawberries down carefully on a nearby pile of antiques magazines.

"Now, Sophy—"

"Don't *say* that. Don't *speak* to me that way—"

He held up a hand. He said, in a voice of great

steadiness, "Sophy, I explained to you. I explained it all. If you didn't choose to hear or understand what I said, that's up to you. But I did tell you, clearly and plainly, why I had to go, why I absolutely *had* to leave."

She leaned forward, eyes blazing, and hissed at him, "But you weren't free to leave! There was me!"

He said nothing. His expression changed from being certain and almost stern to something much more vulnerable. Seizing her chance, Sophy said in the same furious voice, "You dumped me. All those years you took photographs of me and got my breakfast and told me things and read to me and paid me my pocket money and made me believe I could rely on you and then you just *dumped* me."

He said in anguish, "It wasn't you—"

"Well, it was, in the end, wasn't it? I finish up in the same position whether you meant it to be me or not. And you've left me all your mess, all the psychological muddle and chaos, all the grief and half a home and no future. That's what you've done, haven't you? You've done what you wanted and you've messed everything up for me and left me with Mum. I like Mum, I'm sorry for Mum, but I don't want to have to cope with her as well as everything else. Why should I? Why should I do anything for you after what you've done? You taught us how to live one way, you *insisted* on it, and then you just walked off and told us to get on with it without you. And now you want to show me this house and this Tony person as if it was all normal, as if you hadn't wrecked everything, as if you were *free* to live like this!"

Fergus reached out and tried to take her hands but she twitched them away and put them behind her back.

"Don't."

"I love you," Fergus said. He looked older, suddenly, less confident and stylish in his new green shirt.

"Oh," she said.

"I do. You're probably the only person I have ever loved properly, and always will be. You're in me, like blood or air. I never meant it to be like this, I never thought it would be like this. I'd so hoped you'd see—"

"And if I see, as you put it," Sophy shouted, "that means I have to see Mum as you see her, doesn't it, and how do you expect I live with her if I see her like that?"

Fergus nodded.

"It doesn't stop you using your imagination, Sophy. It doesn't stop you seeing that, given my personality and hers, there was neither growth nor harmony to be had between us."

Below them, in the little garden, Tony Turner emerged from the basement kitchen holding a bottle of wine and a fistful of glasses. He raised his arms to them and gestured with the bottle and glasses, grinning. Fergus put up one hand at the window, in return.

"Can we start this evening again?"

Sophy, for the first time, put her hand up to her blue bead.

"How d'you mean?"

"You've said what you wanted to say and I have taken it very seriously and will continue to do so, but could we now put that aside for an hour or two?"

She put the bead in her mouth.

"OK."

Fergus picked up the strawberries.

"You'll like Tony," he said. "I promise."

They ate supper in the garden by the light of special American candles in glass lamps that kept insects away. The men ate from a white plate of lots of different kinds of salami and Fergus had made Sophy her own little pie of spinach and pine nuts and cream cheese, wrapped in filo pastry. There was a lot of wine, and Italian bread and a salad with rocket leaves in it and afterwards the strawberries, served the American way since Tony was half American, with lemon juice, sugar and sour cream. There was also a lot of talking. Both men talked a good deal, about travel and about incidents—some funny, some shocking—in the antiques world, and they kept involving Sophy and asking her opinion of things.

"She has an extremely good eye," Fergus said. "She was a perfectly appreciative visitor of art galleries when she was four."

"Were you?" said Tony, smiling.

"No option," Sophy said, not smiling back, to show that she had not yet decided that she would—if ever—play their game.

After coffee—made in a real miniature espresso machine—Fergus took Sophy up to the first floor. His bedroom was on the garden side of the house and was full of things that Sophy both wanted to embrace and could hardly bear to look at. Beside his bed was a picture of her taken last Christmas, wearing the hooded jersey Hilary and Laurence had given her, which gave her a mysterious air, like the fugitive heroine of a novel set in the eighteenth century.

Behind his bedroom was a little bathroom, blue-and-white and as tidy as a ship's cabin, and next to that another bedroom, with nothing in it but a bed and a white chair and a delicate old table with a lamp on it and a small gilt-framed mirror on the wall behind.

"This is yours," Fergus said.

"Mine?"

"Your bedroom. I hoped that we could do it up together. That's why it's so bare. I didn't want to start without you."

She looked round the room mutely. It was cool and calm except for the cars going past in the street outside. She thought she might be about to cry, which was far worse than the fury she had felt downstairs three hours ago.

Fergus said with a kind of despair, "Oh Sophy, my dearest Sophy, please *help* me."

She took a step away from him and put her basket down on the pale cover of the bed.

"You shouldn't ask," she said.

"But I have to—"

"You shouldn't ask, when I can't even help myself."

There was a pause.

"No," he said, hardly audible. Then, a little more confidently, "Would you like a bath?"

"Yes, please, but—"

"But what?"

"What about the washing up?"

"We'll do that. Tony and me. That's fine."

"I see."

"Sophy—"

"Yes?"

"If—if you let your anger and resentment just burn higher and higher, we'll never be able to talk."

She turned to face him.

"With you," she said carefully, "I don't think talking has much to do with it. It's what you *do* that's so devastating. First our life together, then breaking up our life together, now this. If you just talked, we'd still all be in one piece."

He looked at her for a long time. Then he stepped forward and took her by the shoulders and kissed her exactly as they came level, his mouth on her forehead.

"Good-night," he said. He sounded infinitely sad. "Good-night, and whatever you may think, I'm glad you're here."

She closed her eyes. "Night," she said, and then she heard him go out and shut the door and go quietly down the stairs, past the drawing room, to the kitchen, to wash up the supper things with Tony Turner.

CHAPTER
10

"Do you remember old Harrison at school? My school. He left me The Bee House—"

" 'Course," Gina said.

She lay against him with her head on his bare shoulder.

"I remember him telling us about kingfishers, the halcyons, whom the Greeks believed built floating nests on the sea in the winter during periods of calm. I can actually remember the Greek. *Alkyon.* Aren't you impressed? And the ancients changed it to suit their fancy of the floating nests to *halkyon* as if from *hals,* the sea, and *kyon,* conceiving."

"So," Gina said. "And?" She felt serene and safe, his arm round her, his skin under her cheek.

"I feel," Laurence said, staring at the ceiling, "as if we have built a nest on the sea in a period of calm. It's as if it was all turbulence and unhappiness and storms and suddenly there's this oasis of calm because we've found the answer."

"Do you really feel that calm?"

"Yes."

She raised herself on one elbow and looked at him, his face lying where Fergus's face used to lie and looking perfectly comfortable there.

"Even with all the secrecy and plans and snatched half-hours?"

"Even with those."

She glanced past him, at the bedside clock that still stood, as Fergus had required it to, at his side of the bed. Twenty past four. Ten more minutes, then Sophy might be back or Hilary begin to think that the shopping expedition—only to buy cheeses, after all, and buckwheat flour—was a bit prolonged.

"I don't," Gina said. "I don't feel calm at all. I feel unbelievably happy, but not calm."

He turned to look at her. He raised one hand and ran a finger down the centre of her face, stopping on her mouth.

"Do you feel guilty?"

"Yes. Don't you?"

He thought.

"Yes. But not very." He turned his face away and looked out of the window. "Hilary and I have—"

"Don't," Gina said quickly.

"Don't what?"

"Don't mention Hilary and you. I can't stand it. *Hilary*—"

"If everything was still good between Hilary and me," Laurence said, "I wouldn't be in bed with you. Nor in love with you—" He paused, and then said, "Except I rather wonder now if I wasn't always in love and was simply too ignorant to recognise it."

Gina smiled. She leaned across and kissed him.

"You must go."

"You taste of plums."

"Better than old ashtray—"

"Why on earth," Laurence said, sitting up slowly and swinging his legs to the floor, "should that be the alternative?"

"Don't know. Just being silly."

He looked back at her.

"I love you."

She nodded.

"Don't keep saying it. You'll wear it out."

He stood up and wound a towel round his waist.

"Daft thing."

"Laurence—"

"Yes?"

"When next?"

He closed his eyes.

"Soon. Very soon. Maybe Thursday."

"In between pâté and lemon tart—"

"Yes," he said, smiling, refusing to rise to it. "Something like that."

She got out of bed and picked up her dressing gown.

"Will you tell Hilary?"

There was a pause.

"Will you?"

"Yes," he said, moving towards the bathroom. "Of course I will. When I know exactly what I'm going to say."

The bathroom door closed. Gina picked up her hairbrush and began to brush vigorously.

"I love straight hair," Laurence had said. "Straight, thick, shiny hair. It's amazingly sexy. What is so sexy about hair?"

Everything is sexy about everything just now, Gina thought, brushing. *Everything.* Can't believe it. Can't believe I could go from feeling so discarded to feeling so desired. Can't believe the transformation, the utter, brilliant, wonderful transformation.

"We just came to this place," Laurence had written to her a day or two earlier, "didn't we? We just followed the map we were given when we were sixteen, and after sending us up mountains and through forests and rivers and jungles, it brought us here. All I wonder is why the hell it didn't do it sooner."

He said he'd felt an obscure relief when Fergus left, and couldn't think why. And what an effort it had been, somehow, to like Fergus, which he had supposed then was because Fergus just wasn't quite his type. And how he'd always felt that Sophy was more than just the child of a friend.

"You see?" he'd said. "Stumbling about with a blindfold on all these years and it never quite occurring to me to untie it."

"But there was Hilary. You fell in love with Hilary."

"Yes. But not to the exclusion of you."

"I wasn't there. I was in Pau."

"Why do you always want to qualify my declarations?"

"Because," she said, "I have to be sure you really mean it. I have to be able to rely on you. I can't face another rejection."

Now, coming out of the bathroom, dressed

and redolent of toothpaste, he said, "Do I look too clean?"

She grinned.

"You certainly smell it."

"I'll go and buy some Gorgonzola. Clasp it in my arms all the way home."

"I can't bear you to go—"

He stood looking at her.

"No."

"I can't believe it was ever easy to say goodbye now. I can't think how we've managed it, all these years—"

"B.L. and A.L. Before Love and After Love."

She pointed at him, meaningfully.

"No going back."

"No. Can't anyway. Hopeless case. Canoe went clean over waterfall, hundreds of feet, no chance of getting back."

"Thank God."

He said, smiling, "What'll you tell your counsellor?"

"Haven't thought. No names, certainly. I have to tell her she's right though, about love."

He leaned forward, still holding her hand, and kissed her mouth.

"Good-bye, sweetheart. Laurence Wood loves Gina Sitchell."

She shut her eyes.

"Now buzz off," she said faintly.

• • • •

From her sitting-room window, Vi watched Adam and Gus Wood weeding Dan's flowerbeds. Hilary had sent them round, saying a bit of community service would do them good, and her good to get them out of her hair for a while.

"The unoccupied male," she said to Vi, "is a complete liability. And unimaginably irritating. I wish I had daughters."

"No, you don't," Vi said. "Sons don't patronise you like daughters do."

They weren't doing the weeding very well, not neatly as Dan would have liked, and every time they pulled up a clump they scattered earth all over the path. She'd have to make them sweep it up later, before she gave them tea and the cake she'd made, coffee cake with chocolate icing and walnuts on the top. Funny things, walnuts, like little brains, somehow. It was nice to have someone to make a cake for these days, with Sophy too busy to come and Dan only pecking at what she took him in hospital, like a poor bird with crumbs. He was shrinking, she was sure of it, just shrinking away there in that hospital. Hospital! Workhouse, more like, all rules and hygienic hard-heartedness and food you wouldn't give a dog. She'd be there now, trying to tempt Dan with some morsel or other, if only he hadn't begged her to get the flowerbeds weeded, said that they were on his mind. She worried badly about what was on his mind; hated to think of him lying there trapped with thoughts he could do nothing about. She leaned forward suddenly and opened the window.

"Watch your great feet!"

Adam looked down at his sneakered feet as if amazed to find he was considered responsible for them.

"What—"

"The lobelias!" Vi shouted. "You're crushing the life out of them!"

Adam moved a foot and looked down at the squashed mat of blue flowers.

"Sorry—"

"What's the point of saying that now?"

He stepped off the flowerbed and came up to the window. He liked Vi. She seemed to him both very real and very straight.

"I'm sorry, Vi. Honest. I never meant it. It's just my feet—"

They both looked down at them.

"So I see."

"I'll get a new plant—"

"No," Vi said, relenting. "Don't bother. They've only got a few weeks in them anyway. You seen Sophy?"

"Not today," Adam said. Last night he and Gus had made an imitation Sophy out of pillows and stuffed her down the brass bed at The Bee House. It looked pretty good, except for being headless. Gus had wished for a wig. No one had asked anything and there had been the useful diversion of an argument between Hilary and Laurence, after which

Laurence had gone out at almost midnight, to walk, he said, and cool off. Adam had been uncertain what the argument had been about except for some rather imprecise accusations of insufficiently shared work and obligations. Hilary had used the word "drudgery" several times. None of it had troubled Adam much but Gus had been pathetic and wanted to go over and over what they had overheard and worry about what it might mean. Adam had tried to silence him with a video but Gus hadn't concentrated, had sat in front of the television twiddling his hair and chewing his cuticles until Adam had lost patience altogether and roared at him, and thrown things. That was when Hilary had come in, saying exasperatedly that she had a headache and please would they turn that racket off, and that Laurence had gone off for a walk.

"Why?" Gus said at once.

"To cool off."

"Why?"

Hilary had not seemed to notice that he was upset.

"Why do you think?" she said. "You heard us—"

She'd then gone to bed and George had come home from wherever he'd been and Gus had made some hot chocolate, and they had all three gone to look at the pillow-Sophy.

"Not bad," George said.

Adam said now, to Vi, "I'll probably see her later. Shall I give her a message?"

Vi sighed. She picked a long scarlet thread

off her white summer cardigan and dropped it out of the window.

"No, dear. Don't bother. I just wanted to know how she was."

"Bit down," Adam said helpfully. "Bit stressed. You know."

"Like everyone," Vi said with meaning. "Just like everyone."

Adam balanced on the balls of his feet, stretching his arms in the air so that his T-shirt rose up above the waistband of his jeans, exposing several inches of greenish-white skin.

" 'Cept me," he said. He gave Vi a smile that hadn't a hint of smugness in it. "I'm OK."

In the store room on the top floor of High Place, Gina finally found what she was looking for. It was a box, a sturdy cardboard box that had once held a dozen bottles of burgundy and now contained all her memorabilia of those years in France, postcards and maps and guidebooks, photographs and restaurant bills and a small white plaster statue of Henri IV, in doublet and hose with rosettes on his shoes, which had been given to her by a grateful student at Pau.

"I might go back to France," she said to Laurence during that lovely, unexpected midnight visit. "I've been thinking about it."

"France?" He sounded startled.

"Well, we can't stay here. Can we? And we could both get work in France. I knew Pau really well."

"You met Fergus there—"

"Would you mind that?"

He screwed his face up.

"I might. I mind just about everything this evening. I can't think what I'd have done if I hadn't had you to come to."

"You've always had *that*—"

They were sitting at the kitchen table. In his cage in the window, Sophy's budgerigar had turned his back on them and was asleep, head under his wing. Laurence reached out for Gina's hand.

"I know. But not like now."

"Nothing's like now. Nothing will be like now ever again nor like it was. That's why I was thinking of Pau."

He kissed her hand.

"I'm too dead beat, sweetheart, to think of anything much, except how much I don't want to go home."

He had finally gone about one. They had stood together in the dark garden for a while, holding one another, and then he had let himself silently out of the gate to the street. Gina had made herself some tea, and resolved, with the easy energy of happiness, to cancel her appointment with Diana Taylor in the morning and go and see Vi, and had then drifted up to bed in a frame of mind she could hardly believe to be hers. Outside her bedroom door, she paused and looked up the steep, short flight of stairs that led to Sophy's room. Sophy...Now there was something in the midst of joy that made her stomach plummet like a runaway lift; the prospect of telling Sophy. Well, she thought, with as much resolution as she could muster, we both have terrible tasks ahead of us. Laurence must tell Hilary and his sons; and I must tell Vi and Sophy.

She carried the wine box out on to the landing and put it down under the skylight. It was lovely to think about Pau again, with its wonderful views to the Pyrenees and its absurd, endearing English legacies, like the hunt and the Cercle Anglais, the English Club with its billiard room and bust of Queen Victoria. She'd been so happy there, lodging in an odd little flat, just off the Boulevard des Pyrénées, teaching in a school in the mornings and giving piano lessons in the afternoons, in a tall, quiet room behind the Place de Verdun, where the light from an inner courtyard came filtered through long, lace curtains and there was a maidenhair fern in a Chinese pot, and on top of the piano and never used by Gina, a metronome fashioned like the Eiffel Tower, made of brass and ebonised wood. She had made friends in Pau, spending weekends exploring the Ossau Valley and the Jurançon vineyards, and it was through one of these friends, an Englishman who still kept the villa his grandfather had built when Pau had been a celebrated Victorian spa, that she had met Fergus. He'd come to value some furniture in the villa and Gina had been asked to dinner and found this tall, fair, good-looking man, standing at the open french windows of the salon and looking out at the garden.

"Look at that," he said to Gina. He was laughing. "It's perfect. There's even a monkey-puzzle, the so-called Chile pine. *Araucaria araucana.* Who but a Victorian would have planted such a thing?"

He had watched her all evening, as if he was fascinated. Gina wrenched open the flaps of the box and peered inside. Perhaps it was better not to think of that evening, because the trouble about things going wrong was that they then soured the memory of things that had gone right before. In any case, she didn't want to think about Fergus in Pau. She wanted to think about herself there again, her rediscovered self in that mountain air, with Laurence either with her or coming soon. On the top of all the things in the box lay a postcard, a distant view of Pau with, behind it, the snow-capped backdrop of the Pyrenees. She turned it over. "You should come," she had written on the left-hand half. "It's wonderful and truly bizarre. Utterly French, but there's a hunt with pink coats. Think about it. Seriously, please. Love Gina." On the right-hand half it said, "Laurence Wood, 17 The Leas, Whittingbourne." She'd never sent it. She'd written it quite regardless, seemingly, of Hilary, and then met Fergus and never sent it. She looked at it with a kind of wonder. It was an omen really, another potent little marker on the map.

Hilary saw a glossy photograph of High Place in Barton and Noakes's window, right in the centre, pride of place. "Unique opportunity," it said underneath, "to purchase a historic-town landmark house. Urgent Interest Recommended." The picture must have been taken by someone who had shinned up a lamp post opposite and perched on the top, with a camera, like a desert saint on a pillar, because the view swooped in over the wall and showed the beautiful old stone porch that was never used and which was only ever seen by passing birds. Hilary went in and was given the particulars, not just a couple of photocopied sheets, but a stiff cream paper folder with the photograph on the front and more photographs inside of the panelled hall and stairs, and the garden, with the Gothic seat. The asking price, Hilary noticed, was two hundred and twenty-five thousand pounds.

The presence of the brochure in her carrier bag, along with Laurence's shoes from the mender's and an enormous quantity of sec-ond-class stamps, gave her an obscure com-fort. It wasn't that she wished Gina any ill—far from it—but there was something faintly unsettling about having Gina around without either husband or proper focus, like a loose horse in the Grand National. She had shown no signs of unpredictability, but Hilary was on the look-out for them and was also conscious that Laurence occasionally took or sent some-thing he had cooked round to High Place, a kindness Hilary couldn't possibly object to— indeed thought was quite right—but somehow couldn't feel entirely relaxed about either.

But if High Place was on the market, perhaps, when it was sold, Gina might decide that the time had come for a clean break and leave Whittingbourne. Conscious of sounding like her sister, Vanessa, Hilary told herself that this would be a good idea. Gina and Fergus were one thing; Gina on her own was quite another. And Sophy had another sixth-form year to go, only, and then she too would no doubt form part of the long line of young trailing off into a future which did look, Hilary had to admit, remarkably uninviting.

At the top of Orchard Street, as if by the power of mental association, Hilary met Gina. Gina had been to see Vi, and had gone with her to the hospital, where Dan had been very sleepy indeed and had hardly seemed to recognise them. Vi had been, uncharacteristically, quite silent and Gina had left her at home afterwards with the greatest misgivings, and only because Vi had demanded to be by herself.

"I've got to confess," Hilary said, her hand on her carrier bag.

"What about?"

"I've got the brochure for High Place in here. Nosy-parker, pure and simple."

Gina said, "It isn't a secret—"

"I suppose not. But perhaps I should have asked you—"

Gina looked up at her.

"No."

"It looks great. Very desirable." She paused and then said, with an affectation of casualness she deplored even as she spoke, "Do you know what you will do when it's sold?"

Gina lifted both hands and ran them through her hair in a slow gesture that echoed Hilary's tone.

"I thought I might go back to France."

"Really? To Montélimar?"

"No. To Pau. I liked Pau."

"You met—"

"I know. But I still liked it. And I could work there. It's still very much an idea, though, so perhaps you won't—"

"No, no. Of course not. How's Vi?"

"Very down. She's terribly worried. Dan isn't getting worse but he isn't getting better either, and I do sympathise with her feelings about the hospital. The staff are really nice but it's the institutional atmosphere that freaks her."

"I sent the boys round to do a bit of weeding. Were they any useat all?"

"Not for the garden," Gina said. "But they were for Mum. Ate a whole cake."

Hilary smiled. A small relief, of which she was not proud but which was warming all the same, spread through her like an unaccustomed mouthful of brandy.

"We'd look after her, you know. If you did go to France—"

Gina looked at her again, hard, and there was a small pause before she said, "That's sweet of you."

Hilary bent a little. Her cheek touched Gina's briefly and she had a breath of scent, lemony and clear.

"Nice to see you," Hilary said, released by her relief. "Take care of yourself."

"Yes," Gina said. Her voice was cool, almost impersonal. "I will."

Later that night, after they had closed the dining room, Laurence went to find Hilary in her office. He merely wished to say that he had left Sophy clearing up the kitchen with Kevin and that he didn't much like the look of her. She was always pale, but tonight she looked haunted as well as pale and he thought Hilary ought to say something to her.

"Hil—"

Hilary was bent over her desk. A half-completed work schedule lay to one side and Hilary was scribbling names and times on a piece of scrap paper, juggling them to fit.

"Yes?"

"I wonder if you'd see if Sophy's OK. Looks a bit off-colour."

"She always looks off-colour."

"More than usual tonight."

Hilary said, without turning, "Why don't *you* ask her if she's all right?"

"I'm not a mother."

She whipped round.

"What's that got to do with it?"

"Suppose it's just that she's having a period. She wouldn't want to tell me that."

Hilary regarded him for a while, sighed, said oh, OK then, in ten minutes, and then pulled something from under the work schedule.

"Look at this."

She held out the brochure of High Place. Laurence nodded.

"Very posh."

"Two hundred and twenty-five thousand. I saw Gina today."

Laurence leaned against the wall in the minute space between desk and door.

"Did you?"

"Yes. Coming away from Vi's. She didn't seem very bothered about having to sell the house."

Pause.

"Didn't she?"

"No. Perhaps she's going off the whole idea of living there, now Fergus has gone. I don't blame her. It's like living in a high-class furniture shop. She talked about going to France."

"Did she?"

"Yes, she did. She said she might go back to Pau." Hilary glanced up at Laurence. "Aren't you interested?"

He moved his shoulders slightly and there was some tiny thing in his movement that made Hilary think, startling herself, he's an attractive man. *Heavens,* he's an attractive man.

She said, quickly, to cover her reaction, "I think it would be a good thing, don't you, if she made a new life, and went to France again?"

He shrugged. His eyes were veiled.

"Maybe—"

"I mean, there's nothing to keep her here now, is there? I said we would look after Vi."

Very slowly, Laurence moved his shoulders from the wall, dislodging a calendar, and, equally slowly, closed the door. Hilary watched him and there was something in the way he was moving, something in the sudden atmosphere in the tiny, cluttered room under its single harsh, shadeless light, that prevented her from uttering a word. She simply watched while he turned from the door and came to lean against the edge of the desk beside her, crumpling the work schedule and overturning a jar of pens. She watched them fall and roll across the desktop, and she let them lie.

"Hilary," he said.

She said nothing. She looked up at him, leaning there beside her, his arms in his familiar blue shirtsleeves folded across his white chef's apron, and couldn't speak.

"I did not intend," Laurence said, "to say what I'm going to say now, but the conversation has taken such a turn that I have to. I wasn't going to say anything now because I wasn't in the least certain about how to say it. But I think that there is no way but plainly. I think there probably is no right moment either." He turned his face a little so that he was looking right down into hers, seriously and steadily, almost, Hilary thought, like a father regarding a child, and then he said, in a voice which matched his expression, "The thing I have to tell you is that I have fallen in love with Gina."

There was a silence. It seemed to Hilary both a long and a very alarming silence and one in which neither of them spoke but simply listened, literally petrified, to the words that hung in the air between them. Then Hilary found her hands were scrabbling at her face, at her spectacles, and tearing them off and hurling them across her littered desk. And then she heard a voice screaming something and it was her own voice, coming from somewhere outside her and filling the little, suffocating room.

"Oh no!" she heard herself crying. "Not that! Oh Laurence, not *that*!"

CHAPTER
11

"Mrs. Hennell sent an African violet," Cath Barnett said. "And Mr. Paget's offered to take over the flowerbeds. For now, anyway."

Doug grunted. He had been to see Dan in hospital twice but he couldn't persuade Cath to go.

"You're not to blame," he said over and over again. "If people are going to have heart attacks, they have them anyhow, even lying in bed without a care in the world."

"Mrs. Sitchell doesn't think that."

"You wouldn't expect her to."

"She's making models of me out of candle wax, I bet you, and putting them in drawers, stuck full of pins."

"Well," Doug said comfortably, stubbing out a cigarette, "we'll soon know that, won't we? When your leg drops off."

Cath went to the window overlooking the courtyard and lifted the net curtain.

"This was such a happy place—"

"Don't get morbid—"

"Oh look," Cath said, "there's that poor child."

Doug lifted his head. Under Cath's upraised arm, he could see Sophy Bedford, dressed in jeans and an immense navy-blue sweatshirt. She'd pinned her hair up and it made her neck look startlingly long.

"Nice to see someone young—"

"I think Mrs. Sitchell's out. At the hospital. I'll go and tell her."

Doug spread out the newspaper at the racing page.

"Bring her back, Cath. Bring her back for a coffee."

He looked down at the paper. There was an evening meeting at York. He'd be glad when the flat season was over and the jumping began again—there was more excitement in jumping. Through the window he could see Cath—heavens, the contrast with Sophy made Cath look a right roly-poly and she shouldn't really wear leggings, not with thighs like those—with her hand on Sophy's shoulder. Sophy was a bit taller than Cath and seemed to be standing rather straighter than usual, with her head up in a way Doug would have called defiant in anyone else. She was smiling at Cath but it was a small smile, a courtesy smile. Pretty girl, Doug thought, or at least very nearly, with her hair piled up like that, all casual and soft. Cath often said she thought Sophy had too much to cope with, for her age, but Doug disagreed. He thought you could never learn too early what a right sod life could be, and how best you could cope with it and stay afloat. Look at him and Cath, all those years and years of no-hope jobs or no jobs at all and dismal council flats or bed-and-breakfast hotels. This was the best job they'd ever had, and the best accommodation, and it had taken them until they were over fifty to get it. At least a girl like Sophy Bedford had started in some style, had never had to share a lavatory with eleven other people or feel that life would never be anything better or more interesting than a long series of wet Monday mornings.

He saw Sophy move away from Cath a little, and Cath's hand fall from her shoulder. Then Cath came back towards him, pulling the edges of her crocheted waistcoat together over her front, as if she knew he'd been looking at her bulges. She'd a pink T-shirt on under it, printed with a huge parrot, a good fifteen inches high. Maybe you shouldn't wear pink over fifty either, nor parrots. Yet Vi Sitchell seemed to get away with it, pink and red and purple, the works. Odd really.

"She wouldn't come," Cath said. "Perfectly polite and all that, but she said she'd got a key and was just going to let herself in and have a bit of a think."

Doug lit another cigarette and inhaled deeply.

"Well, if that's what she wants—"

"She made it very plain," Cath said. "In fact, I've never seen her so decided. She had quite a little air about her."

"Yes," Doug said. "Yes." He looked down at the racing page and bent over the day's hot-tip selection. "Cath—"

"Yes?"

"Cath," he said as casually as he could. "You looked in a mirror lately? A full-length one?"

Gus thought his mother looked terrible. She reminded him a bit of the way Gina had looked when she'd come round the day Sophy's father had said he was going, as if she had heard or seen something so awful she couldn't take it in. She was almost white she was so pale, and her eyes looked as if she hadn't closed them for nights, all dead and empty, and her temper was shocking.

"You OK?" Gus had said, standing in the passage outside his parents' bedroom door with a bowl of cereal. "Mum?" Hilary was making the bed, savagely, as if she wanted to tear the sheets.

"No," she said, her back to him.

He slurped another mouthful and said,

through it, "What's up? Anything I can—"

"I have a headache," Hilary said, her voice full of anger. "And a period, and a hotel full of people I don't care about and a son of fourteen who is dripping milk on the carpet like a two-year-old."

"Sorry," Gus said. He rubbed at the milk-drops with his shoe sole and they turned into a small dark stain.

"Don't do that!"

"Sorry—"

"Get a cloth and wipe it properly, you *stupid* child, or it'll smell!"

"OK, I—"

"Hurry," Hilary said, banging pillows down. "*Hurry.* And use some detergent or something."

Later, meeting him in the corridor behind the bar, she had ruffled his hair.

"Sorry, old boy. End of season, or something."

He nodded. He wanted to put his arms round her, as he did Sophy, for his comfort quite as much—if not more—than their own, but neither Hilary nor Sophy was very easy to touch. Dad was easier, oddly enough, even if he wasn't concentrating. He'd always respond, always put an arm back round you. Hilary looked to Gus as if she badly needed an arm or two but was more than likely to fight it off if she got one.

To his amazement, he was longing for term to start again, almost counting the days. It had been an endless summer and a really, really boring one, and the prospect of school seemed to offer occupation, social life, and a blessed return to normality. Gus loved things to be normal; he loved it as much as Adam detested it. Even when Gus broke the rules, he made sure that they were only the normal rules—such as no smoking—and that he didn't exaggerate his breaking of them. He disliked it if things got out of hand, out of control, and just at the moment he felt that that was exactly what was happening. Everyone in his immediate world seemed to have slipped off their rails, somehow, and be sliding about the place, without guidance. What the situation needed, Gus decided, was for something ordinary to happen again, something ordinary that you just had to do which would make everyone go back to being as they ought to be. School would do that. Two weeks more, and school would normalise life again.

"You at a loose end then?" Don the barman said when Gus offered to sweep out the cellar. "You looking forward to school?"

"Yes," Gus said.

"Blimey," Don said. "Never thought I'd hear a modern kid say that. Never thought it. Sure I shouldn't be calling the men in white coats?"

"I suppose," the young woman said, pausing on the threshold of the dining room in High Place, "this could always be a playroom."

Gina studied her. She wasn't exactly pretty, but she was arresting-looking, with hair cut in a sharply angled bob and black clothes and red lipstick. Her husband was a male equivalent, in sunglasses and a blackT-shirt. They ran a design company.

"There's the children, you see," the woman said. "We have two."

"So far," the man said. He almost winked at Gina, as if boasting.

"Our daughter," Gina said, and then quickly, "*my* daughter, always seemed to play in the kitchen. Under my feet."

The woman grimaced.

"These are boys—"

"I thought boys clung to their mothers even more than girls."

The woman went over to the chimneypiece and studied the stone surround, chin on hand, other hand on elbow, as if looking at a sculpture.

"Not *this* mother—"

"Take no notice," the man said. "She's besotted."

They had come an hour before. Gina had made them coffee and found mineral water for Mrs. Pugh—"Zara," she said when she arrived, holding out a white hand adorned with a silver ring as big as a doorknob, "Zara Pugh"—and escorted them round the house in the half-proud, half-pleading way common to most vendors. They'd looked at everything, every last cupboard and corner, and Mr. Pugh had stood in various rooms, gazing at them with his eyes half-closed as if sizing them up for photographic angles. They were the seventh couple Gina had shown round and, even if mildly ridiculous, easily the most promising.

"Good," Mr. Pugh kept saying approvingly at the carefully recessed electrical sockets and the waxed flagstones in the kitchen. *"Good."* Sometimes he took his dark glasses off for a better look.

Gina kept her eye on him. She didn't want him thinking for one second that she was a poor abandoned woman who might easily be taken advantage of in her weakened state. She had put on a jacket, and gold hoop earrings, to indicate that she was not to be trifled with. As she saw the Pughs in the various rooms, so metropolitan in their black clothes, so exotic and sophisticated for Whittingbourne, she was amazed to discover that she hardly minded. All she could think about was how the money the Pughs would—might—pay her would enable her to make a proper home at last, a home dedicated to herself and her inclinations and her loved ones, and not to some abstract principle of restoration perfection. She was beginning to feel—and this was something she had told Diana Taylor—that Fergus had almost done her a favour.

"Be careful," Diana had said.

"Don't say rebound to me—"

"I must. It isn't to be despised, it's only to be watched."

"But you said anything that made things better for me helped me to bear things—"

"There is no change without sacrifice," Diana said. "That's for sure. Just make perfectly certain you aren't making innocent people make the sacrifice."

"Are these beech?" Mr. Pugh said, laying his hand on the kitchen shelves.

"Elm."

"Elm," he said reverently. He looked round. "No Aga."

"No—"

"We'd have to put one in," Zara said. "I have one in Camden Town. It's my dearest friend." She looked out of the open glass door to the garden. "There's a man in your garden. Did you know?"

Gina hurried over. There on the Gothic bench, his elbows on his knees, staring at nothing much, was Laurence.

"Oh," she said, "that's a friend—"

"Doesn't look too good, does he? Do you think he's OK?"

"I'll see," Gina said, sliding past. "I won't be a moment. Do please go on looking."

She raced up the steps on to the little lawn.

"Laurence—"

He lifted his head. Then he held his hands out to her.

"Are you—"

"No," he said. "I'm not."

She knelt in front of him. He looked as if he hadn't slept for weeks.

"I told Hilary. Late last night. I hadn't meant to, but the conversation took such a turn that it was inevitable. So I told her."

"What did you tell her?"

"That I was in love with you."

"Is that all?"

Laurence stared.

"Isn't that enough?"

Gina glanced over her shoulder. The Pughs were not visible.

"What happened?"

Laurence took his hands gently out of Gina's.

"She was devastated. I—I'd thought she was sick of me. Really sick. But it seems not. It seems that she feels in a rut about everything but that she knows that's what it is and she—" He stopped.

Gina whispered, "Still loves you."

"Yes."

She got off her knees and sat beside him.

"I can't be long. I'm showing people round the house. Have you—"

"What?"

She swallowed. "Come to say that Hilary's feelings change yours?"

He swung to look at her.

"Utterly not."

She held one hand firmly in the other to stop them shaking.

"Thank God."

"Gina. Gina. What the hell do you take me for? I only came because it's my instinct to come to you when something happens as bad as this. I don't expect you to *do* anything. I just need to tell you how awful it was, all night, and how—"

"How what?"

"Guilty I feel. Now."

She put a hand over his.

"I'm so sorry. Really I am."

He pulled a face.

"You don't wish for love, do you? But when it happens, you don't seem to have choices any more."

She said, "I wished for it. I wished for it more than anything."

She glanced at the house again. The Pughs were at her bedroom window, gesturing to one another as if describing how the window might be better dressed.

"I'm so sorry, but I think I'd better go—"

"Of course. I'll come later. This afternoon. At least I don't have to pretend I'm buying pink peppercorns any more. Oh Gina, her *face*—"

"Don't."

"Let me look at yours."

She turned to him. He looked at her for several seconds, very seriously, as if memorising her.

"It's always worse," Gina said, "the first shock. It was with me, when Fergus went. I thought I'd die. Literally."

Laurence stood up.

"I don't know," he said. He squinted up at the sky, where big pale-grey-and-white clouds hung in the blue like balloons. "I don't know. I think I dread the fall-out even more."

Sophy slept for two hours on Vi's sofa. She had meant to sit on it only, and fix her gaze on Vi's collage, which hung opposite, of two white brocade swans on a green silk lake among brown velvet bullrushes, thus allowing her mind the

freedom to think. But drowsiness had overcome her, and the slightly stuffy warmth and
security of Vi's sitting room, and she had
lain down with her head on a patchwork cushion and slept and slept.

It had been a drowned sleep. Every so
often, she had been conscious of her mind spinning slowly to the surface, like a fish coming
up for air, and of her not wanting it to, not wanting it to wake, and making it turn slowly
again and slide heavily back down into uncon-
sciousness. She had some peculiar dreams, full
of huge, dark, blossoming images, slightly
threatening, but even they, her sleeping self
told her, were better than being awake.

When she finally woke, it was lunchtime. She
wondered if Vi might come back from the
hospital and whether she should open a tin of
soup, or grate some cheese for toasting. She
went out into the kitchen. A loaf lay on the
breadboard in a sea of crumbs and there was
a jar of marmalade on the table, a tube of arti-
ficial sweeteners, and two tomatoes in a little raffia basket with a green rim. In the sink
stood Vi's early-morning tea mug, unwashed
up. Sophy opened the fridge and squatted
down. It had all the things in it that Vi had
bought for as long as Sophy could remember,
all the things Fergus had so despised, like
sausages and processed cheese and a half-
eaten steak-and-kidney pie in a tin. Sophy took
out the processed cheese and peeled off two
soft, rubbery slices. She rolled one into a
tube and ate it, pressing it against the roof of

her mouth until it dissolved. Then she cut a slice of bread and laid the second piece of cheese on it and ate that too, leaning against the sink, with one of the tomatoes in her other hand. There seemed to be no taste to any of it, only texture. She rinsed out Vi's mug and filled it with tap water and drank it down in great gulps until she felt sick.

By the telephone was Vi's message pad. At the top, "DAN" was written, in red felt-tipped pen, and beside it, the hospital number. Sophy tore off the sheet underneath and wrote on it, "Dear Gran, I came to be by myself a bit here. Hope you don't mind. I ate some cheese and a tomato. I'll come back soon and see you. I hope Dan was OK today. With love from Sophy." She re-read what she had written; it seemed bald and childish. "Sorry," she added, "I haven't said what I meant. More love from Sophy."

She looked round the kitchen. It occurred to her to tidy up a little and then she thought that a) Vi wouldn't notice; b) Vi wouldn't care much; and c) it was interfering. So she wedged her note into the raffia basket, under the remaining tomato, and let herself out of the house.

"She's not here," Lotte said. "She's gone out. Mr. Wood's in the kitchen, if you want him." She bent to pick up the white plastic sack of bedroom rubbish at her feet. "Really quiet today, all of a sudden. Only three doubles

205

booked. Just as well, I think. Mrs. Wood has a headache. My mother used to get headaches like that and the doctor in Boden said it was a migraine and that she should not eat smoked fish—"

"When am I on duty?" Sophy said, interrupting.

"Tonight," Lotte said, "in the kitchen. It's Kevin's night off and Michelle's in the dining room. With my mother it was always the same at the time of the month and worse in the winter when the nights were so long and we only got a little piece of daylight at lunchtime. It was terrible. It was a place to take your own life. I wouldn't go back there for a million pounds."

"No," Sophy said, edging past Lotte and her buckets and bags. "No, I bet not."

"I said to Mrs. Wood, you want to watch how hard you work. She has too much to think of. I said to her you are so like my mother—"

Sophy fled towards the staircase to the flat and raced up it, three steps at a time. Someone had dropped a Crunchie wrapper which Sophy seized, mindful of Hilary's migraine, and from the top came the thud and wail of music from one of the boys' rooms. The kitchen was empty and untidy, and so were Adam and Gus's rooms. George's bedroom door was shut.

Sophy hesitated outside it for a moment, cramming the Crunchie wrapper into her jeans pocket. Then she knocked. Nothing happened and the music went on. She knocked again, harder.

George opened the door. He looked rumpled and only half awake.

"What on earth are you doing knocking?"

"Bedrooms are private," Sophy said.

George stood back, to let her in. The room smelled of bedclothes and cigarette smoke.

"Wish you'd tell my brothers that."

"Can I turn the music down?"

"Yeah," he said. " 'Course." He reached past her and moved the volume control. "I haven't seen you since London, since you went—"

"No."

She moved across the room through the clothes on the floor and the scattered magazines and newspapers, and sat on the unmade bed. She sat, George noticed, upright and not stooped forward as usual, as if apologising for being so thin, for being Sophy, for being there at all.

"Want a coffee?"

She shook her head.

"Maybe later. Were you doing anything?"

He yawned. "Nope. Just lying here, trying not to worry. I've been offered a job at the garden centre. I ought to take it but I'm scared to. Suppose I find that it's bearable, even if not thrilling, and then I get used to it and then I just get stuck."

"You don't have to—"

"No. But it's what happens." He looked at Sophy and then he lay down at the far end of the bed from her, across the crumpled pillows. "What happened to you? In London."

Sophy's whole posture stiffened.

"It was grotesque."

"Grotesque?"

She put her hands up, shaking them, and closed her eyes as if trying to ward something off.

"He's got this house. A very nice house, very pretty, and it's all done up like some newly married couple's house, and he wants to have a cat and there's this man there, this Tony."

George was suddenly very still.

"Christ."

"I don't know," Sophy said, her chin high. "I just don't know. I'm only guessing. But the kitchen was all perfect with gadgets and delicatessen stuff and a really furtive clock, like a fish, all modern metal, and they were— well, they were kind of *cosy* together. They've got bedrooms on separate floors and Dad kept saying how Tony helped him to buy the house, how he'd never have afforded it otherwise, but they seemed kind of *used* to each other."

"Yikes," George said. He wriggled a bit down the bed closer to Sophy. "Oh Soph—"

"I was so *angry*," Sophy said. "I was pretty angry before I went but when I got there and this Tony bloke opened the door and tried to be all kind of smarmy charming on me, I was so furious I thought I'd explode. And then Daddy came back and I wanted him to hold me and I wanted to kill him, all at once. He just seemed to think"—she paused, and then smashed her clenched fists into the billows of duvet round her—"that it was perfectly OK to take himself away from me and give himself to someone else. That he had a right to!"

"Soph, it mightn't *be* that, he mightn't be—"

"Whether he's gay or not," Sophy said, "he's now spending his life with another person and that person isn't me. Or my mother." She swung sideways on to one elbow, so that her face was close to George's. "The house made me sick. And my things were all mixed up with strange things. And my photos are *every*where."

"He might mean that," George said. "He might really want them everywhere. Give the bloke a chance." He paused, and then he said, "Have you told your mother?"

Sophy lay down, her cheek pillowed on the duvet.

"No."

George said nothing. He looked down at Sophy's face, at her cheek and her jawline and the pleasing complementary curves of her eyebrows and eyelashes.

"I thought about it," Sophy said, "in the train, coming home. But I decided against it, at least for now. She's got sort of happy recently, you see. I suppose it's all this counselling, giving her confidence and stuff. I don't want to knock her back and I don't want to have to cope with her reaction. And she always gets the wrong end of the stick about Daddy."

George grunted. Sophy let a small silence

fall and then she said, "Anyway, I don't want her to know that I'm jealous."

"Are you?"

"Of course I am!" Sophy yelled, springing upright. "Of *course* I am! It's all I can think about!"

George looked down and put one hand, for a second, onto the hollow where Sophy's face had been.

"I think I am too. A bit—"

"You—"

"Yes," George said. He looked away from her. "Of your dad, I suppose. It must be amazing to have anyone feel that strongly about you. Like you do about him. *Amazing.*"

She said, almost in a whisper, "I don't think he notices."

"He *must* do. It must affect everything to know you're that important to anyone. I mean, I know Mum and Dad are kind of concerned about me and want me to be OK, but I don't fill their lives. I'd probably hate it if I did but—" He broke off and then said, in a different voice, "They're fighting like cats just now. Dad even walked out the other night. It's probably nothing, but it kind of drives us even more to the edges of things, it—" He stopped again, and put his arm up across his eyes.

"George?"

He shook his head.

"George," Sophy said, edging closer. "George, don't cry—"

"I'm not—"

"OK," she said. "OK." She leaned forward, balancing on her hands, and put her mouth gently on his, under his upraised arm.

He took the arm away. His face was dry except for two tears, halfway down his cheeks. Sophy drew back and looked at him. He said, "You don't have—"

She shook her head. He reached out and touched her face with an unsteady hand. Then he leaned forward and kissed her, a little less gently. She put her arms round his neck and he pushed her sideways into the mounds of bedding until they were lying together, side by side, their faces almost touching.

Sophy whispered, "Will anyone know?"

"No," he said. He looked into her eyes and was astonished to see them so close, looking at him, looking right, deep at him and at no one else.

"No," George said again, pushing himself even closer so that she could indeed see nothing but him, only him in all the world. "No one'll know."

CHAPTER

12

"There's a lot on my mind," Vi said to Dan. She wasn't sure if he could hear her, he'd been so dozy the last few days, but she was prepared to take a chance. Anyway, she needed to tell him.

"It's Sophy. And Gina. What's new, you'll say. And Mr. Paget wants to put evergreen shrubs in the garden, to save maintenance, he said. I said, 'What maintenance?' He said, 'All that weeding.' I said, 'I'd rather weed day and night, Mr. Paget, than have this garden look like a blooming cemetery.' "

She paused and negotiated something with her crochet hook.

"Has Sophy been in to see you?"

From somewhere just below the surface, Dan endeavoured to say not lately. He didn't blame her, mind you, he wasn't complaining, he knew she'd got a job. Gina had been, every other day. When she bent to kiss him and he didn't seem able to open his eyes, he knew it was her because of the scent. She read bits of poetry to him. He didn't understand much of it, but he liked the sound of her reading, her voice slipping over the words like water over stones. Vi said she'd been quite a little actress at school but she'd never gone on with it. Small wonder really, when you thought of the Whittingbourne Players. All they ever did was *An Inspector Calls*, *The Importance of Being Earnest*, and a Christmas panto full of in-jokes that only the cast understood.

"Sophy came round the other day," Vi said. "She let herself in and I think she just went to sleep there, from the look of the sofa. She left me a funny little note. Said she just needed to be by herself. If you ask me, she's been too much by herself all her life, poor scrap. Too many adults, not enough people her own age.

When I was a kid, we played in the street together, the whole street knew each other. We mightn't have had indoor toilets but we had each other." She paused and gave a little snort and tugged the emerging circle of crochet into shape. "Poor Sophy. More toilets than she knows what to do with, and hardly a friend to her name. Do you like this pattern?"

Dan attempted to say, "Very much." Somewhere in the gently moving mists of his memory, he recalled a rhyme he'd known as a child, about a spider called Sammy: "Bright in every way, Except he didn't like to spin, But only would crochet." You had to emphasise the last syllable of "crochet," to rhyme with "way," He'd tell Vi that. It was the kind of joke she liked, a daft, harmless joke. He strained his mouth to speak, and his eyes to get her attention. "Vi," he said, "Vi, I've got this rhyme for you." But she wasn't listening, or she couldn't hear him. She just went on hooking and looping the long white trail of crochet yarn as if he'd never said a word.

There was an eighteenth-birthday party in the reception room at The Bee House. It was for a girl, and at her parents' request, Hilary had done vases of pink-and-white carnations down the buffet table, and hung bunches of pink-and-white balloons, printed with "You're 18 Today!" in silver and tied up with ribbons, all along the walls. The food had to be pink too, salmon and prawns in shellfish dressing and raspberry pavlovas and a sparkling wine described on the bottle as blush. Laurence had cooked it all, taking the list from Hilary's hand without comment and, as far as she could see, without a tremor. Hilary had got the boys to rig up a little makeshift stage at one end for the band, a very small band composed of Steve from the kitchen, on drums, and two friends of his on guitar and keyboard, one of whom could sort of sing. Michelle and Lotte and two girls from a local agency were going to serve the food and drink, and Hilary was going to stay out of the way, because the birthday girl's father, who ran the Whittingbourne branch of a big national building society, and was full of a booming *bonhomie,* had already said how much he and Pat would like the Woods to be included on this special day, as part of the family.

There were only ten covers booked in the dining room that night, all of them quite early. By nine o'clock, at the latest, Laurence would have done all he needed to do in the kitchen, and could safely leave coffee and a few remaining puddings to Kevin and Sophy, which would in turn, Hilary supposed, leave him free to go round to Gina. Pride froze her urgent desire to beg him not to, especially as he seemed to feel that, having confessed, he now had a freedom to behave openly. All she had been able to bring herself to say was that they must, if Laurence was firmly fixed in his desires, tell the boys.

"Of course," he said. He was sitting on the edge of their bed after another night in which they had both, for different reasons, flinched if their limbs accidentally touched. "But together."

"I'm glad you at least have the decency to suggest that."

He said nothing. He got up and moved slowly round the bed and past her, familiar and yet absolutely alien, in his pyjama bottoms only, towards the passage and the bathroom.

He got as far as the door before he said, "I don't just suggest it, Hil, I insist upon it."

"What are you implying?"

"You know perfectly well."

She said furiously, "That I'd take some kind of revenge?"

"Maybe. But I also want the boys to know the truth. From my mouth as well as from yours."

She turned her back on him.

"I can't believe what a shit you've become."

That conversation had been yesterday, and the last one they had had. Hilary had gone to bed before Laurence was back from High Place and had feigned sleep when he slid in beside her, smelling exaggeratedly of soap as if emphasising his desire to keep his new, thrilling life at a safe distance from his old, tired one. He appeared then to slip quite easily into sleep, his back to her, his breathing even, his warmth and smell just as they had always been, in this very bed, for twenty years. Hilary had lain awake until dawn wondering what one did about this kind of pain, wondering if she could even begin to bear it, and if she couldn't, what would then happen. Being consumed with rage at Laurence, grief for herself and—at the moment at least—hatred of Gina was not enough. It left her weak and helpless and in despair at her own impotence. Hour after hour she lay there, staring at the bars of queer apricot light cast by the lamp in the street below through the gap in the curtains on to the ceiling, while her mind went round and relentlessly round, like a beast in a cage, unable either to stop or to progress.

In the morning, dragging herself out of the worst kind of sleep—too late, too heavy and haunted—she had been compelled to act, to say something that would somehow push the action forward, release this terrible deadlock. She had crawled out of bed and was standing there in her old cotton nightgown, holding her arms across herself, looking at his back as he sat on the edge of the bed, turned away from her. She had meant to sound calm and neutral in order to save what shreds of face he had left her, but it didn't work.

And so it was that, in a voice full of strangled contempt, she had said, "If, as you seem to be, you really are intent upon going through with this—this *ludicrous* business, we shall have to tell the boys."

There had been a tiny pause. Then he said, "Of course." He sounded extremely polite. Then there was another tiny pause after which he added, more firmly, "But together."

Of course, he was right, and she resented him for it. Given the current state of her feelings about him, she thought, hunting for the notebook in which she kept her weekly checklist of bedroom faults, spent light bulbs, dripping taps, broken handles, she didn't want him to be right about anything. She wanted for herself the prerogative of good behaviour; it was all she had left. She wanted—I am ashamed of this, Hilary told herself sternly, but equally I can't pretend I don't feel it—the boys to see her situation as she saw it, to see the complex levels of betrayal, the abuse of friendship, the even worse fraud upon love. She wanted them to be outraged for her even while she knew that, if she succeeded, and they were, she would wish she had never said a word, would know she had let herself down. She looked, without interest, at her notebook. "No. 3," it said, "wardrobe door not latching. Chain to plug in handbasin broken. No. 10, cracked windowpane r.h. side l.h. window." None of these items had been crossed off, none had been seen to. She looked up at her office ceiling. A spider hung there, neatly parcelling up something on a line it had spun from the flex of the central light. It moved very slowly and certainly, swaying in the slight draught. From across the garden, in the reception room, came the faint thumping sound of Steve's band, and an uneven voice singing an old Elvis Presley song in a bad American accent. It was singing—wouldn't you just know it, Hilary thought, watching the spider—"Are You Lonesome Tonight?"

• • • •

A little later, she went upstairs. The dining room was cleared and there were only half a dozen people in the bar, comfortably doing nothing with glasses in their hands. Only a few years ago, Hilary thought, I'd have wanted to go in there and talk to them and tell them about The Bee House and ask them tenderly if they'd enjoyed their dinner. Now I don't want to have anything to do with them, I don't even want them here, I want them to get into their Vauxhalls and drive back to Surrey and Yorkshire and Wales. Poor people, poor pleasant, inoffensive people who have no idea what's going on, who simply think they have found a nice hotel in a nice country town run by a nice family. Well, not only is none of us nice, least of all Laurence, but we're hardly a family any more. Or about to be just the remnant of one. She made an enquiring face at Don through the glass panel in the door to the bar, and he grinned at her and briefly jerked a thumb up. She felt a rush of mad affection for him, for a stable, unchanged thing in a crazily tilting world.

She climbed the stairs very slowly. It was not eleven yet and the birthday party was scheduled to end at eleven-thirty, after which she—or Laurence, if he deigned to be back—would have to go across to the reception room and check it before locking it up for the night. Perhaps she had better make herself some coffee, to keep awake. She went into the kitchen and filled and plugged in the kettle.

"I'd have done that," George said.

She turned. He was standing in the doorway, barefoot, in jeans and an old shirt of Laurence's, striped grey flannel and collarless, that they had bought on a long-ago holiday in Donegal.

"We were just waiting," George said. "We were waiting for you, you see. And I was going to make you a coffee. Adam's got some wine—"

"What for?"

"Sorry?"

"What were you waiting for me for?"

George padded past her and retrieved a mug from the upside-down pile on the draining board. He spooned coffee into it.

"We've got to talk."

Hilary turned away to get a bottle of milk out of the fridge.

"I see." Her heart was suddenly jumping, as if she was afraid.

"The others are in the sitting room," George said. He put a hand out to her to prevent her, with maternal arbitrariness, from just bolting in the opposite direction. "Come on."

She followed him. Adam and Gus, slumped on the floor against the sofa, watching television, got up when she came in, as if she had been, she thought, a figure of some fearful authority. Gus leaned forward to turn off the television and she caught something in his face, and something even in Adam's, that made her feel that they had got up, not out of fear or respect, but out of some kind of solicitude.

"Sit down," George said. He pushed a chair forward. "Go on."

"Go on, Mum," Gus said. He gave her a little shove, his hand on her shoulder.

"Oh God," Hilary said, subsiding. She bent her head and her spectacles swung forward, loose on her nose. A hand came in and retrieved them, taking them away. Someone else put a little table by her with the coffee mug on it and a glass of white wine. "If you go on like this, I'll cry—"

Adam crouched by her chair, peering in under her bent head to see her face.

"You cry if you want to. Just so long as you tell us why you're crying."

She shook her head.

"Yes," George said, from very close by her. "*Yes.*"

"I can't—"

"What can't you?"

"I can't, not without Dad. I promised—"

"Too bad," George said. He came to kneel at her other side. "We can't wait till we can get you together. You're never together. Mum—"

"Yes—"

"What's going on?"

She lifted her head. Gus was standing straight in front of her, eyes wide. He looked about ten, rather than fourteen, and some tufts of hair, so carefully persuaded most of the time to lie down nonchalantly in imitation of Adam's, stood up wildly as if registering the anxiety of the skull beneath.

Looking directly at Gus, Hilary said, "Dad's fallen in love with Gina."

She saw their faces, all three, stunned and empty. Then she saw Adam hurl himself away from her and bury his face in the sofa cushions, and Gus dissolve into instant tears, and George grow scarlet, his face heavy and contorted.

"Oh my *God*—"

"He thinks he may actually have been in love with her since school, since they were sixteen. He says it has nothing to do with me, or anything I've done or haven't done. He says that when Gina has sold High Place, they'll probably go and live in France."

Tears were cascading down Gus's face like a waterfall. He flung himself at Hilary, knocking over the coffee and the wine, scrabbling and clutching at her in a frenzy. She put her arms round him.

"Hush, Gus. Hush, darling. It isn't the end of the world—"

"It is!" Gus screeched. "It is! It is!"

Adam turned from the sofa. Like George's, his face was hotly flushed.

"The bastard—"

George jerked his head up.

"The bitch, you mean."

"No," Hilary said. "Stop that. It doesn't help and it isn't—" She paused and then said with a determined effort, "It isn't true."

"Huh," Adam said. He began to bang his fist on the floor, steadily, as if hammering something.

George said, his voice choked, "Does Sophy know?"

"No. Only me and now you."

"I don't *want* to know!" Gus yelled.

Hilary kissed his hair.

"Me neither."

"I'd like to kill someone—"

"Two people—"

"You haven't heard Dad," Hilary said. She adjusted herself in the armchair so that Gus could cram in beside her, his face against her shoulder. "I wasn't supposed to tell you without him. I promised."

George got up from the floor, very slowly, as if he had just woken from sleep. He stood with his back to them all, staring at the wall opposite, where a picture hung that Hilary had given Laurence, a reproduction of a painting of three Irish fishermen pulling a dinghy up a wild, dark beach.

"How long have you known?"

"A week," Hilary said. "No. Eight days."

"It's a shit," George said. "Fergus goes off so Gina thinks she's entitled to some compensation. And Dad's a pushover—"

"I want to throw up," Adam said. He stopped banging the carpet and put his head against Gina's chair and began to swear under his breath, word after word, in a steady stream as if reading a list.

Hilary put a hand out to him and held the back of his neck.

"Don't—"

He took no notice. George said, still staring at the fishermen, "Has he said anything about us?"

Hilary flinched.

"You must ask him that."

"I don't believe this," George said, beginning to shake his head slowly from side to side. "I just don't bloody *believe* it."

Gus said, his voice muffled in Hilary's shoulder, "It's the worst thing, it's the worst—"

Hilary said nothing. The temptation to cry was immense, to cry and have them all come round her and touch her; even cry too. I must not, she told herself, I must not, they must not be required to com-fort me.

"Do you want to cry?" Gus said, looking up at her.

"Yes," she said, "or break things."

Adam stopped swearing and lifted his head.

"You can start with bloody Gina." He thrust his face into his mother's. "Why don't you go and see her? Why don't you go and say she can't just help herself to Dad like this?"

Hilary said carefully, "I don't think I want him unless he wants me."

"Suppose he's just being pathetic and doing what she wants? Go, Mum, *go.*"

She sighed. In the distance, the clock in the tower of Whittingbourne Church struck the three-quarter hour.

"I'll think about it. Right now, I have to go and check up after this party."

"Stay here—"

"We'll go—"

She smiled, struggling out from under Gus.

"You're dears, but I have to. Fire regulations and all that. I won't be long." She stood up, looking down at Gus, huddled where she had left him like a puppet with limp strings. "I wonder where my specs are? Oh, there. Lovely." She paused, sliding them on to her nose with a gesture as effortless and practised as breathing. "I'm sorry," she said. Her voice sounded stiff and bright and not at all as she intended it to. "Really, boys. I'm so sorry." Then she bent to touch Adam and Gus just briefly, and went past George, brushing his arm, and out of the room.

When she had gone, nobody moved, and there was no sound except the odd sniffle from Gus and a car or two going by in the street below. Eventually George turned round, and picked up the glass and the mug and the little table, and went out to the kitchen for a cloth and a bowl of soapy water. The others watched him while he scrubbed, Gus slumped in the armchair, Adam on the floor beyond it, leaning his head on his arm. There was a tattoo on his arm, a new one, a tiny swallow, in emulation of the swallows ex-prisoners wore, to show they'd done time.

When George had finished with the carpet, he came back into the sitting room with a packet of cigarettes and offered them to his brothers.

"Here—"

Gus sat up a little.

"In here?"

"Tonight," George said, "we can do what we bloody well like wherever we want."

Gus leaned forward for a light. He looked pathetic, gaunt, and gawky, like a wet fledgling. He said, his voice catching, "I thought she was a friend—"

His brothers said nothing. He drew unevenly on his cigarette and exhaled a ragged stream of smoke.

"Didn't you? Didn't you think she was a friend? I mean, she always seemed pretty nice. And now she's ruined our lives."

"I told them," Hilary said. She was sitting up in bed with her spectacles on, pretending to read.

Laurence was by the chest of drawers, emptying his pockets in the familiar clinking ritual of keys and coins.

"You what?"

"I told the boys. About you and Gina. I didn't intend to but they asked me."

Laurence said, "How very, very convenient for you."

"No," she said, "it wasn't. But it wasn't to be avoided either."

"I see."

"If you'd been *here*—"

"I see."

"You make your choices," Hilary said, suddenly unable to bear the sight of him standing there, "and then you take the consequences. None of this is *my* choice."

He didn't reply. He unbuttoned his shirt very slowly and pulled it out of the waistband of his trousers. Then he unbuckled his watch and dropped it on to the pile of coins.

"Where are they now?"

"The boys? In their rooms."

"Oh *Hilary,*" Laurence said, his voice thick with reproach.

"Their choice. Not mine. Mine, at this precise moment, is not to sleep with you. Sophy isn't here, so go to the spare room. I can't stand you being in my bed after you've been in hers."

"I wasn't," Laurence said quietly. "We talked in the kitchen. Sophy was there."

"And what does *she* think?"

"I don't know," Laurence said. He unhooked his bathrobe from the back of the door. "She hardly spoke. She was upstairs in her bedroom."

He opened the door to the passage, and glanced back at her.

"Night," he said.

She looked fiercely at her book, seeing nothing.

"Night," she said.

It was drizzling, soft warm summer drizzle that blew before the wind in faint plumes. Hilary, cursing without an umbrella, had to keep snatching off her spectacles to clear them, unable to decide whether blurred wet lenses or her natural myopia was worse. It had taken ages to decide what to wear, ages in which her anger and self-contempt at giving sartorial choices even a second's contemplation in these circumstances mounted and mounted. She had even come close to laughing out loud at the absurdity of it, remembering a *New Yorker* cartoon she had once seen in which a dress-shop assistant was saying to a customer, "And are you the defendant or the plaintiff?" Did one, Hilary thought, wear something sexy, as a furiously injured wife, or something aggressively outdated (of which I seem to have far too much) or a witch's outfit complete with broomstick? In the end, she'd chosen red. Black trousers and a big red shirt, to show that nothing that had happened or might happen would cow her. Women in red signalled that they were not easily to be overcome.

The shirt was damp across the shoulders by the time she reached High Place, and her hair was curling up in misted tendrils. From an upstairs window, quite by chance, Gina looked down and saw her, a formidable black-and-scarlet figure just inside the street gate, rubbing the lenses of her spectacles on her shirt-tails. Gina held the windowsill. She had not bargained for this, not for Hilary just turning up, out of the blue. She'd thought that they'd have to meet sometime, that there would have to be a telephone call, and then a meeting which she had shrunk from visualising, but she hadn't reckoned on Hilary seizing the initiative. That privilege she had assumed to be her own. Now, holding the windowsill tightly, and looking down at Hilary, Gina felt a deep, disabling shaft of panic.

She went out on to the landing and glanced up the stairs towards Sophy's floor. The door was shut as it usually was these days, and from behind it came the long, lavish strains of a recent film theme. Sophy's uncommunicativeness had altered recently. The sullenness had gone, to be replaced by something sadder but also more steely. There was a grimness to Sophy these days, and an air of determination. She was packing up her room, neatly and methodically, with a palpable air of resignation but without resentment. From where she stood, Gina could see several cardboard boxes stacked on the top landing, boxes of books and ornaments and music tapes. Sticking out of the top of one, Gina noticed, was Sophy's hippopotamus, his coy plush face resting on the rim. She would have, she thought, just to take the risk that Sophy would not choose the next half-hour to come downstairs and discover, by Hilary's presence, the very thing that Gina had been putting off telling her.

"I will," she had said to Laurence, "when you tell the boys. We'll tell them all at the same time. It wouldn't be fair, otherwise."

Hilary was waiting by the glass door in the kitchen. She saw Gina come in, and hesitate, but she didn't let herself in. She merely waited, watching, while Gina slowly crossed the kitchen and opened the door.

"Hello," Hilary said.

Gina swallowed.

"Hello." She stood aside just enough to allow Hilary past her.

"Well," Hilary said. She put her hands up

to her hair and ruffled it. Then she took her spectacles off. She looked at Gina, and her eyes seemed wide and young without them.

"Not having done this before," Hilary said, "I don't know how one proceeds, I don't know the *form*."

"No."

"But you can imagine why I've come. How I feel."

Gina closed the door and moved to the table, to the opposite side from Hilary.

"It wasn't deliberate. Nothing was. Neither of us wanted it to happen—"

"No?"

"No," Gina said with emphasis.

"I see."

"It's true," Gina said. "There was no *intention*."

"But there was a connection. Wasn't there? One minute you are utterly devastated by Fergus going, the next minute you're in bed with the man you know best in life after Fergus. No connection?"

Gina leaned on the table. Her silver bangles slid down her arm and clashed softly together.

"I didn't take Laurence, Hilary, to make me feel better about Fergus."

Hilary put her hands flat on the table and leaned across it, towards Gina.

"You did, you know."

"No, I—"

"You listen," Hilary said. "You just *listen*. You've been possessive about Laurence all your life and never ceased to remind me, by

229

inference if not by actual words, that you'd known him long before we ever met. As long as you had Fergus, you could tolerate me having Laurence, but when Fergus went, you wanted Laurence back, you felt he was yours to have. I believe you almost thought you were *entitled* to him."

Gina bent her head and her hair swung forward in glossy wings. Then she flung it up again.

"I did not take him, Hilary. He came. He came *for me.*"

"Nobody does that out of the blue. Nobody comes without signals. Especially not Laurence."

"He did. He sought me out."

"And it never occurred to you to turn him down? It never crossed your mind to say sorry, I love you as a friend but no more, and besides I have an abiding loyalty to your wife and sons which precludes me from even *thinking* about this?"

Gina cried, "I was in love too!"

Hilary straightened up.

"Exactly," she said. "And now how do you feel? How do you feel about wrecking my life and the boys' lives, and Sophy's life, all over again? Can you live with that? Can you honestly go waltzing off to France with all that on your conscience and lead a happy life?"

The telephone rang.

"Leave it," Hilary said.

"No, I can't, I—"

"You're a coward, aren't you?" Hilary said.

"Not just the kind of friend who makes enemies seem preferable, but a craven coward."

Gina snatched up the receiver.

"Yes?

"What? Oh Lord, oh Mum. Yes. When? Of course. Of course I'll come. Hold on there, hold on, I'm coming. Yes, Mum, yes. I know. I know. Ten minutes—"

She put the receiver down, and stood for a second with her head bowed against the telephone.

"Well?" Hilary demanded, but her voice had softened.

"I can't talk to you just now," Gina said, turning. "I can't talk to anyone. That was Vi. Dan's dead." She raised her head and looked at Hilary directly for the first time. "He died twenty minutes ago."

CHAPTER
13

"Don't sit there watching me," Vi said, "waiting for me to slip off my dish."

"Mum, I—"

"It's the look on your face. That *look*—"

"I'm sorry for you," Gina said.

Vi gave a little grunt, contorting her face to prevent more tears. She had a handkerchief in her hands, the kind she always used, spurning paper tissues, with embroidered flowers and a deep scratchy hem of lace, and she was twisting it in and out of her fingers, in a damp rope.

"That nurse," she said, "that Irish one. Couldn't stand her at first, all that talk of Christ Jesus. But she was kind to him, and *respectful*. Mr. Bradshaw, she called him, not Dan or dear. When he'd gone, she said that I was to try and love Cath Barnett in Christ Jesus. 'Must be joking,' I said. 'Love Cath Barnett! Well, if it's anything it's in Christ Jesus, because I certainly don't love her in anyone else.' "

Gina leaned forward to pour more tea. Vi's sitting room was too hot but Vi couldn't stop shivering, even in a cardigan and a shawl Gina had found in the airing cupboard.

"It wasn't Cath, Mum."

Vi wrenched the handkerchief into a tourniquet round one finger.

"I've got to think it's *someone*."

"I know."

"It's too wicked, if it's for no reason—"

"There was a reason, Mum. His heart was weak."

"Oh I know," Vi said, "I know that really." She closed her eyes. "I know."

Gina turned to look at Sophy, huddled in a corner on one of Vi's dining chairs, upright and uncomfortable. She was holding a balled-up wad of tissues and her eyes were red.

"Soph?"

Sophy whispered, "I never said goodbye. I never went to see him enough—"

"That's hard," Vi said. "Hard for you." She

picked up her teacup, looked at the contents, and put it down again. "Grief is hard, though, it's one of the hardest. Because you can't do anything about it. You just have to bear it. Look it in the face and bear it." She got up and went unevenly across the room to where Dan's photograph stood, between two vases of small red roses, like a little shrine. "I look at going on without him," Vi said, "and I think I can't do it. But I know I will, somehow. I'll clear out that flat and I'll take his clothes to Oxfam and I'll pack up all his things from the Navy and send them to that nephew in King's Lynn and I'll let old Paget fill the garden with his dreary shrubs and I'll see someone else come into Dan's flat, and it won't be Dan's flat any more." She put an unsteady finger out and touched the face in the photograph. "I won't give in, though. He wouldn't like that. I wouldn't like it either."

Sophy began to cry again. Gina got up and went to comfort her, holding her as best she could.

"If you don't grieve," Vi said, turning to look at them, "then you didn't love in the first place. It's the being left behind that does it; it's the staying here while they go on."

She came back to the chair where she had been sitting, holding on to passing bits of furniture for support.

"You're amazing, Mum," Gina said.

Vi shook her head. An earring slipped from the hole in one ear, dropping down her front. Vi made a clumsy effort to retrieve it, but gave up almost at once, subsiding into the chair with a sudden relief, as if her legs wouldn't have held her up another minute.

"No," she said, "I was lucky. I got lucky with Dan, didn't I, lucky at a time of life when you don't look for luck." She paused and then said gruffly, almost to herself, "Or love."

There was a sudden silence, broken only by Sophy's sniffing. Gina looked over her head, at the wall where Vi's brocade swans sailed calmly across their green silk lake, and saw reflected in the glass that covered them Vi sitting there, half in and half out of her shawl, lost in her own inviolable remembrance of luck and love.

"God gave us memories," Vi said abruptly, breaking the moment, "so we'd have roses in December."

"Oh Gran," Sophy said, laughing through the sniffs. "Oh *Gran*. They'd be dead by then."

Hilary drove the car north out of Whittingbourne, towards the hills. They were ancient hills, made of limestone oolite, good for sheep but not for crops, where the villages that strayed down the slopes here and there looked as if they had broken through the turf rather than been built upon it. It was high country, open and bleak for three-quarters of the year, and when the boys were small, Laurence and Hilary had brought them out here with kites on wild winter afternoons, they had all returned exhilarated and breathless from battling with the wind. Adam had had a wonderful Chinese kite, a deceptively simple thing made of red and yellow cotton, which flew like a bird, swooping and curving and plunging in response to the smallest movement. He had lost it finally to a dog who had savaged it as it came to earth in a gorse bush, convinced that it represented mortal danger. The dog's poor owner had been mortified. He had sent Adam a replacement kite, a gleaming affair in blue and silver nylon which proved in action, as Laurence said, like trying to fly a pudding. Adam hadn't minded much; he was already obsessed by wanting a skateboard.

Hilary parked the car in a field gateway and got out. It was a quiet, glowing day, and the field beyond the gate was striped with neat lines of blond and buff stubble left by the harvester. It sloped away from her, down a gradual hill, curving as it went, and ending up with a hedgerow full of dark-leaved late-summer trees that surely signified the course of a stream. Beyond that the land lifted again, a steeply rising hill of pasture, dotted with casual sheep who had nibbled the grass almost out of all colour except for harsh, dark clumps of thistle.

It was an unremarkable view, Hilary thought, the kind of calm, dull agricultural view one might find almost anywhere in England, yet strangely soothing because of the timelessness of it, the way it made no demands on you, didn't oppress you with requirements for change, but merely unrolled itself before you and existed. Hilary leaned her arms on the gate and felt the worn wood warm on her skin and the calm air warm on her face, and closed her eyes.

Her sister Vanessa had said come to London.

"Come and stay, Hil. We'll talk and you can say whatever you want to say. Get away from that place. That hotel. Just for a few days."

She hadn't meant to ring Vanessa, any more than she had meant to tell the boys about Laurence and Gina. The impulse to tell Vanessa had been something to do with her aborted visit to Gina, with having the tables turned upon her by Dan's death and having to come home feeling she had achieved nothing but an increase in antagonism and melodrama, both of which she despised. She had gone straight up to the flat and telephoned Vanessa, who had been at work, so she had fretted round the telephone, unable to do anything else, for an hour and a half until Vanessa came home.

Vanessa had been very shocked, Hilary could tell that, not from any comment she made, but from her silence. In that silence, Hilary could hear the unspoken word "divorce" ringing like a knell of doom, recalling Hilary's elder brother's divorce some years before, which the family had treated with the kind of scarcely-to-be-expressed outrageof people who believe such offensive things only happen to others—others, by implication, with insufficient morals and fortitude to prevent them. Then Vanessa had melted.

"Poor Hil," she said. "Poor girl. Poor you."

"I'm OK—"

"And the boys. Poor boys."

"Yes."

"So shocked—"

"Yes."

"So shocking—"

"I'm afraid so. Because it's Gina. I wonder where to put my foot next, for firm land. I mean, a betrayal is one thing but a double one leaves you feeling like that awful screaming Munch painting, especially, as in both cases, no one can hear the screams."

"I can."

"I know," Hilary said, "but Laurence can't."

"Come and stay," Vanessa said then. "We'll talk and you can say whatever you want to say."

Sitting in her neglected sitting room, holding the telephone receiver hard against her ear, Gina had thought, with a childish longing, of the fat security of Vanessa's spare bedroom, with its plump pillows and quilts, its careful lighting and carefully chosen bedside books, its meticulous attention to the details of comfort. Yet even as she pictured it, she knew the pain would remorselessly come too, and would slide in with her between those expensive, well-laundered Egyptian cotton sheets, and go implacably to work.

"I can't," she said. "I'd love to, but I can't. Because of the boys and the hotel—"

"Of course. The boys." Vanessa took a breath. "Bring them with you. Surely someone can look after the hotel?"

"Not easily. We never have had anyone else, you see, we've only been away in the winter, when we could shut it."

"Will you sell it?"

"I don't know. We haven't talked about it. We've hardly talked at all. I can scarcely bear to speak to him, and at the same time, he's the only person I want to be with. I'm terribly confused."

"Hil," Vanessa said.

"Yes?"

"Do you love him? Do you still love Laurence?"

"Yes," Hilary said. "Yes. That's the damnable thing. I may have wanted to kill him recently, but I've never stopped loving him. I stopped loving *me,* which made me pretty unpleasant to live with, but not him. And—"

"And what?"

"He's easy to love. I know you think he's hopeless because he doesn't put on a tie and have a bursting appointments book, but you don't know him very well. He's lovable. He's even sweet. He's gentle and not feeble and he has great passions which you might not see because they're not the same as yours, but they're there. And we like each other. We laugh. No, correction: we used to laugh."

"I know," Vanessa said and then, unexpectedly, "I rather envied that."

She had offered, then, to come down to Whittingbourne. To talk to the boys, she said, to be there, to talk to Laurence, even Gina. Hilary had pictured that, for a fleeting moment,

Vanessa in her pleated skirts and crisp shirts administering brisk, well-meant advice in the squalid bear-pits of the boys' bedrooms, and had almost laughed.

"No," she said. "Bless you, but no. We've got to wade through this bit in the same place together, I think. Laurence hasn't even had a proper conversation with the boys, you see."

That was why she had come out. That was why she was here now, leaning on the gate in order to leave place and time empty for Laurence to talk to the boys.

"I will," he said. "Of course I will. But I'd rather you were there."

"No," she said, seized by some obsessive notion of fair play. "You weren't there when I told them. So I shouldn't be when you do."

She climbed the gate. A broad headland of long tufted grass full of wiry weeds had been left in the field around the cultivated land. She would follow that, she decided, right round the field, down the slope towards the stream and then along it to the furthest hedge and up again, back to the car. That walk, that commonplace mile around a harvested wheat-field on a weekday afternoon, would be the half-hour in which she resolved that, whatever lay ahead, whatever struggle, she would make sure that it had courage and endurance, that it had some kind of *quality*.

The letter was lying on the kitchen table at High Place. Gina had plainly laid it down carefully, marked by the wooden salt and pepper mills and parallel to the edge of the table. Sophy didn't think she had ever had a letter from Fergus before, not in all her sixteen years. There had been no excuse to write, after all, no reason. They'd seen each other every single day, except when Fergus was off at an auction, which was never for more than a few nights, every one of which he telephoned. Gina would talk to him for a few minutes, and then she would hand Sophy the receiver and say, invariably, "Daddy wants you."

Gina had gone out early, to Vi's. She said she didn't want Vi going through Dan's things alone, or eating and drinking nothing all day followed by a whole pot of strong tea and a whole packet of biscuits. Sophy was amazed that Gina didn't mind doing this, after all the years in which she had grown accustomed to hearing Vi spoken of in a tone of faint complaint, as a responsibility Gina was going to bear, but not with particularly good grace. And, Sophy suspected, Fergus had been a little afraid of Vi. He was perfectly civil to her, but from a safe distance, like someone circling with circumspection around an unpredictable animal. When Sophy thought of the way they both lived, her father and her grandmother, she saw them as creatures off different planets. It was that way too, just a little, between her mother and grandmother, which was what made it so odd to see Gina, with apparent cheerfulness, setting off each day to Orchard Close. But then Gina was different. Gina had come

out, almost entirely, of her shell of intro-
verted grief and rage, and was smiling. Amazing, really, if that's what a few weeks of what
Vi called psycho-shrink could do for you.

She picked up Fergus's letter. It was fat, in
one of the long wallet envelopes of cream
paper that he had always used to match the cream
writing paper with the letterhead stamped dra-
matically in black. She looked at it for a bit, wondering if she dreaded opening it or longed to,
and then put her thumb under the flap and ripped
it open so roughly that the whole envelope
tore apart. Fergus would have hated that. Fergus used a paper knife.

Sophy sat down at the kitchen table and
unfolded the thick pages.

"Sophy, my dearest," the letter began.

She put the letter down and tilted her chair
back. If he was going to write guff like that, using
all the endearments he had never used in their
life together, she wasn't going to believe a
word of the letter. She had decided she hated
words like "darling," anyhow, that they meant
nothing, that they were a kind of cop-out for-
mula to delude you into thinking people loved
you, verbally, while the things they actually did
showed quite the opposite. Sophy had begun
to take a lot of notice of action lately, had
begun to think not only that most actions
spoke louder than any words, but also that
they were a way of achieving some control of
your own. That was why she had had sex with
George. She had wanted someone in her power
that afternoon, someone to be surprised into

looking at her differently, seeing her as a person who could affect things, not just be affected by them. The sex itself had been strange, hot and jerky and very quick. But she had quite liked it, to her surprise, and what had surprised her even more was that having done it hadn't haunted her afterwards at all. In fact, rather the contrary. She thought she might do it again in the not too distant future, not necessarily with George. George looked at her differently now, as if wanting something from her, but she was not inclined to respond. She wasn't playing games, she just couldn't tell him—by word or deed—that she felt something she didn't. Her parents' behaviour had taught her that, if she had any say in it, she'd never do that in all her life; she'd rather be brutal than untruthfully, misleadingly kind.

She picked up the letter again and glared at it:

I have spent a long time wondering whether to write this letter and have decided, as you see, that I should. This is for two reasons. I have something to tell you, and something to suggest, and as I know that you burn with scepticism at every word I utter, I want to put these words down on paper so that you have them there, in black and white, to prove, and to use as proof, that they are spoken in earnest.

Sophy stopped reading the letter at arm's length in order to show it how much she mistrusted it, and laid it flat on the table. Fergus's writing was clear, bold and black, written with an italic nib:

The thing I wish to tell you is about Tony. I know what you thought, and I curse myself for not preparing you. The facts are these. I have known Tony for six years, first as a business acquaintance, then as a friend. He is the only person to whom I ever confided my unhappiness with your mother. I love him but I am not in love with him. I owe him a great deal both emotionally and practically, but I am not in his thrall. What is private between us remains private—as I hope you will feel about your own private life, when you have one in years to come— but is not a stealthy secret. I'm your father, and I love you, but I have to have my own life as well.

For all that, although I don't regret what I have done, I regret the way I've done it very much. I didn't think things through and I miscalculated a lot of other things. I owe you an apology and also a recompense. I am moved to do this from the bottom of my heart because your coming here made me feel my loss of you keenly, and your behaviour demonstrated that I hadn't tried to see things sufficiently from your point of view.

My proposal is this. That when my share of the proceeds from High Place comes through, you and I use it to buy a flat

243

together, a two-bedroomed flat for us to live in until your education is finished and for you to have after that. I'd move out of this house, and find a lodger for my half of it to pay the mortgage. I've discussed this all with Tony and although he would be very sad, and he has no children, he accepts that you are my priority. I told you he was a nice man.

Ring me when you can. No one ever seems to be at home these days and the answerphone is never on, either. But I gather that the Pughs had a survey done and the result was satisfactory. So we can begin to do something quite soon. Certainly in time for Christmas. And we can start looking at sixth-form colleges in London.

With my love as ever,
Daddy

Sophy dropped the letter and the pages slid apart and scattered across the table. She stared at them, at the black words on the cream paper, and then she picked up the nearest sheet, and kissed it.

A little later, the envelope hidden between the mattress and the divan base of her bed on the side against the wall, Sophy changed into her waitress clothes and went round to The Bee House. She went in, as she always did, through the kitchen, which was oddly quiet except for cooking noises. Laurence was bent over something in a steel bowl and he glanced up only briefly to say, "Morning, Sophy," before going back to whatever it was with fierce concentration. Kevin and Steve, with elaborate grimaces, caught her eye to indicate that Laurence was in some fearful mood and was not to be spoken to. Sophy looked puzzled. Laurence was never in a fearful mood, he wasn't that kind of man. She opened her mouth to say something but Kevin, flailing his arms like a windmill and then signalling a cut throat with his forefinger, silenced her. She shrugged, walked past them all and up the short flight of stairs outside the kitchen to the bar.

Hilary and Don were leaning on either side of the bar, over several computer-printed invoice sheets. Hilary looked much the same as normal, if tired, and was wearing her usual hotel uniform of straight navy-blue skirt and cream shirt, with a red belt and her red spectacles. Adam had said not long ago that she looked like an air hostess and she had said sharply that that was fine by her since her job was not in the least dissimilar, clearing up after adults behaving like wayward toddlers, in a confined space.

"Hello, Sophy," Hilary said. She looked up from the invoice sheets. She did not appear, Sophy thought, to have slept very well. Perhaps she and Laurance had had one of their quarrels, the ones George had told her about.

"Morning—"

"You look cheerful," Don said to Sophy. He wore a green bow-tie patterned with yellow dinosaurs. "Makes a change round here."

"Thank you," Hilary said. She turned to Sophy. "I'd forgotten I'd put you on the schedule for lunchtime."

"Oh," Sophy said. "Shall I—"

"No. You stay." She paused a second and then she said, "How is Vi?"

"Brave," Sophy said. "Very brave. She's not a bit like she was when he was ill. She's stopped wanting to blame everybody. She's going to have all his favourite hymns at the funeral, all the ones about the sea."

"Good for her," Hilary said. Her voice wasn't quite steady. "We'll all come, of course. Sophy—"

"Yes?"

"See if you can find Gus for me, would you? I've got a job for him. Then check the tables. I want them all laid, but only a third with lunch menus." She gave Sophy a sudden smile, a smile that much startled her since it was not the kind of smile one associated with Hilary but a smile of real sweetness, almost of affection. "You're a good girl, Sophy," Hilary said.

Gus was not in the flat. Nobody was except Lotte, who was trying to subdue the chaos.

"Truly, the way these people live, the way these boys are allowed to be so untidy. Look at these clothes. You can't even walk the floor. When I was growing up, we had to clean our own bedrooms, my mother insisted on it, and of course we always wore slippers

246

in the house because of the dirt. The dirt in Sweden stays outside houses, on outside shoes. Never inside, like here. Have you seen this bedroom, where you sleep sometimes? It is a disgrace. It looks as if ten people had a fight—"

"Have you seen George?" Sophy said.

"He is working. He has gone to his new job at the garden centre. He said to me, 'Lotte, would you—' "

"Or Gus?"

"He went out," Lotte said. She picked up a bucket of hot water from which fumes of disinfectant rose chokingly. "He is not supervised, Gus. At his age he should be in a summer camp, with other boys, like in Sweden."

"We don't have them here. Where did he go?"

"He said something about the garden. He said he might climb a tree. Climb a tree! At his age."

"His mother wants him—"

"Now, she does not look well, Mrs. Wood. Nor Mr. Wood. They are both quite exhausted." She turned towards the bathroom, holding the bucket and a sponge. "It is as well I have a steady Swedish temperament, the things I am asked to do."

Sophy went back down the stairs to the ground floor, and out past Hilary's office through the door to the garden. It was basically a pretty garden, an old, unpretentious, traditional garden of grass and rose beds with, at the far end, a wilder patch with apple trees and a swing and climbing frame for the children of hotel guests, with a slide and ladders. It all looked very neglected. The lawn hadn't seen a mower recently, there were thick ruffs of groundsel under the roses, and the roses themselves needed dead-heading. In the borders along the wall where the bee boles were, all the tall flowers like delphiniums and hollyhocks had faded and fallen over, like long corpses among the smaller things still struggling to live and bloom.

"Gus?" Sophy called. "Gus?"

There was no reply. She walked down the grass, past the tables and benches set out for summer drinks, to the apple trees. She peered up into the bigger ones.

"Gus?"

Silence. She went through the trees to the very far end of the garden, where another wall divided it from some neglected allotments and then the car-park to an office building, and, hitching up her waitress skirt, hauled herself on to the top.

"I'm here," he said.

She turned. He was astride the wall, at the far left-hand side, almost hidden under the stiff dark branches of an old yew tree that hung over it.

"Why didn't you come?" Sophy said. "You heard me—"

"I didn't want to," Gus said. "I'm better here."

"Hilary wants you."

"What for?"

"I don't know. A job, she said."

Gus said, "I haven't seen you for ages."

Sophy swung herself on to the wall and edged towards him astride it.

"Four days, I should think. Come on, Gus. She said to come—"

"I can't."

"What d'you mean, you can't?"

"I can't go back in there."

"Oh *Gus*," Sophy said in exasperation, "don't be so stupid. What's the matter with you?"

Gus said nothing. Sophy couldn't see his face, only his long thin legs in jeans with carefully ripped knees, and the Russian-army belt George had found for him at a Birmingham flea market, and an inch or two of greyish-white T-shirt.

"Come out," Sophy said. "Come out so I can see you." He didn't move.

"Well, I'm going then. I'll tell Hilary you won't budge."

"Wait—"

She leaned back along the wall, her hands behind her for support.

"I haven't got all day."

Slowly, Gus emerged. He came towards her, dragging himself astride out of the whispering branches. His face was filthy, streaked with dark smears from the yew bark. When he was about a foot away, he stopped, and looked at her. Sophy saw that he'd been crying. She sat bolt upright.

"Hey, Gus—"

He stared at her, as mournful as a chastised puppy.

"Gus, what is it?"

"Don't you know?"

"Know what?"

Gus sighed, a huge, shuddering sigh. He put up one grimy hand as if to hide his face and then he said from behind it, "Don't you know that my father wants to leave my mother and marry your mother instead?"

CHAPTER
14

The church was a riot of flowers. Vi had done a deal with her flower-seller friend in Whittingbourne market and had come away with armfuls of dahlias and spray chrysanthemums. Vi loved dahlias. She loved the precision of them and their clear, strong, unabashed colours. The first flowers Dan had ever given her had been dahlias, grown on the allotment he then had at the back of The Bee House, where he grew them in a tidy row, just like his rows of peas and beans and carrots. He'd grown them to enter for the Whittingbourne Flower Show, in one of the pensioner classes, but had decided to give them to Vi instead. She could see them now, the huge, symmetrical, well-defined heads, scarlet and purple and orange and yellow, encased in a cone of newspaper, and behind them Dan's face, quite a small, pale thing by comparison, full of anxious pleasure.

"Lord," she had said. "What are you doing, Mr. Bradshaw? It'll be chocolates next."

It was. A huge box of milk chocolate assortment, just left on her doorstep in a paper bag. Then some vegetables he'd grown, all scrubbed, and then a goldfish in a bowl that he said he'd won, quite by accident, when the fair came through Whittingbourne and camped in the main car-park for two days. The goldfish had been a great success, had broken the ice between them. Vi christened it Fluffy. It lived for two weeks and then suddenly died and Vi found it floating in its bowl, belly up, looking, she said, deader than anything she'd ever seen, even on a fishmonger's slab. But it didn't matter. They didn't need the goldfish any more. They were off by then, and flying.

Vi didn't really approve of church. She thought it stopped people thinking for themselves, and that God was some kind of cop-out, but Dan had thought differently. He seldom went to church, except at Christmas and on Armistice Day, when he wore his poppy and his two small replica wartime medals, but he watched *Songs of Praise* regularly on television and he didn't like Vi to scoff at people who had religion. He said it was ignorant and unfeeling to do that. He said the Merchant Navy had taught him a lot about religion keeping people together.

"Or apart," Vi said.

But she had accompanied him, once or

twice, at Christmas and had liked the crowd and the candles and the singing. When Dan died, she had gone to the vicar of the same little church at the end of Orchard Street and asked rather diffidently about a funeral.

"Of course," the vicar said. "I was expecting it. Mr. Bradshaw was one of our parishioners."

Vi was much amazed. It gave Dan a kind of local status somehow; it showed that other people besides her had noticed him. But then, he'd always looked so smart for church, his suit pressed, his shoes gleaming. And he stood up properly too, back straight, so that even though he was small he had a presence. Vi wished she'd admired him more, to his face. She wished she'd said that she was proud to be seen out with a man like that.

She was pleased with the look of the church. It was small and very old and rather dark, but the dahlias lit it up and there were candles everywhere; she'd asked for them especially. There were flowers beside the altar and either side of the chancel steps and on the font and every windowsill. She'd ordered one arrangement just from her, white and yellow, a long arrangement shaped like a narrow diamond, with lilies in it, and that was to go on top of his coffin when it was carried in. There would be no card with it. There was no need. Dan knew what she was thinking.

Hilary said she wanted to inspect her sons before the funeral. They had made a surprisingly conventional effort, even down to finding ties. Adam wore his at half-mast, but it was a dark tie and he had found a jacket and black shoes.

"Well done," she said.

Adam tossed his hair. He ran a finger round inside his shirt collar as if it was choking him.

"Dan was OK," he said.

George said to his mother, "Are you?"

She nodded. She was wearing a black suit none of them recognised and black high-heels. Adam privately thought she looked pretty good but decided not to say so. Looking too good didn't seem quite right for a funeral; you just had to make sure you didn't look weird. He smiled at her. She was great, carrying it all off like this. She hadn't asked them what their father had said, hadn't given them any hassle. Adam was grateful, grateful that she hadn't been heavy about that or anything else. He never thought he would feel like this, nor that he could even contemplate speaking to his father again. But he could. He thought his father was acting in as bad a way as he could, but at the same time he had admired the way Laurence had spoken to them. Very calm, very steady, very sad.

"I did not look for this to happen," Laurence had said. "I never contemplated it. I can honestly say that it fell upon me, like a thunderbolt, and once it had, I was different and so was everything else."

They had listened to him, all three, in silence. Nobody asked him anything. Even Gus, who usually had no inhibitions about asking questions, said nothing. There was a palpable awkwardness in the air because no one wanted Gina mentioned, no one wanted the existence of that name admitted, no one wanted even to think about the feelings it aroused. It was better, all round, just to consider Dad as Dad, and no more.

"Have you nothing to ask me?" Laurence said. "I'll answer any question as truthfully as I can."

George sighed. He leaned forward in his chair and put his elbows on his knees.

"No," he said.

"Don't you even want to say anything?"

George said, staring at the floor, "Nothing you'd want to hear."

Gus had his eyes shut. Adam knew he was just waiting for this interview to be over, counting the minutes. Was it worse if it was your father? Or if it had happened to Hilary, would they have felt even more outraged, even more that everything they'd been brought up to believe in had just been chucked out of the window? Just like that. And Dad wasn't that kind of bloke, not the kind of bloke you associated with fancying women, going off the rails, talking about love like some third-rate movie. He was one of the most permanent kind of men Adam had ever come across. His friends had always been amazed that he was always there, always part of the family, always easy. There was something about Dad that was comforting. Or at least there had been, until now.

"Vi will be really pleased you're all coming," Hilary said.

They looked abashed. It was difficult to say that for some bizarre reason they quite wanted to go.

"I don't want to see Gina, though," Gus said.

"You don't have to."

"But she'll be there—"

"She'll sit at the front. We'll all be at the back. She's got nothing to do with this. We're going for Vi, boys. And Dan."

"And Sophy."

"Yes," Hilary said, smiling at Gus, "and Sophy."

The church was more than half full. Everyone from Orchard Close was there, including Doug and Cath Barnett, also several cronies of Dan's from all his years in the town, two representatives from the British Legion, and a nurse from the hospital. The front pew was empty. Laurence, who would ordinarily have stood back to let his family file into a pew first, led the way and took a seat as far from the aisle as possible, under a small marble tablet commemorating the short life of a young Whittingbourne man, a soldier, who had lost his life at the Battle of Omdurman. "A noble son," the tablet said. "A steadfast patriot." Laurence knelt beneath it, acutely ill at ease, and stared fixedly ahead.

A few more people came in and settled themselves in the strange midday candle-lit gloom. Ahead of them all, Dan lay in his coffin, a short coffin of waxed wood with brass handles—"Only the best," Vi had said—under a dome of pale flowers. The organ was playing softly "Jesu, Joy of Man's Desiring," and some people were whispering, leaning towards one another with their shoulders touching confidentially. Then there was a small hush. Vi came in, on Gina's arm, dressed in deep purple. She walked very upright, her white hair waved under a little net arrangement. She paused by Hilary, and the pew full of Woods, and Laurence heard the hiss of her whisper. He held his own breath. Gina, in navy blue, was standing very straight and looking ahead.

"Bless you, dear," Vi said, a little louder. She looked along the pew. "Bless you all for coming. Have you seen Sophy?"

They shook their heads.

"She'll be along," Vi said. "Poor dear. She's so upset."

Her smile travelled along their heads and lighted, at the end, on Laurence. He could feel it, like a little glow of warmth, full of the affection, at a time like this, of having known someone like him for thirty years. He was almost part of the family. He bent his head still further. I can't bear it, he told himself, I can't. Dear old Vi. She doesn't know. Gina hasn't told her yet, and she doesn't know.

Sophy had High Place to herself. She had done this deliberately, saying she was going out to buy last-minute flowers for Dan and that she would follow them to the funeral. She had even dressed for the funeral, in a long black jersey pinafore dress over a dark-green T-shirt, and had put her hair up with a slide Dan had given her, shaped like a butterfly, made of dull silvery metal. He had been shy about giving it to her and she had never, while he was alive, liked it very much. Now, she felt violently fond of it. She also put on the bracelet that had been Fergus's last birthday present to her, a twist of rough silver, like a rope. Then she said she was going out to get flowers for Dan.

"We've got flowers," Gina said. "I ordered them days ago. From both of us."

"I want some to be just from me. Some I've bought."

"But not now, Sophy. It's far too late. We've got to be at Gran's in fifteen minutes. You know that."

"I'll be there," Sophy said. "I'll be quick. I'll go straight to the church."

She went out of the glass door and round to the street door, which she banged but didn't go through. Instead, she doubled back into the garden, threaded her way behind a tangled curtain of clematis, and hid behind the summer house. She waited there for some minutes, panting slightly, her blue bead between her teeth, and then she saw Gina come out of the garden door and turn to lock it. She looked very neat, in a dark suit and dark shoes, and she had a little flat bag, like an envelope, under one arm. Sophy looked at her quite impersonally, as if she had nothing to do with her, as if she was just a woman who'd been in Sophy's house for sixteen years. She watched her walk in her high-heels round the house to the street door, and vanish through it on her way to Orchard Close. Sophy spat out the bead, counted to fifty and then fled across the little camomile lawn, past the Gothic bench, and let herself into the house again.

She went straight up to her bedroom. It was almost stripped by now except for her bed and desk and bookcase, and a bag lying on the floor. It was a black canvas bag, new and stiff, which her parents had once given her for school books and which she had spurned in favour of the plastic supermarket carrier bags everyone else in her class used because it looked more casual, more cool. To carry books in an expensive, well-made bag with leather handles might indicate you cared about them, and therefore, Heaven forbid, about school. But the bag was going to come into its own now. Sophy only wished she'd left it out in the rain for a while, or got Gina to drive the car over it once or twice, to take off a bit of its newness.

There was nothing inside it but Fergus's letter and a small pot of strawberry-flavoured lip gloss. Sophy added jeans, knickers, a handful of T-shirts, her Walkman, some tapes, a hairbrush, and the pages of the diary she had kept that summer. She zipped the bag up and weighed it experimentally on her shoulder. She could take more, she decided. She put it down, opened it and stuffed in a sweatshirt, her sponge bag, and the pig Vi had made out of Gina's shadowy father's uniform trousers. She looked at her photographs. There were pictures of Fergus and Gina and Vi, with a tiny one of Dan pushed into a corner of the frame; there were some of the Wood family and some taken at school, and several of herself. There was also one of her budgerigar in which he appeared to be listening intently to something no one else could hear. For a moment, Sophy's hand hovered over the picture of Vi, and then dropped. You didn't need pictures to make you feel Vi was right beside you.

Sophy looked round the room. She had liked it once, been proud of it, had enjoyed being up there in the roof with first the morning and then the evening sun sliding past the windows. Now she felt nothing for it. All the same, she wouldn't leave it without straightening the bedspread and putting her pencil pot precisely beside her blotter, and her blotter exactly parallel to the neat pile of books on her desk. Then she pulled the curtains, as if to indicate to the room that it should now go to sleep, picked up her bag, and went out.

On the next landing, she opened Gina's bedroom door. Very orderly, as it always was, with Gina's small slippers under a chair and her make-up jars shining on the reflective surface of the glass-topped dressing table. Then the bathroom, which smelt so feminine these days, and the spare bedroom where nobody, as far as Sophy could remember, had ever been, to occupy those handsome beds under their crewelwork covers, or stare at themselves in the Spanish mirror bordered with delicate, flattened ironwork flowers. After that, there was Fergus's office—completely empty except for the carpet and a big wicker basket he had used for wastepaper—and a little room which Gina had always insisted no one must touch because it was to be her private place. But she had never done anything about it except hang up curtains of buff linen patterned with stylised tulips and import a table and a chair, which now sat forlorn and without purpose under a pale film of dust. It was a temptation to write "Good-bye" in the dust, and Sophy had to shut the door, with resolution, before she gave in to it.

Downstairs, there was the dining room, the sitting room, and the kitchen. Sophy looked religiously at all three, as if remembering her manners and the need to say goodbye and thank you at the end of a party she hadn't in the least enjoyed. She opened Gina's neglected piano and played a single middle C, over and over, to emphasise her departure by insistent repetition. Then she went into the kitchen and looked at her budgerigar. He hardly moved. She opened the tiny door in his cage and took out his water and seed containers to refill them, and he watched her, without interest.

"You should go back to Gran," Sophy said. "It's better for you there."

The bird gave a minute shrug as if to say that one place or another in this caged life was all the same to him, and then fell to investigating

260

something compelling under one wing. Sophy glanced round the kitchen, at the table where she had eaten so many meals and written so many miles and miles of homework and left so many notes. Well, there would be no note today, not a word. She picked up her bag again, blew a kiss to the budgerigar, and went out of the glass door, locking it carefully behind her.

"I expect she was just too upset," Vi said. "After all, she was ever so fond of him and because of one thing and another this summer, she thought she hadn't been to see him enough. He never thought that. But then he never thought anything but good of anyone he was fond of."

"I ought to get back," Gina said. She leaned forward and put her teacup down beside the plate of sandwiches she and Vi had tried to eat. "I ought to just see how she is."

"It was lovely, wasn't it? Just as he'd have wanted it. And so many people! Even that nephew, Roger Whatsit, thanking me for taking care of his Uncle Dan. All I could do not to laugh. Silly prat, standing there in his boating-club blazer, all solemn and pompous. Dan said he was like that all his life. Never knew such a pompous little boy."

Gina stood up.

"Will you be all right?"

Vi nodded.

"I've plenty to keep me busy. Plenty to think about. You go and find Sophy and give me a ring. Poor Sophy. Tell her from me that she and I can go and say goodbye to him privately another day."

"She just said she was going to get flowers. She never said she'd duck out of the whole thing—"

"Well, she wouldn't, would she? Or you'd have tried to persuade her out of it. I don't blame her. Some things we just have to do on our own."

Gina bent and kissed her. She had taken off her flowered veil and put it, like a frail cage, over the teapot.

"Not sure about that orchid. A bit Ascotish, orchids. You ring me later."

"I will. Bye, Mum. It was a lovely service, couldn't have been better."

"Bye, dear," Vi said. "Tell her I quite understand."

The clouds were gathering as Gina stepped out into Orchard Street, drawing in outlying fragments to make a dense, smooth grey mass, threatening rain. Gina walked quickly, with little steps on account of her skirt and her shoes, up Orchard Street to the junction with Tannery Street, where an ancient lane, called The Ditches, ran up between huddled old dwellings towards High Place. Some of these had been brightly modernised, with new front doors and hanging baskets of lobelia and geranium, but others crouched as they had done for three hundred years, lurking behind low sills and dusty curtains and unwashed windows. From several came the steady, muted prattle of afternoon television.

Gina glanced up at High Place as she approached it. Sophy's bedroom curtains were drawn. Gina, with a pang of pity, saw Sophy huddled on her bed, still in her black funeral dress, clutching the flowers she had bought for Dan, and crying. Poor Sophy, one blow after another. And another yet to come. Gina hurried to the street door, unlocked it and sped through, reaching the kitchen just as the first specks of small rain came drifting out of the sky.

She kicked her shoes off on the doormat and ran towards the stairs.

"Sophy!" she called, hitching her skirt up. "Sophy! I'm home!"

She ran up the stairs.

"Sophy! Sophy!"

Then up Sophy's stairs. Sophy's door was shut, and there was no music. Gina flung it open.

"Darling—"

The room was exceedingly empty. No Sophy, no cushions, no ornaments. Her bed lay smoothly made, the bedcover tucked in under the pillow as in a hotel, and her desk was alarmingly ordered.

"Sophy?" Gina said.

She opened the wardrobe. Sophy's clothes hung there, untouched, over a muddle of shoes and scarves and old jumpers. She looked round again. All her photographs were still in place, but her hairbrush was missing, and her Walkman.

Gina went out on to the landing. There

were all Sophy's boxes, ready for her to evacuate weeks before she needed to, from the oncoming invasion of the Pughs. Gina picked up the hippopotamus and looked at him. She held him against her for a second, soft and resilient, and put her cheek on his green plush head. Sophy had gone to The Bee House. It was obvious. It was also very sad and slightly angry-making that she should nowadays automatically head round there the moment things got too much for her. Gina went slowly downstairs to her bedroom, counted to ten and picked up the receiver.

She held her breath. Hilary answered.

"The Bee House Hotel. Good afternoon."

"Hilary—"

"Yes?"

"Hilary. It's Gina."

There was a short pause.

"What do you want?"

"I wondered—I wondered if I could speak to Sophy?"

"She isn't here," Hilary said. "I didn't put her on today's schedule, because of the funeral."

"I think she is there. Somewhere. Perhaps with the boys. Because she isn't here and she never turned up at the funeral."

"I'll check," Hilary said. "Hold on."

She put the receiver down beside the telephone with a sharp rap, and Gina could hear her steps going quickly away somewhere, and then the sound of a door opening and then her voice, calling. After a few seconds, her steps returned and went off in another direction and there was silence. Finally, she came back to the telephone.

"I'm afraid no one's seen her. I'll send Gus out to check the garden, in a minute."

"Oh my God," Gina said. "Her room looks abandoned, as if she's left it, as if she meant to. Where can she be?"

"Walking, I should think. She's perfectly sensible—"

"Please ring me," Gina said, her voice suddenly breaking. "Please ring me if you find her—"

There was another tiny pause and then Hilary said, "Of course," and put the telephone down.

Gus was back on the wall, under the yew tree. For a while, for some reason, the funeral had made him feel better, had made him feel that something orthodox and accustomed was happening with all the hymns and the prayers and everyone in church clothes. But when they got back, it had all fallen to pieces again. Laurence had gone off to the kitchen without speaking. George had gone back to the garden centre, where they'd only given him an hour off anyway, and Adam had vanished. Gus had trailed upstairs and hung about in Hilary's bedroom while she took off her black suit and put on her hotel clothes, but when she said there were lots of things he could do to help her, which in turn would help him, he had shuffled about and muttered that he'd got stuff to do anyway.

"All right," Hilary said. "As you wish." She gave him a hug as she went past, and the smell of her made him want to cry again. He went into his bedroom and wrenched off his tie and his school shoes and chucked his school trousers on the bed. Then he put on his jeans again, the really wide ones, and a T-shirt of Sophy's that she'd left behind one night, dark blue with a rainbow on the front, and his sneakers, and drifted downstairs, his back rubbing against the wall, kicking every step.

He went slowly out into the garden. It looked as if it was going to rain, but he thought he would like to get wet. He'd get into the yew tree and get wet and dirty with his hair full of bits of bark and he would stay there. Everyone, including—no, especially—Sophy would say he was behaving like a baby but he couldn't see there was any other way to behave just now. Sophy hadn't come to the funeral. Plainly, she hadn't been able to face it. She was probably shut away somewhere, having a good howl, like she did when he told her about Laurence and Gina.

"It isn't true!" she'd said. Her face had gone quite empty, like a moon.

"It is," he said. He wanted to hold her hand. "It is. First Mum told us and then Dad did. It's true."

He had tried to comfort her when she cried. He had got off the wall and clumsily half pulled, half helped her off it too, and then he had put his arms around her even though she was taller than him. She had simply stood there, in the circle of his awkward arms, with her face covered by her hands, gasping with tears. He'd seen them run down under her hands and trickle into the cuffs of her waitress blouse. He hadn't a handkerchief, of course, so after a while he dropped his arms and took his T-shirt off and offered her that instead.

She'd been grateful. "Thank you," she'd said. "Oh Gus. Thank you." He stood for a while watching her crying into his T-shirt and thought he had never felt so awful for anyone else in his whole life. Then she blew her nose and dried her face and her hands and her wrists. Her face was blotched with pink and her eyes were red. She looked absolutely terrible and Gus couldn't take his eyes off her. Then they both sat down with their backs to the wall and Sophy shut her eyes and said, "Do you think that really is the end? Of all these awful things happening?"

Gus didn't know. He had spent some alarming hours before he went to sleep each night trying to imagine horrors that were still left to happen, like Hilary being killed in a car smash or everyone dying except him and the house burning down, in order to create a kind of insurance bargain with fate, and prevent them. He felt tired. He felt tired the whole time and he didn't want to be with anybody, while at the same time worrying about them if he couldn't actually see them. He reached up into the yew branches above him and gripped a springy bough, pulling it up and down like some exercise machine, so that he was showered with dirty bits and his muscles ached.

"Gus?"

He stopped pulling. It was Hilary. He peered sideways out of the tree. She was standing about ten feet away among the old apple trees, and she was looking in his direction.

"Yes," he said, without moving.

"Gus. Do you know where Sophy is?"

"Why should I?"

"Could you come out of that tree? While I talk to you."

He inched along the wall, ducking under the bough.

"She didn't come to the funeral," Hilary said. "And Gina has just rung to say her room is empty and it looks as if she's left it. She thought she might be here. Have you seen her all day?"

"No," Gus said. He swung one leg tiredly over the wall and dropped to the ground. "I haven't seen her for two days."

"Did she say anything? About going away?"

"No," Gus said and then, because the memory of it was suddenly so strong upon him, "She was crying."

Hilary took a step forward. Gus leaned back against the wall and put an arm up across his face.

"Gus," Hilary said, leaning to put her hands on his shoulders. "Gus, what happened?"

"I told her," Gus said. "I didn't mean to. I just did."

"What did you tell her?"

Gus turned his head sideways so that he needn't look at her.

"You know," he said. "About Dad and her mother. About them going to marry each other."

CHAPTER

15

"I'm here," Sophy said.

Fergus stared at her.

"Sophy—"

He held the door with one hand and in the other he held his reading glasses, half-moon spectacles framed in tortoiseshell. His hair stood on end a bit, as if he'd ruffled it while he was thinking.

"My dear, how wonderful. How—it's just that I wasn't expecting you—"

Sophy hitched her bag a little higher on her shoulder.

"May I come in?"

"Of course," he said. "Of course—" He sounded flustered. He stood back, holding the door open for her, and as she went past he made a small clumsy dart to kiss her cheek, and missed.

She went into the sitting room and dumped her bag on a white sofa. She looked perfectly in command. He followed her.

"Did you get my letter?"

"Of course," she said, her eyes widening. "Why else do you think I'm here?"

"It's—it's just that I didn't quite think it would be so soon."

"I had to," Sophy said simply.

Fergus went across to the white sofa and transferred the bag to the floor.

"New covers—"

Sophy made a little impatient noise. She bent over a table with some glass and silver objects on it and re-arranged them, as if asserting her right to do that in retaliation for having her bag shifted. Fergus moved quickly beside her and put his hand restrainingly on hers.

"Sophy. Why did you have to?"

She looked at him. Her glance was oblique. She said maddeningly, "You said we had to look at flats. And schools. Schools start again next week."

Fergus sighed. "Dear one, we can't get you into a new school this term. It would have to be after Christmas—"

"Why would it?"

"It's too late now—"

"But I don't want to do just two terms somewhere. I want to do a proper year—"

"Sophy," Fergus said, seizing both her wrists. "Stop this nonsense. Stop being so damned childish. Tell me why you have suddenly turned up here, out of the blue."

She glared.

"You asked me to come."

"I know. But you know as well as I do that I didn't mean by return of post."

She went over to the window and looked down into the garden. She looked enormously tall and thin and fragile, silhouetted there against the light in her narrow dark clothes, with her long neck and piled-up hair. She also looked rather dangerous, as if she might explode if not handled delicately. Fergus wondered for a moment if he should go up to her and put his hands on her shoulders, in a fatherly way, and decided against it. Instead, he lowered himself on to the arm of an upholstered chair and waited, swinging his spectacles by an earpiece. Please, he begged Sophy silently, please. Be amenable, be reasonable, be even a little pliant. Please.

She stood there for several minutes. At one point, she reached up and took the butterfly clasp out of her hair, shook her hair loose and then wound it all up again more tightly, with practised competence.

Then, after another minute or so, she said, without turning round, "Dan died."

"I know," Fergus said. "Your mother told me. I'm so sorry."

"Then Gus told me something."

"Did he?"

"Yes. Something that no one else had had the guts to tell me."

Fergus was silent.

Sophy waited for a further half-minute and said, "Laurence is going to leave Hilary."

"What!"

"You heard me. Laurence is going to leave Hilary."

"Oh my God," Fergus said, getting up. "*Why?*"

"Because he's in love with my mother."

There was another small pause and then Fergus said softly, "Dear Heaven."

"And she's in love back. They're going to run off to France together. That's what Gus said."

Fergus came up to Sophy and put his arm round her. She shook him off.

"Don't."

"I don't know what to say to you. What does your mother say?"

"I haven't mentioned it to her. I can't. I can hardly bear to think of it, let alone talk about it."

"Oh Sophy—"

"I thought she'd got all happy because of the counselling thing. I thought it was that."

He stood beside her, gazing down into the garden. It looked tired now, heavy with dark late-summer green, and there were a few dead curled leaves drifting wearily about under the white-painted furniture. He felt a sudden surge of real grief, not for himself, but for this child beside him and those other children in Whittingbourne, those three boys, and for old Vi. He swallowed hard. The consequences of some actions were terrifying. Quite terrifying. Uproot one significant tree in the forest, and then the wind gets in and winds its way about and blows down all the other trees, one after another, helpless in the face of it. However much, Fergus thought, you think you are in charge of life, there are always things that happen to you, things you can't avoid, and they can devastate you. Sophy had said that to him, blazing with resentful anger, when last she'd been to London. And he had been, if he was honest, resentful in return, but resentful of her innocence, her passivity, her goodness even. He regretted that bitterly now, bitterly.

She said suddenly, "And something else."

He looked at her. Her expression was set.

"I slept with George."

Fergus bowed his head.

"Did you?"

"Yes. And we didn't have a condom. We didn't mean to do it. Not before we did, I mean."

There was a pause.

"So are you pregnant?"

"I don't know."

"Sophy—"

"I'll know soon."

Fergus found that his hands were trembling, as if they were having their own private anguished reaction to all this. He put them in his pockets.

"How soon?"

"Five days."

"Don't you think we should see a doctor?"

"No," Sophy said furiously. "*No.* Not yet."

"Anything else?"

"No," Sophy said. "Except that I'm not going back."

For the first time, she turned and looked at him. Her eyes were quite clear and almost blank.

"I'll have to get some more things. I didn't bring much, you see, because I didn't want that life all over this life. I can't stand any more of that sort of thing, all that lying and mess."

"Does your mother know you've come?"

"No," Sophy said.

"Would you ring her?"

"No."

"Then I must."

Sophy turned away from him and crossed the room back to her black bag.

"If you want."

She picked the bag up and held it in her arms like a cumbersome baby. He noticed she was wearing a bangle he had given her.

"I'll see you later," she said. "I'm finished. I'm going up to my room."

Gina lay on her bed, fully dressed. It wasn't quite dark, and the room was full of dim ghostly light, like veils. She was wide awake. She had been there for almost an hour, ever since Fergus had rung and said that Sophy was with him.

She had cried. She had leaned against the wall of the kitchen, clutching the telephone receiver, and cried and cried, unsteady with relief.

"Can I speak to her?"

"I don't think so," Fergus said. His voice

was odd, as if he too wasn't quite in control. "She's in her room. The door's shut."

"Is she all right?"

"No," he said.

"Did she—"

"Yes. She told me. Gus told her."

Gina was silent. There was at that moment no fight in her sufficient for her to say, "Well, I expect it's all very satisfactory for you."

In the silence Fergus said, "I don't have an opinion, Gina. At least, as far as Sophy is concerned."

"Maybe that's mutual."

"Maybe."

"Is she coming back?"

"I don't think so," Fergus said. "At least, not immediately."

Gina lifted her arm to blot her eyes on her shirtsleeve. They left an ink-blot spatter of mascara smears.

"School starts on Monday."

"Yes. I don't think I can talk much sense to her just for a day or two."

"She wants to live with you?"

"Yes." He took a breath. "I said I'd buy a flat for her and me, until her education is finished at least."

"I see."

"I'm not doing this for me, Gina—"

She said, interrupting him, "The Pughs want to move in, in October. Their children's half-term."

"And then," Fergus said, "you are going to France."

"Yes," she whispered.

"And had you," he said, his voice suddenly finding authority again, "thought of Sophy in this scheme?"

Slowly, she took the telephone receiver away from her ear, looked at it for a moment or two, and then put it quietly, almost stealthily, back on the wall. Then she counted to ten and, when it didn't ring again, took it off the hook and laid it on the pile of directories near by.

She pulled herself upstairs, using the banister as if it were a lifeline, and crawled across her bed, without even kicking off her shoes. For a while, she lay face down, and then she rolled over, very slowly, on to her back and stared at the ceiling and listened to the rush-hour cars going home, past the high wall, home to supper and evening television and a bit of late gardening in the fading light. She pictured suburban Whittingbourne, with cats on garden fences, and cars in carports, and domestic-evening sounds drifting out of open windows across small lawns and runner-bean rows and discreetly hidden clumps of dustbins. It felt like another world, another planet even, from this wide, lonely bed in a room where she had unquestionably been the happiest and the most wretched in her whole life.

"You can't stop the bad things happening," Vi had said that afternoon, laying down an uneaten sandwich after the funeral. "It's hopeless, that. But it's what you do when they happen which counts."

Gina closed her eyes. I know that, she thought. Her lids felt gritty along the rim, as if each lash was a little spike. But what about the good things? Does one's reaction to them carry exactly the same responsibility? Without opening her eyes, she felt sideways across the bed until she touched the handle of the drawer in her bedside cabinet. She tried to open it, but it required her to sit up to do that, so she rolled over on to one side and stretched out her other arm. In the drawer, lying on top and paper-clipped together, were the postcard she had written to Laurence from Pau and a photograph, a piece of photograph cut from a much larger one, showing Laurence playing Ham in the school play in 1964. He was wearing a tunic his mother had made, Gina remembered, out of some old yellow curtains, and his sixteen-year-old arms and legs and feet were bare. His face had been roughly blacked, as no more than a dramatic gesture, and his features were plainly visible still. Gina unclipped the postcard and the photograph and laid them side by side on the bedcover, and stared at them, with a fierce, greedy concentration, until it was too dark to see them any more.

"Does it really need," Hilary said impatiently, "*three* of you to work out my account?"

The building society branch manager, a friendly young man who looked about George's age and who wore a brush haircut, a collar and tie, and a gold earring, glanced up from his supervision of two girl clerks and said cheerfully, "Won't be a minute, Mrs. Wood. You should see us when we need to change a lightbulb."

The girls giggled faintly, tapping buttons on their keyboards and pushing Hilary's pass book in and out of the printer.

"I really only wanted to know what the present balance is when the interest's been added—"

"Going somewhere nice?" the manager said.

Hilary pushed her spectacles up her nose.

"I'm running away, I think. Where do you suggest?"

One of the girls glanced up.

"You a Pisces?"

"Yes. How did you know?"

"I can always tell," the girl said, snapping Hilary's book out of the machine. "I always know. You ought to go to Portugal. Pisces have an affinity with Portugal."

She pushed the passbook under the protective glass screen. They all looked at Hilary and smiled cosily.

"Have a nice time, Mrs. Wood."

"Mind you run back again."

She nodded. She went out into the market place, where a disagreeable little wind was blowing litter and dust along the gutters and tugging at the awnings above the market stalls. There was a sudden small sharpness in the air too, a first breath of autumn.

Seven thousand, four hundred and twenty-two pounds. Not enough to run away on, or at least, not enough to run away on in a final and substantial manner. And not at forty-five. An adolescent could do it on nothing, but a middle-aged woman with three children and a business couldn't. At forty-five a future consisting only of a rucksack containing forty cigarettes, music tapes, a red lipstick, and a change of nose stud was neither suitable nor practical. At forty-five, you needed a job and some seed money and a landscape of at least apparent solidity. In any case, she wasn't in the least sure she wanted to run away. She just wanted to toy with the idea of it, to tell herself that she could if she wanted to; that she had the option.

"You won't go anywhere, will you," Gus had said, making the remark a statement, not a question.

"No," Hilary said. "And if I did, I'd take you with me."

Gus had then become fiercely involved with the dog clip he wore hanging from a belt loop on his jeans, from which was suspended a whole lot of keys and discs and a grisly little hand made of bright-green rubber.

"Mum—"

"Yes?"

"Will—will Dad take Sophy to France?"

"Oh my God," Hilary said. "I never thought of that."

"But will he?"

Hilary looked at Gus. His face was averted but the expression on it was evident from his whole attitude.

"Gus. I don't know."

His mouth was working.

"It seems," he said unsteadily, "it just sometimes seems all too crazy to be happening. Doesn't it?"

He had gone back to school today. At breakfast, Hilary noticed how all his clothes were too small, even though he himself was quite small for fourteen. He had looked relieved, spooning up his cereal, his tie badly knotted and askew. Adam wasn't wearing his tie. It lay, Hilary knew, in a screwed-up string in his pocket and he would, like all his group, put it on with elaborate defiance as he sauntered through the school gates. He wouldn't eat breakfast. He drank two mugs of black coffee in noisy gulps like a dog, and groaned. Hilary saw them both off with a feeling very like the feeling she had had with all three of them that first day of primary school, delivering her pink-kneed, bat-eared, shaking child to that roaring playground.

"Take care," she said idiotically to her sons of fourteen and sixteen. She had a lump in her throat.

Adam clumped her on the shoulder.

"No," he said, "not us. You. You take care."

The whole building had felt eerily quiet when they had gone. There were only half a dozen guests, and they had eaten their breakfasts and taken themselves off, leaving the strange, impersonal chaos of their bedrooms to Lotte's attention. Hilary had gone into her office, and looked for some time at the computer she had bought in the spring and vowed to master in a month, and decided that, if there was a day in which to start tackling it, this was not it. So, avoiding the kitchen, she went out into Whittingbourne to do various errands and assess her personal assets.

On the way back, she paused outside the estate agent's window in the market place. There was the brochure of High Place, propped up on a little wooden easel, with a scarlet sticker across one corner, proclaiming "SOLD." A couple from London had bought it, Michelle had told Hilary, and they were setting up a design studio on the industrial estate and were advertising already for cleaning staff. She gave a huge sigh and looked with loathing at the little regiment of salt and pepper pots on the dining-room sideboard in The Bee House. She thought she might apply, she said, not looking at Hilary. Only fair to warn you. And of course Lotte wasn't really satisfied either. It was probably speaking out of turn to mention it, but she might as well. Only fair, after all.

Only fair, Hilary thought now, turning away from Barton and Noakes's window. Only fair to say that at least two of the regular staff were off, at any minute, to take other jobs whose only advantage was a brief novelty. And what was the alternative to "Only fair"? Just walking out, perhaps, mid-meal one day, leaving a note saying, "I've gone. Sorry. Michelle." Or no note at all. There was no fairness in these things, no more than there was in Laurence falling in love with Gina and causing such violent turbulence and distress. If you looked for things to be fair, relied on them to be so, you'd go mad. Yet you didn't, on the other hand, have to lie down and simply take unfairness. You needn't be passive. Hilary, during that queer afternoon walk round her solitary, sloping field, had come very much to that conclusion. Things of a devastating kind might have happened to herself and to her sons, but even if she had, in the end, to succumb to them, she wasn't going to do so without a fight.

The bar of The Bee House, which also served as its foyer, was full of people and suitcases when she returned. A small elderly coach party, dismayed by the powerful aroma of curry and drains which affected the hotel on the edge of Whittingbourne into which they had been booked, were pleading for accommodation. Laurence was dealing with them, in his chef's apron, and the sight of him, calm and friendly in this sea of agitation, smote Hilary in much the same way that the boys had, going off to school that morning.

He saw her. He raised a hand and smiled.

"Orphans from the storm," he called. They laughed in relief. "Fourteen of them. Seven doubles. Can we?"

She hurried forward.

"This is my wife," Laurence said. "She is the soul of competence. I'm sure she won't abandon you to the gutter."

• • • •

In the afternoon, having shut seven double-bedroom doors on relieved and contented cluckings within, and found a room at the Brewer's Arms in Orchard Street for the coach driver, Hilary went down to the kitchen. Laurence was alone, slicing racks of lamb into cutlets with deft, quick blows.

"All settled?"

"Poor old things. In a panic they might get upset tummies as well as nylon sheets."

Laurence grunted. He laid the cleaver down and wiped his hands on a cloth.

Hilary said, "I see High Place is finally sold. There's a red sticker on the brochure in Barton and Noakes's window."

"Yes."

Hilary sat down at the chair by Laurence's desk. She looked at his row of notebooks, battered and tattered, some held together by rubber bands. They made her feel strange, and rather unsteady, as if they were living things she was about to lose. She stretched out a hand and picked up Laurence's grey marble egg.

"Michelle says it's some London couple with a design consultancy or something. They're renting studio space on the industrial estate. She thinks she'd like to leave us and go and work for them."

Laurence grunted again. He took down an aluminium canister of breadcrumbs, and began to shake it evenly over a large, shallow dish.

"If High Place is sold," Hilary said, holding the egg in both hands, "then the new people will be moving in, in a couple of months. Won't they?"

Laurence broke two eggs into a bowl and began to whisk them.

"Laurence—"

"Yes?"

"Would you stop doing that and come here just one minute?"

"Why?"

"Because I need to see your face. I need to look in your face."

Slowly, Laurence lowered his right hand until the whisk rested against the rim of the bowl. Then, in the gesture she knew so well, he wiped his hands across the belly of his apron, and came towards her. He pulled a chair away from the kitchen table and sat astride it, his arms folded on the back, his face turned her way. She put the egg down carefully beside Gus's dragon.

"I suppose," Hilary said, "that the new people will come about October."

He shrugged. "I should think so."

"So does that mean that in October you are going to France?"

There was a pause. His gaze never left her face. After a while he said, "I don't know the actual date."

Hilary put her hands together in her lap.

"I went to the building society today. To see how much money I have personally. It isn't much, about seven thousand. The thing is, I have to plan. If you go, I have to decide whether to try and stay on and employ a chef or whether just to sell the whole thing."

He was watching her.

"It's your house, I know; it was left to you. But the business is ours and I think you'd be honourable about my share of the house."

"Of course—"

"Laurence—" She leaned forward, her elbows on her knees, holding her hands clasped together to keep them steady. "Laurence, I want you to think about all this. I want you to think about The Bee House and me and the boys and our future. You can't just walk out on us all."

"I never intended to. At least, not in the way you imply."

"And while—" She stopped.

He waited. The kitchen was very still.

"While you're thinking about that—"

"Yes?"

"I'd like you to think about something else too."

He raised his head a little.

"Tell me."

"I want you to think," Hilary said slowly, giving every word weight to keep her voice steady too, "I want you to think—about us. I want you to consider the possibility, which I think is a probability in fact, that our marriage isn't over." She swallowed. "I know I still love you. I think you may well love me. I may often have wanted to murder you, but I've never wanted to divorce you. And I don't now."

She stood up, holding the edge of the desk, looking down at him. He sat motionless, his arms in their blue rolled-up shirtsleeves crossed on the chair back, his face still turned to where her face had been.

"It isn't the end, you know," Hilary said. "Our marriage isn't dead. It never was."

And then she turned away from him and went out of the swing door and up the stairs to the bar.

Sophy sat on the floor of her London bedroom. She wore new black jeans Fergus had bought her and a long-sleeved grey T-shirt and her silver bracelet. She had also had a haircut and the result was that her hair felt thicker and better. She wore it loose, tossed to one side, in a way she had never worn it before. At Fergus's request, she had taken her blue bead on its leather thong off from round her neck and wound it round her wrist instead. He had said it might stop her putting it in her mouth. It did, but she kept fingering the hollow at the base of her throat where it had lain, and missing it.

On her bedroom walls were several new posters bought from the shop at the Tate Gallery. Fergus had said that, if they were going to live together, there had to be a few rules that each insisted on, and one of his was that any kind of adherence to pop culture happened outside the house. Sophy didn't really mind. She made a token fuss, but her new posters were both beautiful and adventurous, and totally unlike anything she had had in Whittingbourne, and she felt a secret pride in them. Fergus had also bought her several floor cushions covered in ikat-printed cotton, an ink-blue silk shirt, and a cream-coloured dressing gown shaped like a kimono and patterned with flying cranes.

It had been a very good few days. The thing was, Tony was away, working in some stately home for a week, so they had the house to themselves. Apart from shopping, they cooked together and went to a film and there was a breath of excitement to it all because it wasn't in the least, in atmosphere, like life at High Place together had been. Sophy felt older now, less the child, the dependent one shackled by homework. Fergus hadn't mentioned school. Nor had he mentioned a flat nor the possibility that Sophy might be pregnant. He had simply talked to her about London things and his work. He had asked her if she wanted to talk about Gina and Laurence and she had said no. Not in the least. Well, you will, he'd said, and when you do, you must tell me. It's too big a thing to keep to yourself.

That afternoon, he had taken her with him to a huge, grim, grand house in St. John's Wood, to look at some furniture. The house belonged to someone who was never there, and a housekeeper showed them into several great, shrouded rooms where Fergus examined a tallboy and several chairs and a long looking glass with a gilded eagle crouched at the top of the frame. He had also spent a long time inspecting some tall, graceful blue-and-white vases that reminded Sophy, in design if not in shape, of the Chinese vases that had sat on the landing windowsill at High Place. After that, they had driven slowly round the circle of Regent's Park so that Fergus could show Sophy the architecture, and then they had come home—"Risotto tonight, don't you think?" Fergus had said. "With all different kinds of mushrooms. And a bottle of Mâconnais"—to find that Tony had arrived, two days early.

"It was hopeless," he said. "They employ me as the specialist, and then they stand over me all the time, second-guessing everything I'm doing and saying what a disaster the last restoration was, in 1928. So I said send the damn thing to me, or I won't do it at all."

He had kissed Sophy, and smiled at her.

"Nice to see you. I like the haircut. Having a little breath of civilisation before school?"

"No," she said. She tried to make her voice sound light and unconcerned. "I've come to live here. To live in London."

There was abruptly something rather alarming in the atmosphere, like the unnatural echoing stillness before a breaking storm. Fergus cleared his throat. Sophy felt that she neither could, nor wanted to, look at Tony.

"Sophy—"

"Yes?"

"I wonder," Fergus said and his voice sounded quite different to the way it had sounded all afternoon, "I wonder if you'd be sweet and just leave us for ten minutes."

She gave her new haircut a toss.

"OK," she said.

She went out of the sitting room and up the stairs to her bedroom, and closed the door, loudly, so that they could hear her. Then she went over to the space of floor at the end of her bed, where her new cushions were, and sat there, holding her ankles, her head back and her eyes closed, trying with every muscle of her body and imagination not to consider what might happen next.

CHAPTER
16

"You should have told me," Vi said. "You should have told me before."

She sat at the kitchen table in High Place, one hand on a mug of tea, the other holding the turquoise pendant Dan had given her and which she wore round her neck on a silver chain.

"I couldn't, Mum. Because of Dan. You were so worried."

"I wonder," Vi said, "I wonder if *you* weren't a bit worried about telling *me*. I wonder that."

Gina leaned forward over her own mug and looked at the coffee in it and thought what a horrible colour it was.

"Yes," she said.

Vi had caught her still in her dressing gown that morning, at almost ten o'clock. She hadn't telephoned, she had simply come in, unannounced, a thing she hadn't done more than half a dozen times in all the years Gina had lived in High Place. Gina had overslept because Laurence had been there until after one in the morning, and when he had gone, she couldn't sleep. They hadn't made love.

"I can't," he had said. "I can't even think about it. Not tonight. The sadness of everything is just overwhelming."

She had been very afraid, and the fear had made her angry. She had shouted at him that he was being bullied by Hilary, by his children; she had accused him of being like any old weak-principled politician who, caught with his trousers down, then did whatever he was told to by the last strong-minded woman he had spoken to. When she had finished screaming, she wanted him to hold her, and he did, but with a hint of absent-mindedness that fanned the dying flames of her anxiety and anger back into a blaze.

"Don't you think I feel guilty?" she had shouted. "Don't you remember that I felt guilty long before you even troubled to get round to it? And don't talk to me about all there is to lose, Laurence, don't insult me with that. *I'm* the one whose child has run off to her father! I'm the one who failed to tell her the truth early enough and who's got to pay for that omission, over and over!"

He had turned to her then, and held her properly for the first time.

"We can't use our children as excuses for what we do," Gina said. "They'd never forgive us. They may hate us just now but they'd hate us even more later if we said that you'd only stayed on in your marriage for their sakes. It isn't fair to burden them with that. That's our burden."

Laurence said softly, "Don't *you* make excuses."

"I'm not—"

"Yes, you are. You're trying to justify things. The only justification we have, Gina, is that we want to do this thing, and it's not a justification that has, or can possibly have, any appeal for anyone but us."

She had pulled away from him then.

"I think you'd better go."

"Can I ask you something?"

"Of course."

"Do you intend Sophy to come with us?"

She picked up one of the glasses of wine she had poured and which neither of them had touched.

"I did. Of course I did. But she seems rather to have put paid to that. Why do you ask?"

"Because she's a person," Laurence said, suddenly angry. "Because she's a player in all this, poor girl, whether she likes it or not, just as my boys are. Because I've started trying to see things as other people see them and now I've started, I can't stop."

He got off the edge of the table, where he had been perching, and went across to the door. She put the glass down with a shaking hand and a little tongue of wine leaped out and fell in a pale pool on the table.

"Laurence—"

"Yes?"

She bent her head. She would have given anything not to have to ask him, but the need was too great to stop herself.

"Do you still love me?"

He paused by the door and turned back to look at her.

"You know I do. I love you, I have always loved you and I always will."

Then he had gone out into the dark and she had gone to bed and lain there, tormenting herself with the fact that he hadn't kissed her goodnight, until she heard the clock on the church strike five and a heavy, unnatural sleep came to claim her.

She hadn't woken until almost ten, and was downstairs in the kitchen muzzily plugging in the kettle when Vi appeared at the glass door.

"I think it's time you told me," she said without preliminary when Gina let her in. "I've been awake since four, thinking, and I decided it's time you told me why Sophy's gone to her father."

Gina had made them tea and coffee. Vi said she didn't want tea, she wanted the truth.

"It's Laurence, Mum," Gina said. "Laurence and me."

Vi had picked up her pendant then, and begun to stroke it between finger and thumb as if to comfort herself with it.

"We want to go away together. To France. We wanted to take Sophy."

"I don't understand you," Vi said. "Sometimes you seem to me like someone I've never met before."

"I knew you'd be angry—"

"I'm not angry," Vi said. "I've learned lately what it's worth getting angry about and this isn't it. But I'm shocked."

"If it's any comfort," Gina said, "I'm a bit shocked myself. But I'm happy and he's given me my confidence back."

Vi picked up her mug and took a sip of tea.

"I used to wonder if you two would end up together, long ago. He'd have been good for you, Gina. He'd have made you work hard and you wouldn't have had a minute to get into all these states. No wonder he was so odd at the funeral. Couldn't look me in the eye." She put her mug down and Gina suddenly saw how old her hands had become, almost uncertain. "But you can't do it," Vi said.

Gina pulled the sash of her dressing gown tighter.

"We can. We're going to."

"There's all these children—"

"They're big children, Mum."

"Only in size," Vi said. "And Sophy hasn't the temperament for this. Any more than you'd have had, at her age. You 'only' children aren't like others. You find families in things and people to make up to yourselves for not having one of your own. You may hate your family if you have one, but it's better than not having one at all. Families is where you do your learning." She pushed her tea mug away. "If you'd told me sooner, I could have done something."

"No, you couldn't," Gina said. "No one could. We've loved each other all our lives."

"Just because you love a thing," Vi said, "doesn't follow you've got to have it." She stood up and leaned heavily on the table, her pendant swinging forward out of the neck of her blouse. "I suppose I see why you did it. I suppose I do. But can't you see that there are some things that can't be cured by your ways, or by any other way for that matter? And because they can't be cured, Gina my girl, they just have to be borne."

Gina swallowed.

"People don't think like that any more."

Vi snorted. "No need to tell me *that*. But it doesn't mean *you* have to follow the herd, behave like all the others—"

"I love him," Gina said. "I told you. I've loved him all my life."

Vi moved slowly towards the door.

"That's not enough," she said without turning to look at Gina. "It's not enough to give you the right to do as you please."

Outside in the fresh air, Vi felt suddenly dizzy. She moved slowly to the little steps that went up to the camomile lawn and sat on the low wall that bordered them. She was just out of sight of the kitchen door, so couldn't see Gina. Just as well, perhaps. She didn't, for the moment, much want to see Gina; it was better just to think about her and not have that pretty, neat face framed in its smooth dark hair opposite her and looking, because of what was being said, like an entire stranger. She couldn't be angry. She could be, and was, sad and anxious and shocked but, since Dan's death, she couldn't be angry. Gina wasn't a wicked girl. She might be confused and a bit spoiled and behaving in a way that in others you'd condemn as bad or silly, but she wasn't wicked. Of course she shouldn't have married Fergus Bedford, but then of course she, Vi, shouldn't have believed that Corporal Sy Dunand was going to marry her and take her back to Avenel, New Jersey, where his mom, he assured her, would be just as pleased to see her as if she'd been a lifelong sweetheart on the next block. She'd never mind, Sy had said, that Vi was six years older than he was. Not when she met her. And now, baby, how's about a bit of comfort for a hard-working soldier?

Vi put the heels of her hands into her eye sockets and pressed. Who knew what Gina had inherited, down all those dark mysterious channels of reproduction, from Sy Dunand? Not much of his looks, certainly, but perhaps something in the temperament, something of wanting easy pleasure, the pleasure of the moment. And her childhood had been an odd affair, by modern standards, not a cosy time, God knew, with her, Vi, working all hours with only Sundays off, when she liked to turn the house out and do the accounts. Years of that, there was, years. Perhaps they made Gina hungry. Perhaps they made her so hungry she kept asking things of Fergus Bedford he couldn't possibly give her. She should have had more children after Sophy, of course she should. Four children and she wouldn't have had a moment to ask herself all the time whether she was happy or not.

Well, it was no good wishing for four children now. Vi got up off the wall and tested herself. She felt much steadier. She looked up at the back of the house and reminded herself of how much she had always disliked it because of the airs it gave itself. "Bye," Vi said to it, and walked to the gate to the street and let herself out.

She turned away from High Place and made for The Ditches. Some of the inhabitants there, in the low, squat cottages, were on the waiting list for flats in Orchard Close. Vi didn't blame them. Full of history those cottages might be, but the ceilings crumbled into your tea and there was no sunlight and the damp was shocking. Better by far to get your history off the television and live with some kind of convenience, even if that convenience did entail Cath Barnett. Vi had forgiven Cath Barnett but she hadn't told her so yet. She was biding her time, and while she waited, she watched Cath take the long way round the courtyard every morning, in order not to pass the door of number seven.

At the end of The Ditches, Vi turned left into Orchard Street. Almost opposite her The Bee House stood with its painted signboard and two tubs of geraniums flanking the front door, dispirited now at the end of summer. Vi crossed the street and passed in front of the dining-room windows, through which she could see the tables already laid for dinner. Something awfully depressing about dining rooms, she thought, especially with no one in them. Like empty cricket pitches or theatres. No point to them with no one there.

She turned into the yard. A wine merchant's delivery van stood there with its back doors open and one of the boys who worked in the kitchen, in his blue-checked trousers and white tunic, was lounging against it and chatting to the driver. Vi peered at him. It was Kevin someone. She recognised him. Sometimes, in the old days, she and Dan had seen his Aunt Freda having a Saturday-night drink in the Brewer's Arms.

"Mr. Wood about?" she said.

Kevin took his shoulder away from the side of the van.

"Yeah," he said. "He's in the kitchen. Help yourself."

The kitchen door was open. Vi had never been inside The Bee House kitchen. It looked forbidding, with its long central table and all the stainless-steel-covered work surfaces

and the great cooker thing like a ship's boiler.
She stood on the threshold and peered in. There
was another boy, sorting a crate of green stuff
in one corner, and beyond him, sitting at a desk
and working at something, sat Laurence. He
wasn't dressed like the cook boys, but just had
a white apron on, over his clothes. Vi cleared
her throat. No one seemed to hear her.

"Laurence," Vi said.

He looked up and stood up, immediately.
"Vi!"

She stepped into the room. He came out from
behind his desk and hurried over to her.

"Vi," he said again, stooping to kiss her.
"How are you?"

"Not so bad, all things considering." She
looked round the kitchen. "Have you got a
minute—"

"Well," he said. "It's a bit awkward. The
hotel's suddenly full again—"

"It'll only take a minute," Vi said. She put
a hand out and held his arm. "Just a minute,
Laurence. Somewhere private. There's something I've got to say to you."

"Are you saying I can't stay?" Sophy said.

They were in the car, heading out towards
Richmond, to see a dealer.

"No. No, I'm not saying that. But we did have
a slight, well, row—"

"I know," Sophy said. "I heard you."

She had been in her room and had heard
them quite plainly, Tony's voice raised

298

sometimes in something that was almost a scream. She couldn't hear exactly what they were saying, and a mixture of pride and disgust prevented her from pressing her ear to the door, or even opening it a little, but she had heard Tony cry out, "But you promised! You promised!" and had felt for him, against all her inclinations, a small sympathy.

"You mustn't doubt," Fergus said, "where my priorities lie. But I can't pretend I'm not in something of a dilemma."

Sophy held her stomach with one hand. It was perfectly flat. Her period had been due to start the day before, and hadn't. Also, the day before, she had a conversation with Gina in which Gina said that the law of the land required her to go to school, and that term had now begun and her headmaster had been on the telephone twice asking to know where she was. Gina had, she said, promised that Sophy would be back in a few days.

"It isn't an option," Gina said. "It isn't something you can just do or not according to whim. It's something you have to do, Sophy. You have to come home and go back to school."

Sophy had reported this conversation to Fergus. He hadn't mentioned school again, nor her period. She gave him a lightning glance out of the sides of her eyes. She wondered if he was actually thinking about either of her problems or whether he was preoccupied instead with his own. To her dismay, so used had she recently become to being fuelled by anger, his absorption in his own difficulties did not make her feel furious and jealous, but merely alarmed. She had a feeling that if she were to say now, "Dad. About being pregnant—" he would frown and put on an air of forced concern to hide his inner wish to be distanced from such things and repeat his brutally practical suggestion that she should go and see a doctor. Sophy didn't want to see a doctor, or at least, not in an atmosphere of impatient adult exasperation with her incompetence. She wanted someone to focus on her, to understand why she had had sex with George and why, given the distracting quality of both their lives, they had been so careless. She pressed her stomach again, and surreptitiously crossed the first two fingers of both hands.

"I suppose," Fergus said, frowning, "I had better tell you everything."

Sophy looked out of the window. They were going down a long, wide road lined with red-brick houses with blue-slate roofs which some people, optimistically but hardly successfully, had tried to improve with fake Georgian front doors and imitation-leaded windows and thick coats of pebbledash.

"All right," she said.

"You must try and respond in as adult a way as you can," Fergus said. "And with dispassion."

She said nothing. She put her crossed-fingered hands under her thighs and pressed them down hard.

"Tony is gay," Fergus said.

She waited.

"And I am not."

"Oh," Sophy said.

"I love him, but he is in love with me, which makes it very hard for him indeed because I do not wish to sleep with him."

Out of the window, Sophy saw that one house had a stone cat on the roof, creeping down the slates as if stalking a bird. It was a very crude cat, painted in grey-and-black stripes. You could tell it was a fake from yards off.

"That's why he has to be away sometimes, you see. I am very conscious of how difficult it is for him and I don't want to make it any harder. He says he would rather live with me on my terms than with anyone else, but inevitably there are tensions."

They reached some traffic lights at the end of the road and pulled up. Sophy took her hands out and uncrossed the fingers and flexed them as if she were concentrating on nothing else.

"I had promised Tony we would go to Italy together, for a month, before I started looking for a flat for you and me. I have to go back on that promise now, of course, and he is terribly distressed. He sees my commitment as a father, but he is in love with me. To be in love with someone and know you must always come second with them is very hard. I'm sure you can see that."

Sophy turned sideways, propped her elbow up on the back of the passenger seat, and regarded her father. She tried to imagine being in love with him. She looked at his good, regular profile, and his longish fair hair—thinning a little, she observed, and receding just a fraction at the temples—and his neck rising out of his open shirt collar, and then she looked at his arms and his hands on the steering wheel and all down him, past the leather belt at his waist and his legs—a bit thin—under his chinos, and then at his ankles above the black suede loafers he had taken to wearing. His ankles were good, at least. She remembered looking at all these things in a devouring kind of way, with possessive pride. She remembered too saying once to Adam, during a quarrel, that at least her father had *style*. And elegance. Adam had been helpless with laughter. He had rolled about on the floor guffawing and chucking cushions around.

"Elegance!" he'd shouted in a camp shriek. "Oh my *dear*! Elegance!"

The car began to move forward again.

"So you see," Fergus said, "I have a few things to smooth out before I can really make decisive progress with you. On our life together, I mean."

It's odd, to say the least, Sophy thought, finishing her scrutiny of him, and turning back to sit straight once more, to have you asking for my understanding for an almost stranger, to help you, when it didn't cross your *mind* to give me such consideration—your own daughter—when you left Mum. She waited for a familiar surge of anger to give her the impetus to say this out loud, but it didn't come. There was just, instead, some fatigue and a bit of boredom and this new fear which lay, coiled and cold, at the pit of her stomach.

"Sophy," Fergus said, changing gear with accomplished smoothness and swinging the car round a sharp corner, narrowly missing a dawdling boy oblivious inside the cocoon of his personal stereo, "could you at least have the courtesy to respond?"

She felt for her blue bead. It wasn't there.

"I'd wondered," she said carelessly, "if you were gay."

"I told you. I'm not. My inclination now, to be truthful, is to remain celibate. But at the same time, I don't want to live alone. I never have. I like a domestic life and Tony and I have domestic tastes in common."

Sophy waited a moment and then she said, "But he was crying, he was pleading with you. I heard him. He sounded just like Mum."

Fergus said, under his breath, "He isn't the least like your mother."

Sophy began to pick at the knot of the thong that bound her blue bead to her wrist.

"You ought to take him to Italy," she said.

"That's very sweet of you, but I wouldn't think of it. As I said, you are my priority."

Sophy unwound the long strip of leather from her wrist and slid the bead up and down it.

"I don't want the responsibility, you see. I don't want to be the one to blame for you not taking Tony to Italy—"

"You wouldn't be."

"Yes, I would."

Fergus pulled the car into a small lay-by at the side of the road, intended for buses, and stopped it.

"Sophy—"

"I've got problems," Sophy said. "There's Mum and Laurence and there's my future and—" She paused, suddenly unable to mention that her period hadn't come. "And there's you. But I don't want your problems. They're yours. You deal with them first. Then we'll see."

"But I thought," Fergus said patiently, his hands resting on the steering wheel and his eyes staring straight ahead, "I thought that's what you didn't want. I thought you wanted me to drop everything for you. So I did."

"But I didn't know what there was to drop. Did I? I didn't know about these layers. I didn't know you were going to ask for my *sympathy*." She lifted the bead on its thong and tied it back again around her neck, and then she said, quite suddenly and startling herself, "At least Mum never does that. She's never asked me to be sorry for her."

There was a little silence between them. Fergus took his hands off the steering wheel and put one on Sophy's knee.

"I love you," he said. "That'll never change. But this bit is very hard."

"OK," she said, "OK." She felt a little tearful. "But maybe it isn't the time for that just now."

"Oh my dear—"

"I think," Sophy said, moving her knee very slightly so that his hand slipped from it, "that we'd better not start looking at schools and flats. Not now. I think—" She paused and gave a little sigh. "I think I'd better go home," she said, and picked up the blue bead and put it in her mouth.

The kitchen at The Bee House was tidy, quiet and dark except for the line of work lights that hung over the central table. At it sat Laurence, with half a glass of Chablis in front of him and a piece of scrap paper on which he was doodling complicated patterns, patterns which grew out of a small, neat, central hexagon and spread into increasingly uncontrolled mazes with spirals and zig-zags and explosions. He stopped every so often to look at his hands, examining them as if he were going to make an inventory of every nick and callus and hangnail. When he had done that, he would look up at the door for a few seconds, as if he were waiting for someone to come in. No one did. It was almost midnight and everyone, even Adam and George, this being a weekday, was in bed.

He had not been to see Gina that evening. He had telephoned her and she had sounded better, more optimistic. She said Sophy was coming back.

"Thank God. Did she ring?"

"No," Gina said, "Fergus did. How's your day been?"

"Recipe as usual—"

"Not for much longer."

"No," he said.

"But no alarms and excursions today, at least—"

He laughed. It was not a very relaxed laugh, but he found he could not say that an odd little thing had happened, a tiny five-minute thing which had shaken him much more than Vi's visit. He had been crossing the bar on his way up to the flat in the middle of the afternoon when he had caught sight of Hilary through the little glass window set into the dining-room door, talking to Michelle. She looked exactly the same as usual, her short dark hair slightly ruffled, her red spectacles, her cream blouse and dark-blue skirt, all utterly familiar, as was the way she stood, one arm across her waist, the other balanced on it at the elbow so that her fist fitted under her chin. It gave her a slightly hunched stance, and pushed her face forward. It certainly wasn't graceful, it was gawky, awkward even, and for some reason it absolutely smote him to the heart. He stood there for several minutes, transfixed, on the worn carpet of the bar, with Don polishing glasses and whistling behind him, and stared and stared at Hilary as if it wasn't flesh-and-blood Hilary at all but just the essence of her, the concentration of her personality and his knowledge of it, embodied in this tall, slim, forceful figure who had no idea of image, who had no capacity to be anything other than herself and scorned the wiles necessary even to try.

"You OK?" Don said.

"Yes," Laurence said. "Fine. I was just watching something."

Don came out from behind the bar still twisting a cloth into a sherry schooner.

"A row?" he said hopefully. He joined Laurence.

"Don't think so," Laurence said. "Just looked as if there might be one brewing."

"Pity—"

Laurence looked at him. He had taken to wearing little round spectacles framed in emerald green and to bleaching a few front strands in his hair.

"She's looking a bit better," Don said. "Mrs. Wood, I mean. I thought for a few weeks we were going to have a real case on our hands—"

"A long summer—"

"You ought to take her away," Don said, returning to the bar. "In the winter. Somewhere nice. We'll hold the fort for ten days or so."

"Nice of you," Laurence said. "Thank you."

Don picked up a pint glass and held it up to the light, squinting for smears.

"You think about it."

Laurence went on up to the flat. He climbed the stairs very slowly and when he reached the top, he couldn't remember why he had come up in the first place, remembered only the strange sensation of watching Hilary through the glass of the dining-room door. He went into their bedroom, where she had now slept alone for some time, and stared at the bed. It was

307

made, but there was a dent at one side, where she had sat on it, perhaps to put her tights on.

Since she had asked him to think about their marriage, she had said nothing further on the subject. She had spoken to him, certainly, in quite a businesslike way about businesslike things, and smiled, but not with any special meaning or pleading. He went over to the chest of drawers where her make-up pots and his brushes and keys had lain together for over twenty years in a companionable muddle of dry-cleaning tickets and photographs of the boys and lone earrings and buttons and pins. His brushes now lay in the spare bedroom, but Hilary hadn't moved her things to occupy the space his had left. She had simply allowed the space to remain as if, in a way, it did not matter. As if it might even be filled again.

When he had returned to the kitchen to begin on the preparations for dinner, the atmosphere of the tiny episode had stayed strongly with him. Hilary had come in once or twice and he had looked at her with a kind of awe, as if she had revealed herself to be something other than his long-term assumptions about her. And yet at the same time, he longed to see Gina, to remind himself of her presence and warmth and reality, to reassure himself that everything was really as he knew it was, in his heart of hearts. Why was it, he thought, during those long hours of stirring and slicing and instructing the boys, that if one chose one love, it seemed to invalidate all others, even if you felt them still? Why did the age-old arrangement of society, two by two in an endless procession, force one to be so ruthless?

When it came to it, he didn't go round to High Place. Eleven o'clock struck, and he didn't, as was his custom, go. He thought of it, he wanted it, but he stayed where he was until the boys had burnished the last surface and closed the last cupboard, and then he telephoned.

"I'm knackered," he said, dreading her disappointment. "I'm on my knees."

"It's all right," she said, and her voice sounded as if she meant it. "It's all right, Laurence. Sophy's coming home."

So here he was, sitting with his bottle-end of Chablis at the kitchen table, drawing mad patterns, and waiting. No one came. He reached the edge of the paper, finished the wine, and no one came. The church clock, calm in the night, struck a quarter past midnight. Laurence got up and fetched the bottle of Bulgarian wine with which he'd been cooking earlier in the day and poured half a glass.

The door opened. He looked up, his heart jumping.

"Hi," Adam said.

He wore black trackpants and a misshapen purple T-shirt and his feet were bare.

"I thought you were asleep—"

"Nope," Adam said. "Couldn't. Looked in your room and you weren't there so I looked out of the window and saw the kitchen lights were on."

Laurence said softly, "Thank you."

"Thought you might have gone round there—"

"No."

Adam moved towards the table and slumped in a chair. He picked up Laurence's wine glass, took a swallow, and made a face.

"Ugh."

"It's been open two days."

Adam looked up at his father through the floppy tongues of hair that fell over his forehead.

"Hi," he said again.

"Hi, Adam."

"I just thought," Adam said, "when I saw those lights, I just thought I'd come down and hang around with you for a while. OK?"

CHAPTER
17

Sophy walked very slowly. Her bag was heavier, on account of the new clothes it contained, even though she had left all the posters and the crane-patterned dressing gown in London.

"Please," Fergus said, "please don't take everything."

"I wasn't going to."

Neither man had known quite what to do with her, Sophy had noticed. Tony had been rather irritable, but that might well have been, she thought, because he now owed her something and didn't want to admit it. Fergus had been simply sad, and in his sadness, she could see he loved her and was going to miss her, and although she was pleased about this, and touched by it, she wasn't pleased as she once might have been, rapturous and demanding.

"I'll be back," she said. "Weekends and things."

Fergus nodded.

"But not if you go to France—"

"I won't go to France," Sophy said.

"But if your mother—"

"There's Gran," Sophy said, "and there's school. And there's Hilary and"—her voice faltered as her mind shied away from George—"the boys. You know."

Fergus had tried to give her some money, several twenty-pound notes rolled up into a little tube like a cigarette and tied with a plum-coloured ribbon which said "Fortnum and Mason" on it, in gold letters. Fortnum and Mason was where Tony bought their tea. They were very particular about tea.

"No," Sophy said. "No thank you. Honestly."

He had driven her to the station. All the way she had held her stomach, as she had become accustomed to doing the last five days. Fergus had never again mentioned her period and Sophy wondered if he had forgotten it. She hadn't. She thought about it all the time. That morning, standing in Fergus's pristine bathroom and staring at herself in his shaving mirror while she brushed her teeth, she wondered if she felt sick. She had then felt better after breakfast but that was no consolation. Early-morning sickness was often helped by eating something. It had said that on the leaflet enclosed with every pregnancy-testing kit her schoolfriends had bought and also it always said, in capital letters, "It is essential to consult your doctor." Sophy dreaded that. But it was probably the next thing, the next thing she did before she told Gina. Or Vi. Or George. Of all those three, the person she wanted to tell least was George.

Fergus put her on the train with a newspaper and two magazines.

"Ring me. Please."

"Of course I will."

"No, I mean often. Not just a once-a-week catch-up call, but every day or every other day. I want to know what you're doing."

He had kissed her good-bye, on the mouth. He had never done that before and afterwards she wondered about that mouth and whether it had also kissed Tony's. He stood outside the carriage window on the platform until the train went, and for the first time in their life together, Sophy thought he looked as if he wasn't quite in command, as if he too was feeling that alarming helplessness of being on the receiving end of actions rather than being their perpetrator.

To her amazement, she slept almost all the

way to Whittingbourne and woke up dazed, with a stiff neck and an embarrassed consciousness of having been asleep with her mouth open. There was a school party on the platform, an excited party of little chattering children being taken off to Birmingham to see some exhibition. They had lunchboxes with Snoopy pictures on the lids and little backpacks shaped like teddy bears or tigers, and there was a beautiful black boy in the middle, a little taller than the rest, with huge liquid eyes, whom the others were jostling to be next to. For a second, Sophy considered joining them, just asking one of the teachers if she could come too and have the diversion of that excited journey. She smiled at the nearest teacher. She grimaced back, mock-despairing.

"Must be mad," she said. "Must be out of my mind. Three of my own at home and I choose to do this all day."

She tapped her head, as if there was something the matter with the mechanism inside. Sophy smiled again.

"Have a good day—"

She decided to walk. She was tired, in a way, despite having slept, but a taxi would make her feel silly, and in any case, the route taxis took from the station would go through the market square, where all the people from school who played hookey regularly gathered to smoke, and shout at nothing much, and they might see her. She hitched the bag on to her shoulder and set off, stooping slightly, the strap of the bag pulling her T-shirt away from her neck.

When she reached High Place the glass door to the kitchen was open and Gina had hung the budgerigar in his cage outside it, on a bracket intended for a hanging basket.

"Hi," Sophy said to the bird.

He eyed her, first one side and then, swivelling round, the other.

"Poor bird," Sophy said. "Poor bored bird."

She gave the bell in his cage a little push, to make it ring. The budgie took no notice.

"Sorry," Sophy said. "Didn't mean to patronise you."

She looked into the kitchen. It was empty and tidy, except for a mug on the table and a scatter of that morning's post. From a little distance, the sitting room probably, she could hear Gina's voice, unmistakably on the telephone. She stepped into the kitchen, put her bag on the table and crossed to the door to the hall.

"I'm so sorry," Gina was saying. "I'd love to see both children again but my plans are so uncertain at the moment that I feel I shouldn't take any pupils on just now. I may not even be staying in Whittingbourne, you see."

Sophy tiptoed across the hall and leaned in the sitting-room doorway. Gina was sitting on the floor, as was her wont, with the telephone in front of her crossed legs. Her head was bent. Sophy cleared her throat.

"Mum," she whispered.

Gina looked up and her face was illuminated. She waved frantically, indicating the telephone.

"Mrs. Whitaker, would you forgive me? I really have to go, but I promise you that I'll be back in touch about Rachel and Emily if I feel there's enough time to give them more proper tuition. Yes. Yes, certainly. Thank you. Good-bye." She flung the receiver approximately towards the handset and scrambled to her feet. "Oh Sophy!"

Sophy moved away from the doorframe to be embraced. It was peculiar, being embraced by Gina—it hadn't happened for years, not a proper hug like this anyway, a holding hug where she could feel Gina's shirt buttons pressing through her own T-shirt into her flesh.

"Oh Sophy," Gina said. "Oh Soph. Thank God you're back."

She had tears in her eyes. Sophy bent her head.

"It didn't work."

"You don't have to tell me," Gina said. "You don't have to say anything if you don't want to."

"Maybe one day. I don't know. It was just—"

Gina drew Sophy towards an armchair and pushed her gently into it.

"That's a lovely haircut."

Sophy touched it.

"Dad—"

"Yes. He's good at that sort of thing. Would you like some coffee? Or tea?"

Sophy shook her head. Gina went back to her cross-legged position, close to the armchair.

"I'm worn out," Sophy said. She bent her

head again and put her hands over her eyes. "I'm worn out with being angry with you all."

"I should have told you. I should have told you about Laurence and me. I was waiting; we were going to tell all you children together and then it slipped out before we were ready and I never did it."

"Gus told me."

"I know. I rang him to say you were coming home."

Sophy took her hands away from her eyes. She said incredulously, "You rang Gus?"

"Yes," Gina said. "Laurence told me he's been absolutely miserable the last few weeks, and when you went to London he was inconsolable—so I rang him to comfort him. He thinks the world of you."

A bright, unnatural spot of colour appeared in both Sophy's cheeks. She put her right hand flat across her stomach.

"Shall I talk to you about Laurence?" Gina said. "Do you want me to explain?"

Sophy shook her head.

"You don't need to."

"I was afraid to tell you," Gina said, leaning forward and crossing her wrists to grasp her ankles. "I was afraid that you'd be so angry you would never speak to me again. You were so angry about Daddy, you see. You thought it was my fault."

Sophy said wearily, "Some of it was."

"Yes."

"I'm exhausted by it all," Sophy said. "I

couldn't tell you if I'm angry or not any more. I just feel like someone who's been knocked down by a car and every time they try and cross the street afterwards, they get knocked down again. I'm not interested really in who's to blame or who wants what. I can't even be very surprised any longer. I don't have any curiosity left about what's going to happen next." She paused, pressed her stomach with her hand and then said in a low voice, "I just have dread."

Gina uncrossed her legs and came to kneel by Sophy's chair.

"About going to France, you mean? About coming to France with Laurence and me?"

Sophy looked at her steadily.

"Oh," she said, in a very reasonable voice, "I couldn't come to France."

"You couldn't—"

"No," Sophy said. "Whatever happens, I couldn't do that."

"But, darling, you can't stay here without me. We'd send you to a *lycée,* you see, you could do a baccalaureate—"

"No," Sophy said, "I couldn't."

"Because of Laurence?"

"Oh no," Sophy said, almost amazed, as if she had forgotten his existence. "Not because of him. Or you. Or France, for that matter."

"Then—"

"Mum," Sophy said, closing her eyes as if with the effort of explaining something very simple to someone extremely stupid, "*Mum.* We can't both leave Vi."

• • • •

On the way home from school, Gus broke away from the group he'd been scuffling along with and dived into the Abbey grounds. He avoided the familiar benches where people he knew lounged about smoking and kicking idly at the paintwork, and made for a clump of bushes close to the arch. He knew that it was idiotic to do this because bushes like these were where weirdies lurked. One of them had exposed himself to someone Gus knew only the week before and the someone had boasted he'd shouted, "You lousy perv!" so loud that several passers-by had heard, and given chase. Gus wondered about this, but it was only one of a dozen miserable things to wonder about, so he hadn't given it long. He wanted to be somewhere dark, and private, on his own, where no one would find him for a bit and ask if he was OK. Of course he wasn't OK, but what the hell could he or anyone else do about it?

He crawled a little way into the darkness under the bushes over a carpet of whispering dead leaves and litter. There was a small clearing about eight feet in, with some old newspaper in it and an empty milk bottle. Gus settled himself there, his back against a narrow dark trunk of a shrub, and got out his Marlboros. He took one out of the packet, lit it, and began to cry.

He had intended not to cry, but to think. He had cried most of the night before, after

318

his conversation with George, his face crammed into the pillow and his throat bursting with sobs. He and George had been in the kitchen, making bacon sandwiches, and he had said, in a burst of confidentiality, "I just wonder what's going to happen next. I wonder what I don't know."

George had been spreading tomato ketchup across the slices of bacon.

"It isn't always a good idea to know everything."

"It is," Gus insisted, "it is. If you know everything, then there's nothing left to scare you. No more shitty surprises."

"Do you really think that?"

" 'Course I do," Gus said. He took two slices of toast out of the toaster and offered them to George. "I think that all the time. I keep waiting for the next whammy otherwise."

There was a pause. George put the toast on top of the half-made sandwiches and pressed down hard, with the heel of his hand.

"OK, then," George said.

"OK what?"

"I'll tell you."

Gus stared at him.

"What—"

"I'll tell you the last thing there is to know. The last bloody thing of this bloody summer. The reason Sophy went to London."

Gus said, "But that was me, me telling her—"

"No," George said. He picked up one

sandwich and held it out, oozing ketchup, towards Gus. "Here."

Gus shook his head.

"No—"

George sighed and put the sandwich down again.

"She went because of me. We had sex, Sophy and me. That's why she went. She was so upset."

Gus stood there. He looked at his brother and tried to see him. He looked at the sandwiches lying on the table-top and tried to see them. He opened his mouth once or twice but nothing came until he heard a voice, a rather high voice, say "Sex?" as if it was a question.

"Yes," George said. "One afternoon. Here." He shrugged. Even through his distress, Gus could see that the shrug was not quite relaxed. "Her first time."

Gus put his hand on the bunch of keys at his waist, and held them hard.

"Come on," George said, "have a sandwich."

Gus shook his head.

"What's up?"

"Not hungry."

"But you said—"

"Not hungry!" Gus shouted. "Can't you hear? Gone fucking deaf?"

"Gus—"

"Shut up!" Gus screamed. "Shut up, shut up, shut up!"

He lifted one foot and kicked the nearest

kitchen chair so hard that it crashed away from the table and thudded into the fridge. Three bottles balanced on the top fell over.

"Hey!" George said. He came round the table and tried to take Gus's arm, but Gus wrenched himself free and whirled to the kitchen door.

"You shit!" Gus yelled. "You shit!" and then he raced down the passage to his bedroom and plunged inside, slamming the door behind him.

He had still been in his school clothes, which made it worse. When he began to cry, he couldn't get his tie off, or his shoes, and he had to wrestle about on the floor, choking with pain and tears. He wanted to kill people. He wanted to kill George and Sophy and his parents and Adam and everybody at school and everybody in Whittingbourne. He wanted to stab them and bash them and yell and scream at them. He wanted there to be an agony for everyone as great as his was. He wanted to die. When George came to try to talk to him, he howled, "Fuck off! Fuck off, will you?"

He had crawled into bed finally, wearing his underpants and an old rugby shirt. All his other clothes were on the floor in a tangle. He lay and wept and wept and when Hilary came later and tapped and called to ask if he was all right, he stifled his face in the pillow so that she'd think he was asleep. She'd opened the door and put her head in and he'd held his breath and lain as still as a stone.

"Gus?" she'd said.

He didn't budge.

"Sleep well," Hilary said, and closed the door.

He had gone to sleep in the end, but had woken towards dawn with his face stiff and swollen and a raging hunger. He went along to the kitchen, without turning the lights on, and got several slices of bread out of the packet and took them back to cram into his mouth under the duvet. Remembering hung over him like a black cloud, a witch, a terrible bird of prey. He had lain there, in tears again, while the light grew stronger through the curtains and the bread lay wretchedly inside him in great undigested lumps.

In the morning, they were all very quiet with him. George had tried to say sorry, but this was unbearable. Gus had turned on him such a face full of fury that George had subsided into silence. Hilary put her arm round him.

"Want to talk? Just to me, privately?"

"No!"

"Sure?"

"Yes!" Gus shouted.

He had refused to walk to school with Adam, and had sat all day, slumped and feeling like death, while maths and social studies and practical English passed in a nauseous blur. Now, in the furtive privacy of these grimy bushes, he felt less full of rage and sickness but more full of a despairing sadness. Sophy. Sophy of all people. When he'd thought about her so much and wanted to be with her and all those flowers and stuff. It was a betrayal hardly to be borne. He drew quiveringly on his cigarette and stubbed it out violently on the sour earth under the leaves.

Someone was hovering on the edge of the bushes, stooping down every so often and peering in. Gus sat up. He could see legs in jeans and feet in sneakers and they were going up and down, quite leisurely, in the light beyond the leaves. He got on to hands and knees and crawled rapidly in the opposite direction, where the bushes were much thicker, catching his clothes and hair on twigs and small sharp branches. It seemed a long way to the daylight.

"Hello," the man said.

Gus scrambled to his feet. Apart from jeans and sneakers, the man wore a dirty green polo shirt stretched over a beer belly.

"Saw you in there," the man said. He put a hand out and seized Gus's arm. "Got a cat in there, I have. I was looking for my cat. You want to help me look for my cat?"

"No," Gus said. He tried to pull away.

"Come on," the man said. "You're all upset, I can see that. I'll make you better. You come with me and I'll make you feel better."

With a supreme effort, Gus tore his arm free and gave a wild, plunging shove in the direction of the man's belly. There was a wheezing grunt and the man staggered backwards.

Gus fled. Careless of who saw him, streaked with dirt, he pounded down the paths to the entrance to Orchard Street, gasping, "Sophy, Sophy, Sophy," to himself as he ran.

• • • •

Sophy said she wouldn't stay up and see Laurence. She and Gina had eaten supper together with a semblance of normality both of them found hard to credit. They had talked, carefully, about practical things, about how Sophy could have the little bedroom at Orchard Close in term time, with some weekends in London, and how she could then come out to France in the holidays. Perhaps the boys would come too, Gina said, and they could all travel together. She stopped herself from saying that it all might be quite fun. It was too soon to dare to do that. Sophy ate her pasta and had a brief, unsuccessful attempt at visualising a French kitchen (in a flat? in a house? in a town?) with herself and Gina and Laurence and perhaps Adam or Gus (but not George) in it. Gina said she would get teaching work, like before, and Laurence would of course get a job as a chef. She told Sophy a great deal about Pau and Sophy listened and held her stomach with the hand she wasn't eating with.

"What'll happen to Hilary?"

Gina said quickly, "She's staying here. She'll get a chef for The Bee House and go on as before."

Sophy wound strands of spaghetti round her fork.

"Hard on her."

"Yes," Gina said.

Sophy eyed her. Her face looked very set. She must feel awful. She *ought* to feel awful.

At least she hadn't confided how awful she felt to Sophy and asked for understanding. At least she was getting on with the awfulness alone.

"Laurence comes round most nights," Gina said. "About eleven."

"I don't want to see him."

"No."

She pushed her plate away.

"I'm exhausted, anyway. Bombed."

"I know. You go to bed. I got some of your stuff out again. Your room looked so sad."

"Thanks."

Sophy got up and took her plate over to the sink—oh, the ritual of years—and rinsed it under the tap.

"Sophy—"

"Mmm?"

"It—it means all the world to me that you've come home."

Sophy paused. She looked only at the sink. She considered saying, "But not enough not to go off with Laurence," and decided against it. She was beyond that now, beyond saying such things and almost beyond even thinking them. People didn't do things for other people, even if they loved them; they did them for themselves. Not necessarily because they were horrible and selfish but because that's how people were made, how they got through, survived. Gina wasn't trying to hurt Hilary— even if she had—she was trying to survive. Sophy sighed. None of that seemed a problem just now, anyway. Nothing did. Not, that is, beside her own problem which she carried about with her like a cold dead weight.

She put her rinsed plate on the draining board and stooped to kiss Gina.

" 'Night."

" 'Night, darling. Sleep well."

Much later that night, in the darkest hours, Gina heard Sophy moving about. She thought she could hear music playing faintly and little thumps, as if Sophy was investigating the boxes on the landing she had packed with such ferocious precision only ten days before. She sat up in bed. She wondered if she should go up and see Sophy, and decided against it. She mustn't interfere, mustn't patter round Sophy beseeching communication of some kind, any kind. She must let Sophy come to her, and if it took ages—or for ever—well, that was what happened if you put your own need for love before everything else. And she had. And it had changed her whole life.

Laurence had been so tender. He had held her that evening as if she was really precious to him, as if he was savouring all of her, body and personality. He hadn't said much, had let her talk and had simply held her for long, quiet times. She had been enormously happy. To be in this house with Sophy asleep upstairs and Laurence's arms round her and brochures from French estate agents on the kitchen table made up a kind of huge, steady happiness she hadn't dared hope she might feel again. She had laid her cheek against Laurence's shoulder and revelled in her feeling, and when he had gone, and she had come to bed, she had fallen at once into the most sweet and tranquil sleep she had known for weeks.

Until Sophy woke her. She decided she would let the music and the thumps go on for a little while, and then she might go upstairs and gently suggest that both activities could perhaps wait until the morning. She lay down again and watched, in perfect contentment, while the little green illuminated hands of her bedside clock crept round the invisible dial. She didn't even want to think.

After ten minutes or so, Sophy must have left her bedroom door open, because the music grew louder. Gina waited. Five minutes passed and then Sophy's feet came down the stairs from the top floor and went into the bathroom, shutting the door loudly. Gina sat up again, preparing to call out when Sophy came out of the bathroom. She was ages. Gina heard the lavatory plug and then the basin taps and then a clatter, as if several things had fallen out of the medicine cupboard. Then, at last, feet came out again, and stopped.

"Mum?"

"Yes!" Gina called. "Yes! I'm awake—"

The door opened, silhouetting Sophy against an oblong of electric light.

"Hello," Sophy said.

"Hello, darling—"

"Mum—"

"Yes?"

"Oh Mum!" Sophy cried, hurtling into the room and casting herself across the bed in a sudden burst of rapturous relief. "Oh Mum! I'm not pregnant!"

CHAPTER
18

"What's this," Hilary said. "What's this about you and Sophy?"

George groaned. He rolled over on his bed, draggingthe duvet with him as protective covering. Outside his closed bedroom window— "You revolting boy," Hilary said—the Sunday morning bells rang complacently from the tower of the parish church.

"You will be nineteen in a fortnight," Hilary said. "You aren't fourteen, you know. You are a *man*. Well, technically at least. You have absolutely no business playing around with someone younger than you in an acutely vulnerable state."

George thought of saying resentfully that he was in just as vulnerable a state as Sophy. His head, this morning, contained several extraordinarily heavy weights which slid agonisingly about his skull if he so much as moved. He had meant to drink the night before but not that much. He remembered lying finally on his bed while his feet seemed to swirl uncontrollably up into the air, and reflecting, through the waves of nausea, that he was so drunk he'd probably drowned.

Hilary sat on the edge of the bed and yanked the duvet from his grasp. He felt her eyes boring into the naked flesh of his side and back.

"We are, in a way, responsible for Sophy, George. We always have been. What's happened to us may be as painful as what's happened to her, but we've got each other. She's got no family besides parents and Vi. If you needed some poor creature to vent your adolescent lust on, George, Sophy was the last person you should have chosen. If you haven't got any principles, where the hell at least is your *compassion*?"

George didn't move. He stared at the wall, at the stretch of cream emulsion paint scarred with tags of tape he had used to put up posters, now discarded. He considered saying that Sophy had wanted the sex as much as he had; had, in fact, practically initiated it because she was terribly upset by going to see her father in London and discovering that he was living with another man. George, whatever he might swagger to Gus, was under no illusion about what Sophy had wanted that afternoon. She had wanted to dominate, to overwhelm, and she had succeeded, and he had wanted her to. They had come together with a queer, raw, unarticulated understanding of one another that wasn't about love in the least, but about anger and bewilderment and loneliness. He suspected that they might never mention the afternoon to one another again—or not for years and years—but at the same time, neither would forget it. It struck him that the importance and privacy of this was to be kept safe. They both knew the truth after all, and that was all that mattered. No one else needed to know.

He rolled over and looked at his mother.

"OK," he said.

"What d'you mean, OK?"

"I mean, lesson heard and understood. Shouldn't have done it. Very sorry."

Hilary said, "Have you seen her since?"

"No—"

"I think you should—"

"No," George said. "No, Mum. Leave it. It won't happen again. Neither of us wants it."

Hilary sighed.

"Was that really why she ran away to London?"

George propped himself on one elbow and retrieved a corner of duvet to cover his chest.

"I dunno. Maybe as well as—the other."

"Yes," Hilary said.

"Mum—"

"Yes?"

"Mum, what's going to happen? I mean, what are the plans?"

Hilary was silent a moment, and then she reached out and took George's nearest hand and gripped it.

"I hope—oh George, I'm just hoping about them. I'm just holding my breath and *hoping*."

He sat up further and peered at her.

"Do you mean—"

"I don't know," she said, shaking her head.

"I don't know anything. Except that I haven't quite"—she gave him a small, anxious smile—"quite given up."

Vi stood in the doorway of her second bedroom. You could hardly call it a bedroom really, more a cupboard with a window. There was only room for a bed with a little chest of drawers at the foot of it, and a chair and a table with a lamp. Where'd Sophy put her clothes? And her books? Dan had put a shelf up above the bed, and a mirror, but the shelf was already full of all the things Vi had made the winter she took up pottery at evening classes. They weren't much good, all those vases and mugs and bowls, but they'd been a treat to make. Vi had loved the feel of the clay under her fingers, loved it. Maybe they could all go into a box under the bed. Except that Sophy would have to keep her clothes under the bed. Or on the back of the door. Vi looked. Two brass hooks only; already heavy with clothes on hangers, including an old naval boat cloak she had once bought Dan, in a charity shop, and which he wouldn't wear because he said it was meant for an officer and anyway, it was too showy.

Vi went slowly downstairs again and into her kitchen. It wasn't that she didn't love Sophy dearly, nor wish most earnestly to help her, but she was weighed down, for the first time in her life, by the feeling that she simply could not cope with her. Since Dan died, she had had this feeling quite a lot, the knowledge that she didn't want anything extra in any day, nothing new, nothing that demanded her exertions. But what could she do? Sophy and Gina had come to see her—with flowers, as a sort of propitiation, which had disgusted Vi—and had asked her, outright, their eyes fixed on her face.

"Just term time," Gina said. "Just for a year. And only the weekdays, really."

Just a year! Vi had almost snorted. A year was a precious thing at eighty. She'd heard a discussion on the radio recently, talking about hundredth birthdays, and one of the contributors had said, "Honestly, I can't really imagine it. Who'd want to be a hundred?"

"Somebody of ninety-nine!" Vi had shouted at the set. "Someone of ninety-nine!"

She had looked at Sophy. She'd had a new haircut, much shorter and fuller, and it made her look less perky. The expression in her eyes wasn't as pleading, it wasn't even anxious. The idea wasn't crossing Sophy's mind, even for an instant, that Vi would be other than pleased and relieved to take her in. She probably thought she might be some kind of consolation for the absence of Dan. It was hopeless, quite hopeless. Before Dan died, she'd have flared up in anger and called them cheeky to take advantage of her. But not now. She had, now, smiled at Sophy and said of course, dear, lovely, and you can have the little room.

She stood at her kitchen sink, holding on to the edge, and looked out of the window above it at her bird feeder, where the tits clung so endearingly. Quite apart from the physical effort of having Sophy here, there was something else that troubled her, something more elusive and precious. After Dan's death, when his nephew Roger had been and organised his possessions—an operation requiring the control of Vi's temper as it had never been controlled before—she had come away with all the little things Roger had rejected but which Vi knew Dan had valued, photographs and carnival prizes and funny little souvenirs from those far-off Navy days he had never forgotten. She had put them all round her maisonette, mixed up with her own things, so that they were as properly interwoven as Vi and Dan had been, and they had brought with them a bonus Vi had not looked for, which was a palpable sense of Dan's abiding presence. It was so palpable, in fact, that Vi had taken to talking to Dan, peaceably and companionably, and asking him things. It was a communication which had proved a quite unspeakable comfort. But if Sophy came, with her possessions and her life, and was there, in the flesh, however quietly, bless her, might she not drive away that potent but fragile sense of Dan's propinquity upon which Vi's very existence had come to depend?

The bar at The Bee House was drowsy with the somnolence of Sunday afternoon. The dining room had been almost full, and although a few people had drifted out to the garden, there was still a replete form in every armchair in the lounge bar, sleep imperfectly camouflaged by newspapers. Hilary went stealthily among them and through the door at the back that gave on to the short flight of stairs leading down to the kitchen.

Laurence wasn't in the kitchen. Steve and Kevin were there, clearing up, with a girl called Patsy who had been taken on to help with washing up on busy days. She had a baby, whom she left with her mother while she worked, and she was saving up for a holiday in Disneyland.

"OK?" Hilary said. "Everything OK?"

They nodded. Sunday had a bad atmosphere as a workday and nobody wanted to be here.

"Have you seen Mr. Wood?"

"Yeah," Kevin said. He was wearing a white baseball cap in the kitchen, back to front, and it gave his broad pink face an air of blank stupidity. "In the yard."

"Thank you," Hilary said, and to Patsy, "All right?"

She nodded. She had seven separate jobs to do, all over Whittingbourne, and this was one of the more cheerful. The boys were a pain, but then boys always were. She liked Mr. Wood, though. He had manners.

Outside in the yard, in the quiet September afternoon, Laurence was leaning against one of the store rooms, once a stable, his hands in his trouser pockets under his apron, gazing, apparently, at a tired clump of groundsel growing in a crack in the cobbles.

"Laurence—"

He gave a little start, and then he smiled.

"Hello."

She went across the yard and stood next to him. She observed that the hair above his ears was going grey and that he had cut himself, shaving, on his neck, just beside his Adam's apple.

He said gently, "Did you want something?"

She shook her head.

"Not really. I just came."

"Good," he said.

He took his hands out of his pockets and put them on her shoulders.

"Shall we go somewhere?"

She said, startled, "Where?"

"Oh, I don't know. Just somewhere. Anywhere. Away from here, anyway."

She stepped back a little so that his hands fell from her shoulders.

"Why?" she said warily.

"To get out of all this. To get away, even for an hour. To talk."

Hilary said carefully, "I know a field—"

"Just the one?" he said.

She smiled.

"You're not *joking*," she said. "Not after all these weeks—"

"Where's your field?"

"Out near Adderley Ridge. Where the boys used to fly their kites."

"Good," he said. "Let's go."

"But we can't—"

"We can. Kitchen's finished. Don's here. Is George?"

"Yes. I've just been ticking him off. About Sophy."

Laurence's face clouded.

"Oh God."

"It's all right, I think. No harm done this time. Except I ought to make sure Sophy's OK—"

"Not now."

"No."

"I'll go and tell George and Don," Laurence said. "You find the car keys."

"Laurence—"

"Yes?"

"Laurence," Hilary said, gathering her courage and taking off her spectacles so that she could imagine his face rather than see it. "Laurence, I will talk. I'm happy to, I'd like to. But it mustn't be another interim talk. I can't bear any more of those. It mustn't be another don't-know, haven't-decided talk. It's got to be the final one, you see. It's got to be the real thing."

It was some time before Gus noticed her. He'd been watching the cricket on television, turned up very loud, not so much because he liked it, but because there was no one else in the flat to object, so he could do what he liked. He didn't know where Adam was; George was downstairs on duty and Laurence and Hilary had, for some reason, gone off in the car together. Perhaps, he thought gloomily, to find some empty field to have a good loud row in. Laurence had asked him if he'd be all right on his own, before they left, and he'd said fine, fine, without looking up from the television. He didn't even like cricket very much but it was at least some kind of distraction as well as being a means of getting other people into the room, impersonal other people who were company without wanting something from you.

"Gus," Sophy said.

She had to call it, really, over the sound of the commentary. He whipped round. She was standing in the sitting-room doorway looking very grown up, with a new haircut and a silk shirt on. She was holding a flowerpot.

"Can I come in?"

He nodded. He lunged at the remote-control panel and hit the volume button with unnecessary force. The room went suddenly silent.

"I brought you this," Sophy said. She put the flowerpot down on the coffee table. It was full of black earth and nothing else. "It's an avocado stone. I planted it for you. It'll grow into a little avocado tree. At least, I hope it will."

Gus said nothing. He pulled himself back on to the sofa and sat there, hunched. He wasn't a bloody kid, to be placated by broad beans on blotting paper in jam jars. He wasn't a *baby*.

"I ate the avocado last night," Sophy said. "I've never eaten a whole one before. I felt incredibly full."

She sat down on the sofa beside him, but at a little distance.

"I'm not going to France," she said.

He didn't react.

"I'm staying here. I'm going to live with Gran in term time, in her little room. It's about the size of a phone box."

Gus picked up a cushion, punched it once or twice, and then bunched it against his stomach and leaned over it.

"I expect I'll go to London some weekends." She paused. "You could come, sometimes, if you want to."

He shook his head, very, very slowly.

"Gus—"

He went on shaking his head.

"I didn't go to London because of George. I went because of what you told me. I just couldn't stand any more."

Gus laid the cushion on his knees and bent right over it until his face was almost hidden.

"What George and I did," Sophy said uncertainly, "wasn't anything. I mean, it was, but it didn't mean anything. We don't even fancy each other. It was just—everything else, all the parents, all that." She put her hands together between her knees and squeezed them hard. "I thought I was pregnant."

There was a small convulsion in Gus's cushion.

"But I'm not."

Silence.

"I'm not telling George that. I'm not telling him I thought I was or that I'm not. I told Mum because I was so relieved I couldn't help it. I sort of told my father, but he wasn't listening. I'm only telling you so you know it all. So there's nothing left to know. The way you like it."

Gus raised his face and stared straight ahead, woodenly, at the picture of the Irish fishermen on the wild, dark beach.

"And I don't love anyone," Sophy said. "A boy, I mean. I'm not keen on anyone. I—really like you, Gus. I always will. But we're kind of practising, aren't we, seeing what it's like. You'll have heaps of people after you." She paused and looked at his profile for some seconds. "You're really good-looking."

Not a muscle twitched. She went on watching him for a while and then she got to her feet.

"I'll be at school on Monday. I'm a bit scared, because of last week. Mum says I don't have to explain but I don't know what to do instead. I suppose I could say family crisis, couldn't I? It's true after all. You and I must know more about them than anyone, after this summer."

She stood looking down at him for a moment, as if she was uncertain quite what she should do next. Then she said, "Bye, Gus. See you at school. See you around," and went out of the room.

After she had gone, he sat on for several minutes, quite fixed and still. Then he drooped a little and picked the cushion up and put it over his face and lay back on the sofa. He stayed like this for a while, then he sat up and looked at the flowerpot. It was a real one, made of terracotta. He stuck a forefinger into the earth and felt the avocado stone below the surface, smooth and round and hard.

He got up, wiping his earthy finger on the seat of his jeans. He bent down and picked up the flowerpot in both hands and carried it into his bedroom. The windowsill, narrow anyway, was crowded already with the model aeroplanes he had once so loved to make and the commemorative mugs he collected from all the football teams. There were also a lot of curled-up foreign stamps and defunct ball-point pen innards and dead flies. He put the flowerpot on the floor and cleared a space in the centre of the windowsill, pushing things aside with both hands so that various objects fell to the floor. Then he picked up the flowerpot and put it dead in the middle, between a Spitfire and Manchester United, and watched it for a long time, as if by very willpower he could make it grow.

Hilary's field had been ploughed.

"Winter wheat, no doubt," Laurence said.

The wide headland round the edge was still untouched, and the grass on it was even longer and more rough and bleached and the weeds now looked tough enough to survive a desert.

"I start here," Hilary said, putting a hand on the gate. "And then I go down that side first, and then along the bottom where there's rather a choked stream full of brambles, and then up this side."

"I see," Laurence said. He climbed the gate and turned, balanced on the top, to give her a hand. "Well, today, shall we do it the other way about?"

She looked at him.

"Do you think we ought?"

"Yes," he said, "I do."

She landed in the field beside him.

"Is that where we flew kites? Up there?"

"Yes."

"And the dog ate Adam's?"

"Yes. That poor man—"

They set off unevenly side by side, stepping over the rougher clumps.

"I'm shaking," Hilary said.

"Would you like to hold my hand?"

"Not yet," she said. "Perhaps later, when I know."

"Of course," he said. "I'm not spinning out the agony. I just don't know where to begin."

Hilary stopped.

"I can't," she said. "I can't walk *and* worry."

She subsided into the grassy tussocks. Laurence waited a moment and then he sat down beside her, facing her.

"Hilary," he said, "would you let me stay?"

She couldn't look at him. She gathered up the folds of her skirt and wrenched them tightly under her knees, making a sort of bandage, against feeling.

"You were right," Laurence said, "about our marriage, about still loving you. Our marriage isn't dead, it just had a severe illness. And

I do love you. Still. I think I can't do without loving you. You're sort of in the fabric of me. When I tried it wasn't just that I couldn't imagine life without you, but that I knew there wouldn't be one. Well, there *would*, a kind of life, a kind of limping life, but not the one I've led, the one I need and want."

He paused. A little wind blew against them and dropped a feathery ball of seeds in Hilary's lap, greyish down speckled with black.

"But I'm right too," Laurence went on, "and this bit's harder. I love Gina. I wasn't making any of that up. When I said I'd always loved her, that was true too. Is true. But I don't love her enough to have her instead of you. And even I, from my male have-your-cake-and-eat-it depths, know I can't have both. I don't even want both; I'd rather not have the dilemma, to be honest. I would like to stop loving her, bang, just throw a switch, turn the light off. I think, if I didn't see her, that would happen, and I will strain every sinew to make it happen, I swear I will. But that's why I have to be tentative, you see. That's why I can't just blow up balloons and throw a party and say it's all over, folks, my mistake. I know, with my whole heart, that if you'll have me I want to stay. But I also know, given how I feel about Gina, that I've no right to expect to be allowed to. It's bloody unfair that it's your decision, I know that. But I don't know what else to ask you."

He stopped again. Hilary picked the seed ball out of her lap and held it up in the air, plucking it apart so that the little black specks blew away in the breeze.

"Can you," Laurence said, "forgive me enough to let me stay with you, and bear with me while I get over Gina? I don't know if I could do it in your place, so I'm not expecting miracles."

Hilary said slowly, not looking at him, "I might be horrible."

"I know."

"I might not be able to help myself. I might be unable to resist venomous little remarks. I might not be able to bear to be touched."

"Yes."

"I don't know, Laurence. I longed with all my being for you to say this, and now that you have, I don't know. I feel full of desolation."

"Oh my darling," Laurence said. "Oh Hilary, I'm so sorry."

She bent forward and put her forehead on her knees.

"I want to want it," she said. "I *long* to want it. But I can't seem to reach the feeling."

He said, "Could you take me on trust? Could you stand that? Because I love you with my whole heart."

"Maybe—"

"It's a gamble. I know that. I also know I've got to work harderthan you."

"Don't," she said.

He bent so that he could see something of her face.

"Do you love me?"

He thought she nodded.

"Do you?"

She lifted her head.

"Perhaps," she said. "I think so. At this precise moment, I can't quite remember about love. I can't remember what it feels like."

"You will. You will remember."

He put a hand out and laid it on both hers, clasped around her knees. He waited for her to take hers away, but she didn't. It occurred to him, out of his own need, to push her for a proper yes, an unmistakable one, but he thought better of it. Instead, he simply stayed there, his hand on hers, and watched her.

CHAPTER

19

Gina had found a possible-sounding flat. The particulars said that it was on the right side of Pau for a view towards the Pyrenees, that it had four bedrooms, a salon of great elegance and a roof terrace. There was a photograph of the building it was in, a tall nineteenth-century apartment block, and someone in the French estate agency had stuck a luminous red-paper arrow in the top left-hand corner, to show where the flat was. The price was good. It would mean using all her share of the proceeds of High Place, but that didn't take into account the money Laurence would have when the equity in The Bee House was sorted out. There would be enough for them to travel, to have the children out as often as they could come. Gina bent over the photograph with a magnifying glass, and tried to imagine some personality into that line of long blank windows across the top of the building in Pau.

It was mid-afternoon. In an hour or so, Sophy would be back from school unless, she said, she stayed for drama club. She had appeared the day before with a determined, red-haired girl called Lara, whom Gina had never seen before, and they had disappeared up to Sophy's room with a bottle of mineral water and a jumbo packet of crisps, leaving Gina downstairs feeling rather out of things. Lara had been perfectly friendly but Gina couldn't help wondering what Sophy had told her, how much Lara knew. She had bold eyes under her bright bush of hair, and a robust, unafraid presence. They had been closeted upstairs for almost two hours, and then Lara had come down, collected her bag of books, said, "Nice to meet you," to Gina, and sauntered off.

Gina bent again over the particulars. Two of the bedrooms looked extremely small and there was only one bathroom. She wished there was a photograph of the roof terrace, which might be the thing that made all the difference, or might simply be a bare concrete space, with a washing line. If it was, of course, they could make it into a bower with pots and trellises and tubs. Whatever it was like, the view was bound to be wonderful. She looked out of the glass door of the kitchen to the garden and saw, as she always saw, the low wall below the camomile lawn, and the careful planting, and the Gothic bench. She was tired, oh so tired, of living without a view. A pretty prospect was one thing but it wouldn't, in any way, compensate for not having a view.

As she watched, she heard the street gate bang shut. Sophy, early for some reason. She picked the French flat brochure up quickly and slid it under a nearby newspaper. Then she cupped her face in her hands and waited for Sophy—and perhaps the faintly disconcerting Lara—to come into view. She didn't. Laurence did.

"Oh!" Gina cried, springing up. "In the afternoon!"

He came into the kitchen and took her in his arms and kissed her on the cheek. Then he held her for a second or two.

"Look," Gina said, breaking away. "Look at this!" She pushed the newspaper aside and seized the French brochure. "Do look. It's a flat. It's a rooftop flat with views!"

He took it. He looked just as usual, she thought, if a bit tired. No wonder he was tired. The strain of things at The Bee House must be terrible.

"Ah," Laurence said, flicking through. "*Un salon très élégant*, I see."

"And a roof terrace—"

"Yes."

"What do you think? Do you think it looks possible?"

"I think," Laurence said, laying the brochure down on the table again, "that it looks very French and rather forbidding."

"Laurence!"

"Well, you asked me. And I told you."

He wandered past her into the hall.

"Do you want some tea?"

"No," he called. "No thanks."

She hurried after him.

"What's the matter? Why are you so rest-less—"

He was standing in the sitting room, stand-ing behind an armchair and leaning on the back. She noticed his hands particularly, the fingers grasping the padded cushion.

He said, "My dear Gina, my darling Gina, I am not coming to France."

She stared at him. He left the armchair, and came to where she stood, just inside the sit-ting-room door, and took her hands.

"This is beyond apology," he said. "Way beyond."

She went on staring, straight ahead at the point where his throat rose out of his open shirt collar.

"I'm staying here," Laurence said. "I'm staying with Hilary. I love her and she's my wife and I'm staying."

Gina whispered, "Did she ask you?"

"No," Laurence said. "She only asked me to think very seriously about our marriage before I declared it dead."

"But you did that!" Gina cried. She tore her hands away. "You did that, ages and ages ago, and you thought it was! You said so!"

"I know," Laurence said. "There was a time when I did think it. When I thought Hilary felt it too. But it isn't dead. I don't want to say these things to you, I *hate* saying them. But there's no way of not hurting you."

Gina put her hands to her head as if to reassure herself it was still there.

"Don't you love me any more? Don't you? Don't you?"

He said quietly, "Yes. I love you."

"Then why all this? Why all these horrible things you're saying, going back on your word, throwing me back into the pit—"

"Because," Laurence said, and stopped.

She seized his arms.

"Because what?"

He looked right at her.

"You don't want to know—"

"I do! I do! You must tell me, you must, you must—"

He sighed.

"I can't love you, you see, without Hilary."

She gave a shrieking scream, as if he had slapped her, and beat at him with her fists.

"Liar, liar, liar! What utter crap, what utter, stupid, heartless, lying crap! You loved me long before Hilary, long before, there were years and years before her—"

He took her flailing wrists and gripped them.

"There were. But then I met her and learned to love her."

"It's the boys, you're staying for the boys—"

348

"No. I'm not. I'm staying because I want to mend my marriage. If I can. If Hilary can take it."

Gina pulled free and retreated a few steps.

"And what about me?"

"Gina—"

"Where does that leave *me*? I'll tell you where it leaves me, you lying coward—it leaves me without love or a home or a future. D'you hear me? No love and no future. How can you do this to me? How could you do this to your worst enemy, let alone to me?"

He said nothing.

"You started it!" Gina shouted. "You began all this! It was you who kissed me and told me you were in love with me! It wasn't my idea!"

"No ideas like this are unilateral, Gina—"

"So you want to defend yourself, do you? You want to watch my life fall into utter ruins and explain that it has nothing to do with you? Is that what you want? How disgusting can you get, how base and vile and wicked—"

"Stop that," Laurence said.

She cried, "But I can't believe you don't even feel guilty!"

"I do," he said. "I haven't any words to describe how I feel. But I didn't think it would help if I told you how I felt—"

"So instead you came to tell me that you love Hilary more than me."

He was silent.

"Say it."

He shook his head.

"*Say* it."

"I love Hilary more than you."

She turned away from him and crumpled up on the floor by an armchair, putting her face into her folded arms. He saw her shoulders shaking. He went across to her and put a hand on her. Her head whipped up.

"Please don't touch me."

He took his hand away.

"I can't believe it," Gina said, her voice choking. "I can't *believe* that two men could do this to me. In the space of three months."

A small impatience, of which he was not proud, rose in Laurence.

"I shan't plead with you," Gina said. "I shan't abase myself to your repulsive level. I suppose Hilary is full of triumph."

"Far from it. She's as full of confusion as I am—"

"Oh," Gina said. "*Poor* Hilary."

"Shut up," Laurence said.

She bent her head down again. He looked at the back of her neck, exposed by her hair as it fell forward, and thought how unchanged it was from the sixteen-year-old neck he had sat behind in that long-ago school bus going up to London to see Paul Scofield play King Lear. How you could hate love sometimes, how you could loathe its slimy, seductive trails, how you could despair of yourself for ever having thought it was the key to all happiness and believed its piecrust promises. He sat on the arm of the chair above Gina's bent head.

"I shouldn't have done it," he said. "I shouldn't have started it. But I thought I had no choices; I thought I was following some path laid down for me along all these years, an inevitable path. You know that. You understand what I'm saying. You felt it too. I don't underestimate any of the damage I've done. I daren't."

She raised her head and looked at him.

"How do you know you won't get tired of this frame of mind? As you have of me?"

"I'm not tired of you," Laurence said patiently. "I'll never be tired of you. But you aren't where I belong."

She sat up a little straight and ran her forefingers under her eyes, where the tears had collected.

"Belong—"

"Yes."

"I don't—belong anywhere."

He said nothing. Gina gave a great sigh and rose to her feet. She turned her back to him.

"Please go," she said. "Now. Right now, when I'm not looking."

A little later, she sat in the waiting room of the counselling service, and looked out of the window at the supermarket roof on which rain was falling, making the brown tiles gleam dully. They had said Mrs. Taylor's appointment book was quite full that afternoon and Gina had pleaded and pleaded—she had been quite startled to hear herself—until Diana came on the line and said she could see her, just for half an hour, at the end of the day.

Gina had left a note for Sophy and had torn the French brochure into a hundred pieces, savagely, and thrust them into the kitchen rubbish bin, among the grapefruit skins and the teabags and the discarded salad leaves. She had then gone up to the bathroom and had a fierce shower, noticing as she did so that she was shaking almost too much to manage the controls. After the shower, she wrapped herself in a towel and lay on the bathroom floor, shivering, and abandoned herself to despair.

Perhaps she lay there half an hour, on the pale-grey carpet Fergus had chosen, with a draught from the landing blowing cold and levelly across her bare shoulders. She didn't know. It didn't matter. When she got up at last, her hands were stiff and mauve-pale and her feet were blue. The sight of her painted toenails— "Cherry toes," Laurence had said—revolted her.

It took ages to dress. She put on jeans and a winter jersey, an old soft cream wool jersey with a high neck and long sleeves out of which her hands protruded like the hands of a very old woman. She didn't put on any make-up, she couldn't even bear to look in the mirror, and she brushed her hair, slowly and draggingly, with her back to it. Then she put on her red ballet shoes and went out for her appointment with Diana Taylor.

"I haven't seen you for weeks," Diana said. She looked healthy and rosy brown.

"No."

"Do sit," Diana said. "There, if you like. That's the chair you like, isn't it?"

Gina crouched in it.

"It's all gone wrong."

Diana waited. She had a pad of paper on her knee, and a pen in her hand, but she made no move to write.

"Laurence has gone back to his wife. He came today, to tell me. He says he loves me, but he loves her more."

"Yes."

"Don't they all say that?"

"Yes," Diana said. "And most of them mean it."

"So I've got nothing," Gina said. "I've got even more nothing than when Fergus left. I've never had so much nothing in all my life."

Diana said, in a voice that was kind but not tender, "I'm so sorry."

"One of the reasons I did this," Gina said, leaning forward even further over her knees, "was because you said it would be a good thing."

Diana said, "I don't think so—"

"Yes!" Gina insisted. "Yes! You said it to me, quite plainly! You said that in my self-healing you thought love was a very good place to start!"

Diana laid her pad and pen on the floor beside her chair.

"I probably did say that. And in general, it's true. But in your case you looked for love where you probably wouldn't be able to keep it."

"Oh!" Gina cried. "Why don't you just say I've come a cropper for trying to take someone else's husband!"

"I'm not here to be judgemental—"

Gina gave a cry and flung herself back in the chair.

"And I never promised you a rainbow. People hate thinking there are situations about which nothing can be done, hate it."

"But you said that was never the case, you said that we could always change things, improve things, you said we all had the power to make our lives better lives—"

"I don't think I did."

"Well, you implied it! You implied to me that I could reinvent myself to make both myself and my life happier, more positive!"

"If it helps to blame me," Diana said, "then—"

"I don't want to blame you! I just want you to see what happens when you tell people the things you tell them! I just want you to see the consequences."

"I do try," Diana said carefully, "not to let people become too dependent. I am trying to make them independent of both me and their problems."

"So you tell them to start with love."

"No, I—"

"When I'm loved," Gina said, "I can love other people. I *know* I'm a better person when I'm happy. Is that wrong?"

"I don't really talk about right or wrong—"

Gina sprang up.

"Well, it's time you started!"

Diana rose too. She stood looking at Gina gravely.

"Can you tell me why you came?"

Gina said, "You had to know. You had to know what had happened."

Diana nodded.

"And," Gina said fiercely, "I had to sign off."

Hilary stood at the entrance to Bishop Pryor's School. There were virtually no other mothers there, and past her trailed a ragged procession of boys and girls on their way back into Whittingbourne. It was a dull building, functional and drab, and Hilary couldn't blame most of the pupils for having dressed and cultivated facial expressions to match.

She was not waiting for Gus. Gus had gone off that day on a geography field trip and would be delivered back to the town centre later in the evening. She was waiting for Sophy. Sophy had not been near The Bee House, and Hilary, in her strange state of weary relief and confusion, had found herself thinking, over and over again, that she must make the time to see Sophy, to talk to her. So here she was, standing by a spindly cherry tree in the centre of a worn grass plot, watching the main doors of Bishop Pryor's School.

It was almost twenty minutes before Sophy came. As she was in the sixth form, she was not in school uniform but instead in the accepted garb of the sixth form, which amounted to a uniform. She wore a very short black skirt, a long ragged grey tunic sweater which almost reached the hem of her skirt, black tights and heavy black shoes with thick soles. Her hair, shorter now, and bobbed, fell over one side of her face and she had sunglasses on, small and round and very black.

"Sophy—"

Sophy stopped. She said, "Oh *God*," and took her sunglasses off.

"Do you mind?"

"No. No—I was just surprised—"

"I couldn't think where else to find you."

Sophy looked confused.

"And I wanted to see you. To see if you were all right."

Sophy put the glasses back on again.

"I'm fine."

Hilary took her arm and began to walk her towards the gate.

"I don't want to pry, but I've been thinking of you—"

"Really," Sophy said, "I'm fine."

"I did say something to George—"

"Please—"

"I was worried you'd got hurt."

Sophy looked round wildly. Lara was several feet away, dressed precisely as Sophy was except that the hem of her skirt almost touched the ground. She was waving.

"Hilary," Sophy said, "I think I've got to go. I'm really sorry. Please don't worry. I'm OK, I promise I am. And—and kind of relieved."

"Yes."

"I've got a friend, you see. I'm going home with a friend. And then maybe to the movies—"

"All right," Hilary said, "I see."

Sophy said hastily, "It was nice of you, really kind."

Hilary leaned forward and kissed her. Their spectacles clashed.

"Take care of yourself."

"Yes," Sophy said. "Yes, I will," and fled away to Lara.

Hilary walked on alone through the trudging hordes, to her car, which she had left parked outside the gates in a small lay-by beneath a sign which said, "Please Do Not Even Think Of Parking Here." There was no furious notice on it, however, only a large bird dropping, and she got in and drove thoughtfully back into Whittingbourne, down the long main road past the sports centre where the swimmers cavorted silently behind their great screen of plate glass. Turning up by the high and ancient wall of Whittingbourne Park, she noticed a parking place between two trucks— much sought after, this stretch of road, for parking, as there was no fee—and manoeuvred the car in. Then she got out, locked it, and set off with resolute steps, following the wall of the Park towards High Place.

The street door still had its "For Sale" notice nailed to it, with a triumphant "SOLD!" in scarlet, across it at a diagonal. Hilary pushed it open and looked inside. The garden appeared as it always had, tranquil and a little too carefully planned, but much improved by the addition, without Fergus, of a few weeds. Hilary shut the door behind her and walked, with deliberate steps, around the house to the kitchen door, and peered in.

There was no one inside. Hilary knocked and, as no one came, turned the handle. The door wasn't locked.

"Gina?" Hilary called. She wasn't sure how her voice sounded, or ought to sound.

There was no reply. Hilary crossed the kitchen—there was a typewriter on the table, and a scatter of papers, and a mug beside a plate bearing a banana skin—and went into the hall. Ahead of her, in front of the sitting-room fireplace, and standing quite still as if she was waiting for her, was Gina.

"Hello," Gina said.

Hilary paused in the doorway.

"Hello."

"May I ask," Gina said politely, "why you've come?"

"I went to see Sophy, at the school. To see if she was all right and so on, after the George episode. I did see her, but she wanted to be with a friend. So I came to see you."

"Why?" Gina said again.

"I don't really know. Perhaps because I couldn't bear not to."

Gina said, "Would you like to sit down?"

Hilary moved to the nearest armchair and sat on the arm.

"Thank you."

"It was here," Gina said, "in here, that

Laurence told me he was staying with you. He stood behind that chair, the one you are now sitting on, and said that he wasn't coming to France."

"Will you still go?"

"No. There's no point now. Is there? And anyway, there's Sophy and there's Vi."

Hilary resisted the temptation to say that there always had been.

"Gina—"

"Yes?"

"I think we may be leaving."

Gina went very stiff.

"After something like this," Hilary said, "nothing can be the same, nothing can go on as before. And I think we had better go, all us Woods."

"Where?"

"I don't know. We've hardly talked about it. But I think it will happen, wherever it is. I thought you should know. In case you were making plans."

"Oh," Gina said, "I am."

Hilary stood up. She hesitated a moment and then she said, "It's all taking some courage, isn't it?"

And Gina, looking past her out of the window where the high wall shut her out from the town, said, "More than ever before."

Gus got back after dark. As it was a weekday night the hotel was quiet and Don had virtually closed the bar, even though it was only ten o'clock. As Gus came through, Adam came up from the kitchen, grinning as if on the tail-end of a joke and eating a piece of quiche, messily, with both hands.

"Well," he said, "how were the little toads and the furry squirrels?"

"It was water," Gus said, "sewage and stuff. Boring." He dropped his bag. "Where are Mum and Dad?"

Adam jerked an elbow towards the dining room.

"In there."

"In there?" Gus said in amazement. "Why in there?"

"Having dinner. Suddenly decided."

"But they never eat in there!"

"Well, they are now."

Gus went over to look through the window let into the dining-room door. Alone in the room, Hilary and Laurence faced one another across a table for two. They were in their hotel working clothes and there was a lighted candle on the table and a bottle of wine. Hilary had taken her glasses off and was fiddling with them.

Adam crammed the last lump of quiche into his mouth. He said, round it, "George has got a new job promotion."

Gus grunted. "How long have they been in there?"

"Dunno. An hour?"

He stopped to peer with Gus through the little pane. Gus said, almost in a whisper, "Are they going to be OK?"

For a second, Adam's arm brushed his brother's.

"I don't know," he said. His voice was sober. "I don't know. I mean, it's like someone sticks a knife in your chest." His arm came back and pressed into Gus's. "You can pull it out," Adam said. "You can pull the knife out again, but you've still got a bloody great hole there. Haven't you?"

CHAPTER
20

Sophy's bedroom faced west. It was a dull room, square and modern, with a single window looking over the Abbey grounds towards the tower of Whittingbourne Church and, beyond that, the ancient tall trees in the Park.

Sophy liked it. It asked nothing of her and allowed itself to be made into anything she felt like. What she felt like at the moment was a rather ethnic disorder bordering on mess. The bed was heaped with dark cushions, with tiny pieces of mirror let into the covers, and bits of rough Afghan embroidery, and she had taken, instead of keeping her clothes in a cupboard, to hanging them on knobs and hooks and the corners of pieces of furniture, or leaving them on the floor. All the surfaces in her room were covered in things, pieces of jewellery and pottery, cinema-ticket stubs and old envelopes, mascara wands and half-eaten tubes of glucose tablets. The only thing that wasn't cluttered was her desk. Her old High Place desk stood under the window in a state of perfect order, complete with an anglepoise lamp. Sophy was serious about her desk. From her desk, she had resolved, she would go to university to read Russian and French (because of the literature, she told Gina) and then she would go on to become an interpreter for the United Nations in New York. Or the Red Cross in Geneva. Or at the European Court, in Strasbourg. What she was not going to do, she informed Gina, was to stay in Whittingbourne.

"No," Gina said, "of course not. I never meant to, either."

They had bought the flat because it was on the first floor of a seventies-built block and had space around it. There were dull gardens too, squares of lawn and lines of path, but Gina and Sophy ignored those. From their windows, their square modern windows, they could see distance, even a hill or two to the north, and sky. Gina had painted everything white, to make it seem bigger, and on bright days, the light came in, in great floods, and made the whole flat seem insubstantial, as if it might just melt away in the brilliance. Sophy knew Gina was thankful to be free of the wall, free of the endless mysterious obligations exacted by High Place.

Gina had pupils now, every day, some of them as young as four and some of them older than

Vi. She taught for six or seven hours, and the sound of the piano went relentlessly on, through the thin walls of the flat, and Gina's voice, saying, "No, no, third finger." There was a little Indian papier mâché pot on the piano, full of twenty-pence pieces, to reward the little ones with. At the end of her day, Gina went out to one of her new classes. She was learning to draw and to speak Italian, and on Thursday nights, she did an advanced cookery course and came home with dishes of things both she and Sophy silently remembered Laurence making, quenelles and boned stuffed poussins and little puddings in cages of spun sugar. Sometimes, at the weekend, she went to a film with a man she had met at her cookery course. He was called Michael, and he was younger than Gina and ran a picture-framing business. Gina liked him, Sophy could see that, but not with any electricity. There was nothing between Michael and Gina of what Sophy's friend Lara called factor X. In Gina's bedroom, wedged into the corner of the mirror above her dressing table, was an old postcard, badly printed in uneven colour, of this place called Pau, in France. Gina still said, now and then, that she would go there again.

"When you've left home," she said, to Sophy. "When Vi—"

Vi was quieter now, but then Sophy thought Gina was too. They were both more sober. Sophy took Lara, and some of the others, Greg perhaps and Maggie, to see Vi. Vi liked that. She made one of her cakes and showed them Dan's mementoes and put the boat clock on for them. In return, they changed light bulbs for her and put the rubbish out. Sophy's budgie hung in Vi's kitchen window and talked all day, with beady intensity, to the bluetits on the feeder through the glass. Vi was knitting Sophy a cardigan. It was dark red— the best compromise they could reach between Vi's desire for scarlet and Sophy's need for black—and very long, and Vi was going to put wooden buttons up the front.

On the way to Vi, of course, they had to pass The Bee House. The brewery that had bought it from Laurence and Hilary had turned it into a pub, a themed pub, called The Beehive. There was a new signboard outside, and the garden was full of tables and chairs and red-and-yellow parasols with the brewery name printed across them in black. Inside, it had all been refitted. The dining room was a family room, and all the downstairs offices had been knocked through to enlarge the bar area. The kitchen was full of fryers, huge stainless-steel fryers into which breaded chicken legs and potato chips were dropped all day long before being served on brewery plates with plastic cushions of sauce. Don was in his element. He had been taken on by the brewery, to run the bar side of things, and had instituted a blackboard on which he could write, with flourishes, the day's drink special. Any minute, Sophy thought, she might meet him in Orchard Street, humming audibly and dressed in a bee costume, complete with wings.

She had told Gus about it. Sometimes, during her weekends in London, she and Gus met in the Hard Rock Café in Piccadilly. Gus had changed. He had got bigger and broader and had taken to dyeing his hair a little, just in the front. He had a girlfriend, called Tina, and the last twice Sophy had called him up and suggested the Hard Rock Café, he said he couldn't make it, he was busy. His voice had changed, not just in depth, but in accent. Sophy supposed it was his new London school.

"It's OK," he said.

"And the others?"

"Adam's going to Australia," Gus said. "Next year, after school. And George is going to do this horticulture thing. At some college, somewhere in Kent." He paused and took a deep swallow of Coca-Cola. "Mum's going to college too."

"Is she? What for?"

"Babies and stuff," Gus said. "You know."

Laurence was working in a restaurant in Chelsea. He was head chef. Gus said Laurence didn't like it much because the kitchen was almost underground. He wanted his own place again. They'd bought a house in Hammersmith, in a street that joined one that ran down to the river. Gus said it was brilliant, really close to Hammersmith Broadway Tube Station.

"London's great," Gus said. He grinned at Sophy. "Poor you."

"I don't mind," Sophy said, tossing her hair. "I really don't. Not now."

On the mornings when she was late, Sophy caught the bus to school, but on other mornings, when she got up the first time Gina called her, and not the third or fourth, she walked instead. She took the path through the Abbey grounds, over the green uneven space with its little outcrops of square stone, where the Abbey had once stood, and past the arch which Dan had so loved, and along the path between the bushes and the seats and the litter bins to Orchard Street. Then she would walk up The Ditches, admiring the china cats in bonnets and the starved spider plants that stood on the windowsills in defiance of accepted good taste, and come out by the wall of High Place.

Even half hidden by its wall, High Place looked different now. The upper windows had blinds of bleached canvas and split cane, instead of curtains, and the street gate had been painted matt black with a new latch and handle of brushed steel. Mrs. Pugh was to be seen shopping in the market sometimes, examining melons and avocado pears with a professionalism that disgusted the stallholders, and it was reputed that she still went to London every few weeks, to have her hair cut.

Sophy always paused, on the opposite pavement, and looked at High Place. She could look at it quite easily now and without even a twinge of longing or regret. It had been her childhood home after all, the home of a certain, now finished, period of her life, the place where she had lived all those years before she grew into herself, before the friends began.

A NOTE ON THE AUTHOR

Best known as the author of eagerly awaited and sparklingly readable novels often centred around the domestic nuances and dilemmas of life in contemporary England, Joanna Trollope is also the author of *The Choir*, *A Village Affair*, *The Rector's Wife*, *The Men and the Girls*, and *A Spanish Lover*. Joanna Trollope was born in Gloucestershire and still lives there.